ASHES

PRAISE FOR THE PROJECT EDEN THRILLERS

"Sick didn't just hook me. It hit me with a devastating uppercut on every primal level—as a parent, a father, and a human being."—**Blake Crouch**, best selling author of Run

"...a gem of an outbreak story that unfolds like a thriller movie and never lets up, all the way to the last page. Absolutely my favorite kind of story!"—**John Maberry**, *New York Times* bestselling author

"...not only grabs you by the throat, but by the heart and gut as well, and by the time you finish you feel as if you've just taken a runaway train through dangerous territory. Buy these books now. You won't regret it."—**Robert Browne**, best selling author of Trial Junkies

"You think Battles was badass before? He just cranked it up to 500 joules. CLEAR!"—**PopCultureNerd.com**

"Brett Battles at his best, a thriller that also chills, with a secret at its core that's almost too scary to be contained within the covers of a book."—**Tim Hallinan**, author of the Edgar-nominated The Queen of Patpong

ALSO BY BRETT BATTLES

THE JONATHAN QUINN THRILLERS

THE CLEANER
THE DECEIVED
SHADOW OF BETRAYAL (US)/THE UNWANTED (UK)
THE SILENCED
BECOMING QUINN
THE DESTROYED
THE COLLECTED

THE LOGAN HARPER THRILLERS

LITTLE GIRL GONE
EVERY PRECIOUS THING

THE PROJECT EDEN THRILLERS

SICK
EXIT 9
PALE HORSE
ASHES

STANDALONES

THE PULL OF GRAVITY
NO RETURN

For Younger Readers

THE TROUBLE FAMILY CHRONICLES

HERE COMES MR. TROUBLE

ASHES

Brett Battles

A PROJECT EDEN THRILLER

Book 4

ASHES

For more information about the author, please visit www.brettbattles.com.

What Came Before

THE UNTHINKABLE HAS happened.

Using an extensive network of specially equipped shipping containers, Project Eden has unleashed the Sage Flu upon the world, intent on wiping out over ninety-nine percent of the human population.

Despite its best efforts, the group known as the Resistance was unable to stop this horrific act from happening, and found itself under attack by a squad of Project Eden commandos.

Caught outside the Resistance's hideaway, Brandon Ash raced through the woods in search of safety. But all he found was a woman dealing with her own demons, and he was forced to move farther and farther away from his friends.

Twenty-four-hour curfews spread around the globe as people everywhere did what they could to keep themselves and their families safe.

Martina Gable and her family headed for a cabin in the Sierra Nevada Mountains in the high desert of California, desperately trying to isolate themselves from those who might be carrying the disease.

In India, after Sanjay inoculated Kusum, the girl he loved, he reluctantly took her back to her family in Mumbai. He then went in search of more vaccine, while Kusum led the others out of the city. Once Sanjay found what he was after, he, too, went back to the country, where, after a panicked night apart, he found Kusum again.

And then there was Project Eden itself. Its leadership apparently dead, a new principal director emerges, one who has no intention of ever conceding the job to anyone else.

In a desperate race back to the Resistance headquarters from where he'd witnessed the destruction of Bluebird—Project Eden's base above the Arctic Circle—Captain Daniel Ash arrived only to find his son missing. Out searching for Brandon, he came across a house in the wilderness that Brandon had visited earlier. But while his son had been able to get away from the woman who lived there, Ash was caught in the explosion that destroyed her house. He was rushed back to the Ranch, barely clinging to life.

Meanwhile, throughout the world, the sound of coughing grows louder and louder…

Earth to earth, ashes to ashes, dust to dust…

—Book of Common Prayer

December 24th

Christmas Eve

1

TEMPORARY OFFICE OF PROJECT EDEN'S PRINCIPAL DIRECTOR
NB219, LAS CRUCES, NEW MEXICO
8:53 PM MOUNTAIN STANDARD TIME (MST)

PEREZ HIT PLAY.

It was the fourth time he'd watched the video. He wasn't one hundred percent happy with the piece, but changing it at this point would mean an unnecessary delay of at least a week.

"Fine," he said to Claudia, his assistant. "Approved."

"And the proposed date?"

It was three days away.

"Also approved."

"I'll let the communications team know," she said. "Do you want this on automatic or would you like to activate?"

He gave it only a second's thought. "When the time comes, we'll do it from here."

"Very good, sir."

2

PCN BROADCAST
11:13 PM EASTERN STANDARD TIME (EST)

"FIREFIGHTERS BELIEVE THE blaze started in a grocery store on 22nd Avenue before it quickly overtook the surrounding buildings," Candice Mandel said.

She was reporting from St. Petersburg, Florida. The camera revealed flames rising from nearly every building along the avenue. Firefighters ran up and down the street, pulling equipment from trucks and spraying water on the flames, but it was clear their efforts would not be enough.

"One official we were able to speak with said that the rapid spread of the fire indicated it had been set intentionally." The camera panned to the left until Mandel was in the picture. With her free hand, she adjusted the surgical mask covering her mouth and nose before adding, "A mandatory evacuation of the residential area directly behind the fire has already begun. Unfortunately, the effort is hampered by residents' fear of leaving their homes."

The image of Mandel cut to prerecorded shots of the evacuation.

Police wearing gas masks normally used in riot situations were knocking on doors and moving people to buses parked along the street. Before they boarded, the evacuees were handed masks similar to the one Mandel was wearing. While most people seemed to be cooperating, a few could be seen struggling with the officers.

The picture cut to a shot of a front door as police

knocked on it. It opened an inch, but no more.

"Sir, how many people are in the house with you?" one of the officers asked.

"Just me and my wife. Why?"

"You both need to come with us."

"Are you kidding me? We're not going anywhere," the man said. "Not with that bug out there."

"Sir, there's a fire on 22nd Avenue that's threatening to spread this way. We need to evacuate the entire neighborhood."

"Sorry, buddy. We ain't leaving!" The man started to close the door, but the officer jammed a foot across the threshold.

The image cut back to Mandel standing in front of the fire. "That couple was eventually escorted to one of the buses, but the man wasn't the only one to express that kind of sentiment." She paused. "Choosing between running from a fire or exposing themselves to the Sage Flu virus now spreading around the world is not what these people thought they'd be doing on Christmas Eve. Back to you in New York, Henry."

Mandel was replaced on screen by PCN anchor Henry Nash. "There have been reports of looting and acts of destruction throughout the country, but so far these have been isolated events that authorities have been able to stop." Nash fell silent for a second, his eyes becoming momentarily unfocused. When he looked back into the camera, he said, "We're going to take you to the White House briefing room and correspondent Shelley Barnes. Shelley?"

The new image was a wide shot of an empty podium with the White House seal hanging on the wall behind it. In front of the podium were several rows of chairs, each filled with a member of the press. Most were wearing surgical-type masks, while a few went as far as donning full gas masks.

After a second's delay, the unseen Shelley Barnes said, "Henry, we've been told that a White House spokesman will be delivering an important update on the situation at any moment. So far, we've only been hearing—" She paused as a door at the front of the room opened. "It looks like the brief is about to start."

There was a rustle in the crowd as four men entered and spread out on either side of the podium. As soon as they were in position, the president himself walked out. He was followed by the majority and minority leaders of both the House and Senate, and the chief justice of the Supreme Court.

A murmur of surprise arose as all the reporters stood until the leader of the United States was behind the podium. The president's normally vigorous and youthful face looked drawn and tired. He stared at the gathered press for a moment before he began.

"Ladies and gentleman," he said. His face turned even grimmer. "In the last hour, I have received confirmation that deaths in the US directly attributable to the Sage Flu are in the thousands and climbing rapidly. I wish I could tell you these were confined to a particular location, but I cannot. The cases are spread throughout the country. In addition to the dead, tens of thousands more have already reported suffering from flu-like symptoms.

"I have been in touch with leaders in Asia, the Middle East, Africa, and throughout Europe, and, without exception, all are experiencing similar outbreaks.

"I have told the director of the CDC that there is no higher priority than the creation of a vaccine to defeat this deadly virus. All resources of this government are at their disposal, and I have been assured scientists in labs throughout the world are working around the clock until that goal is met. Something that I am confident they will achieve.

"It will take time, however. Months. Perhaps up to a year. My mission is to see that you, the citizens of the United States, are still here to receive the inoculation." He glanced over his shoulder at the congressional leaders who had joined him, then said, "As a first step to make sure that happens, and in consultation with both parties in Congress, just moments ago, I signed an executive order suspending the Constitution of the United States, extending the twenty-four-hour curfew indefinitely. The only people exempt are those needed for essential services—military; emergency personnel such as police, firefighters, doctors, and nurses; those needed to maintain utilities such as power and water; and others in positions critical to maintaining the health and safety of our nation. Anyone outside of these individuals found breaking curfew or otherwise risking the safety of others will be arrested and forced to spend the duration of our state of emergency in a holding facility as a guest of the United States military. Food and other needed items will be dispersed in an organized, scheduled manner, with strict instructions on how these items are to be retrieved. We ask that everyone please be patient and understanding.

"We are all in this together, and together we will see this through."

SITUATION ROOM, WHITE HOUSE
11:16 PM EST

EVERY CHAIR SAVE the one usually occupied by the president was filled, all eyes on the monitor at the front of the room displaying the press briefing.

All, that was, but Dr. Michael Esposito's. He was glancing at his boss, Dr. Marston, head of the CDC. The man looked thoughtful and supportive as he watched the president speak, an expression Esposito couldn't bring himself to match.

Dr. Marston had been in Washington advising the president since not long after the shipping containers found around the world began spewing their deadly cargo. He had then flown Esposito up that afternoon on a government plane. Esposito had protested, saying he needed to stay at the labs while his team continued trying to find some way to combat the Sage Flu virus. The new strain, which they were calling Sage Flu B (SF-B), was subtly different from the SF-A virus that had broken out in California the previous spring, and Esposito's team was just beginning to make some progress on what those differences might mean.

"The work won't stop if you're not there," Marston had told him. "Get on that plane and get up here now."

Upon arriving in DC, Esposito was rushed to the White House by a police escort, an unnecessary step given that the streets were all but empty. There, he'd been led to an office his boss was using.

Marston immediately stood. "Finally. Come on."

"Where are we going?"

"To brief the president."

"I could have done that over the phone," Esposito said, unable to hide his annoyance.

Marston pressed his lips tightly together, then said, "No, this is *not* something you could have done over the phone."

Esposito held up a hand in defense. "All right, all right." He dropped his jacket on the guest chair and followed his boss to the door. "So what are we supposed to be talking about?"

Marston's hand was on the doorknob, but he paused without turning it and looked back at Esposito. "A vaccine."

"What vaccine?"

"For the Sage Flu. What do you think?"

"There *is* no vaccine."

"I know that, and so does the president. What he wants to know is, when will it be ready?"

Esposito gaped at him, hoping this was some kind of joke. "You know I can't put a date on it. Maybe it'll take a couple of months, maybe it'll take twenty years! Look at HIV, for God's sake. How long have we been working on a cure for that?"

"We both know it will probably take less than a year."

"No, we don't."

"*Yes*, we do. And that's what you're going to tell him."

"You brought me up here to *lie* to the president?"

Marston stared at him for a moment. "What do you think is happening here?"

"I'm not sure what you—"

"Here. In the world. Right now. What do you think is

happening?"

"Um, you mean with the flu?"

"Yes, with the goddamn flu!"

Esposito had never seen his boss so angry. He resisted the urge to moisten his suddenly dry lips. "Someone is trying to kill a lot of people."

"Someone is trying to kill more than just a lot of people. You know what the death rate was for the initial victims of the SF-A outbreak!"

Everyone at the CDC was well aware of that number. Nearly a hundred percent. The only reason there were survivors was because the virus had been tailored with a built-in cutoff so only those in the first few generations received the killer variety. That was a bit of info they hadn't shared with the public.

"And can I assume you've read the report on the deaths we've already seen this time?"

"Of course," Esposito said. So far, the death rate had been the same. "But it's still possible that SF-B will have the same generational cutoff as SF-A. We're still working on finding that out."

"Really? Because the reports I've read from your team indicate that the cutoff trigger identified in SF-A is missing in SF-B."

"That's true," Esposito said. It was one of the first things he and his colleagues had looked for. "But we're hopeful it's just being expressed in a different way."

"Hopeful? Think, Michael, think! This is a terrorist attack. Both strains were purposely released. The limited boundary of the spring release was because they knew it was going to burn out. It was a test. Don't you see that? This time, they're pumping it into the air *everywhere*, not just in a small geographical area. This is the big attack. What they planned for. Do you really think they've included some kind of biological timer? Do you?"

As soon as Sage Flu had been identified as the virus in the containers, Esposito had thought about all the different possibilities, including that given the scale, there would be no cutoff this time. But because of what that would mean—the near annihilation of the human race—he hadn't been able to bring himself to believe anyone could be that ruthless.

He hesitated, then nodded, forced to admit the truth.

"We have one job right now," Marston said. "One. And that's to keep as many people alive as possible." He paused, the look of anger that had taken him dissipating. When he spoke again, his voice was softer, conciliatory. "If people think there is a vaccine coming, they'll cling to hope, and cut down on exposure to one another. There's an excellent chance, then, that some *will* stay alive long enough to receive the vaccine I'm sure your team will develop. But if we tell them we don't know when or even if the vaccine will be ready, we're all but admitting we're condemning everyone to death. That's why we need to give the president a definitive timetable. If *he* believes, he can make everyone else believe. Do you get it now?"

When they entered the Oval Office a few minutes later, and the president asked Esposito how long until a vaccine would be ready, the doctor said, "A year at the outside. Hopefully sooner."

And now, there he sat in the conference room, his eyes avoiding the television screen as he listened to the president spread the fictional timeline.

His throat dry, he stood and walked to the back of the room where several bottles of water sat on a counter. As he took one and opened it, a man in an army uniform walked up and grabbed another bottle.

The officer started to drink, but suddenly pulled the bottle away and coughed.

Already on edge, everyone in the room whipped around and stared at him.

He held up a hand and said in a hoarse voice, "Went down the wrong tube."

That seemed to mollify the crowd. As the others returned their attention to the monitor, Esposito said, "You all right?"

"Fine," the officer replied. He put his hand in front of his mouth as he cleared his throat. "Hate when that happens, you know?"

"Yeah," Esposito said.

On the screen, the president was finishing up, which meant he would be joining them soon. Walking back to his seat, Esposito noticed a few droplets of water on his hand that must have popped off his bottle when he'd opened the top. He wiped them off, and took another drink.

Unfortunately for him, and for everyone else in the room, the drops didn't come from his bottle. They were from the army officer's cough, one that hadn't been caused by water going down the wrong pipe.

3

MONTANA
9:37 PM MST

THE STORM HAD grown steadily worse. The snow, at first a light dusting on the road, had begun to accumulate into a growing blanket of white, making it more and more difficult for Chloe as she drove south on the motorcycle.

As if that weren't enough to heighten her anxiety, each mile she traveled took her farther from the Ranch, adding to the time she would take to return with the help Daniel Ash needed.

An explosion at a house where he had been searching for his son had left Ash unconscious and seriously injured. Billy, the Ranch's doctor, had been killed several days earlier, leaving the Resistance with a nurse who could tend to Ash's visible wounds but was untrained to diagnose and treat anything more severe. Knowing timing was critical, Chloe and two others had raced away on motorcycles in different directions in hopes of finding a doctor who could help. Not just any type of doctor; they needed a surgeon. Chloe had blown through two towns already, but each was too small to support that skill level. The nearest place she might find what she was looking for was Great Falls.

On a sunlit, summer day with no one else on the road, she could have made it there in little more than an hour. But it wasn't daytime or even close to summer, and the darkness and snow were more than doubling the normal travel time.

She checked her watch. Almost a quarter to ten.

Dammit! I should be on my way back by now.

She resisted the urge to increase her speed, knowing she was already pushing her luck, but she couldn't help feeling that every lost second might be crucial to Ash's survival.

The road took a wide turn up ahead. If she remembered correctly, once she was around it the highway would straighten out for the final run into Great Falls. *Maybe a few more miles an hour then.*

Her hand tightened on the grip, ready to sprint the final distance to the city as soon as she finished the turn, but instead of accelerating, she immediately reduced her speed. Fifty yards beyond the turn, a pair of wooden barricades was set across the road. Parked behind it was a military truck. Dual, portable floodlights were set up on the asphalt, lighting up the area.

A roadblock.

The front wheel of the motorcycle wobbled as the bike slowed. Chloe fought to maintain her balance as she brought her ride to a stop ten feet shy of the barricade.

Two men in military uniforms popped out of the truck. They were wearing full biohazard hoods, and armed—one with an M4 rifle, and the other with a handgun, probably a Beretta. By what she could see of their faces through their faceplates, they seemed as surprised to see her as she was by them.

"Hold it right there," the shorter one ordered.

"Does it look like I'm going anywhere?" she asked.

"Ma'am, are you aware there is a curfew in effect?"

"I'm trying to get home, that's all. Why are you guys out here?"

"The president has ordered anyone violating the curfew to be detained."

"When did that happen?" she asked.

"The order came through thirty minutes ago."

"Well, I was on my bike thirty minutes ago. How was I supposed to know? Look, I'm just trying to get home to my kids, all right?"

The other airman gave her a skeptical look. "You *live* here in Great Falls?"

"What does it matter if I do?" She thought there probably weren't that many African-Americans living in town, but there would be a few. "Come on, let me through. My kids are scared to death with all this stuff going on. They need me. I'm sure you can understand that."

The short one hesitated. "Can we see your ID, ma'am?"

She made a show of reaching into her jacket, and then, in a fake panic, padding her other pockets. "*Dammit*!"

"Ma'am?"

"I don't have it."

"You don't have it?"

"No," she said.

The tall one with the rifle raised it a few inches.

"Jesus," she said. "Just because I don't have it with me doesn't mean you have to shoot me! I left it at my friend's place in Concord. I forgot it, that's all."

Neither man said anything.

"Look, you want to drive me to my house so I can prove to you who I am?" she asked. "There's nothing I'd like more than a warm ride at this point. I'm freezing my ass off."

A few more tense seconds passed, then the two men huddled together for a moment. Finally, the first one said, "I'm sorry. We can't do that, ma'am."

"So, what? I stand here and we stare at each other? I gotta see my kids! Come on. Please!"

He studied her for a moment. "What's your name?"

"Megan Adams," she said, using the name of someone back at the Ranch.

"All right, Ms. Adams, we're going to let you go home. But head straight there and stay inside. You get caught out again, you'll be arrested. No questions asked."

"Thank you," she said.

The two men moved one of the barricades out of the way so that she could walk her bike through. The look on the taller one's face made it clear he didn't trust her, and that if he'd been in charge she wouldn't have gotten off so easily.

"Thank you," she said again as she hopped on her bike.

Within minutes, the town of Great Falls started appearing through the falling snow, streetlights at first, then strings of colored Christmas lights outlining a few of the homes.

She stopped under the awning of a gas station and pulled out her cell phone. To find a surgeon, she needed to find a hospital. A quick search told her the major medical center in town was Benefis Hospital. She navigated to their website, and tapped on the "Find a Doctor" tab. She was given the choice of looking for a physician by name, specialty, or keyword. Chloe found "General Surgery" under specialties and selected it. Nine names appeared, some with pictures, some not. All the doctors with photos appeared to be between thirty-five and fifty. If this had been a big-city hospital, she would have expected stern, serious poses, but the surgeons of Benefis looked friendly and approachable.

She flexed her fingers, fighting off the cold, and considered her options. Approaching someone at the hospital would be difficult at best. The facility would undoubtedly be one of the few places in town where people were still working, and, given her experience with the roadblock, there was a good chance that more airmen had been assigned to guard it. Better if she could find a doctor at home.

She looked down the street, half expecting a police car or military vehicle to drive by and catch her standing there, but the only movement came from the snowflakes falling to the ground. Still, to be safe, she walked the bike around the side of the gas station, out of view, then called the general number for the hospital.

"Benefis Hospital," a female voice said.

"Can I speak to someone in the surgical unit, please?"

"Is this an emergency?"

"Ma'am, I'm calling from Malmstrom," Chloe said, invoking the name of the local air force base.

"Of course. One moment."

Instrumental music filled the void, a violin-and-piano version of some old pop song Chloe recognized but couldn't name.

"Nurse Reynolds. Can I help you?" The voice was male and sounded rushed.

"Is this the surgical unit?"

"Yes, it is."

"Mr. Reynolds, I'm Captain Lauren Scott. I'm part of the emergency operations team over here at Malmstrom."

"Yes?" the nurse said, sounding unimpressed.

"I need the names of your surgeons currently on shift, on call, and those who will be coming in next."

"I'm not sure I'm allowed to give that out."

Chloe hardened her tone. "We are in a state of emergency. That means when my office calls needing something, you give it. Understood?"

The nurse fell silent.

"Mr. Reynolds, did you hear me? We are all trying to save lives here. I'm sure you don't want me coming down there in person. That would take time, and I would not be very pleasant when I arrive. Now, please, can I get your cooperation?"

A moment, then, "I'm sorry. Hold for a second. I'll check."

There was no music this time, only the sound of someone using a computer keyboard.

"Okay, here you go," Reynolds said. He read off the name of two doctors who were at the hospital and one who was on call, then gave her the name of the three surgeons who were scheduled to report in the morning.

"Thank you," Chloe said. "Appreciate the help."

As soon as the call disconnected, she brought up the list of doctors again. Eliminating the six names she'd been given left her with the three surgeons who weren't expected in anytime soon. She called Information.

The first name had only a home phone number. The second and third, though, produced addresses as well. She looked at the map. The closest of the two, a Dr. Bradley Gardiner, lived less than half a mile from her current position.

She memorized the route, and put her phone away.

"RUN! RUN!"

Brandon Ash's lungs burned as he pushed himself faster through the trees. He could hear the *boom-boom-boom* of his pulse as blood rushed by his ears.

"Run!"

He glanced back over his shoulder, toward the voice—Mr. Hayes's voice.

"Keep moving!" the man yelled.

Brandon couldn't see him, but knew Mr. Hayes couldn't be far behind. As he looked back in the direction he was headed, his foot slipped on a rock and his leg flew out from under him. He tumbled, slamming against the ground over and over as the slope of the hill prevented him from stopping.

Whoop-whoop-whoop.

The rhythmic sound was slow and distant at first, but as it gained speed, it also increased in volume. The louder it got the more he felt each *whoop* in his chest, as if the sound itself had replaced the beating of his heart.

With a final skid through the dirt, he came to rest on his back. Above him was blue sky peeking through the tops of the trees. Then the blue turned black as the source of the sound moved into view.

"Run!" Mr. Hayes shouted.

Brandon wanted to do that more than anything, but the sight of the machine in the sky paralyzed him.

"Run!"

A helicopter, giant and black, hovered directly overhead.

Brandon felt something drip down the side of his face. He touched it, thinking it must be blood. But it was cold, not warm.

He was cold.

His eyelids fluttered, then opened. He sucked in a deep, frightened breath, and pushed himself partway up before he realized there was no helicopter above him, no blue sky. The only thing over his head was the makeshift lean-to he'd built to shelter himself as he slept.

Mr. Hayes, he thought. Mr. Hayes was dead.

Brandon pulled inside his sleeping bag, and used his flashlight to check his watch.

10:12 p.m.

So it was still Christmas Eve. He turned so he could look out the opening of his lean-to. The snow had yet to stop, and was piling up around the lower part of his shelter. He wondered if enough would fall to cover the entire thing by morning. The former kid in him would have thought that was cool, but not this Brandon. Not the Brandon who was just trying to survive.

He had spent most of that day following the road south. Not once did a vehicle pass by. In the afternoon, the snow had begun to fall, making him not only tired and cold, but wet. What bothered him most, though, was the eerie silence that enveloped him as more snow stuck to the ground. It made him feel like the last person on Earth, destined to walk forever alone. Finally, when he'd been unable to find a structure where he could spend the night, he had made the lean-to and set up camp.

A snippet of the dream came back to him—the *whoop-whoop-whoop* of the helicopter—and he suddenly wondered if the noise had been more than a part of his dream. The cold, after all, had definitely been real.

He pushed his head out of the sleeping bag, and moved over to the opening of the lean-to where he could listen better. Earlier that evening he'd heard a motorcycle drive by, but had rushed over to the road too late to get the driver's attention. Maybe it was coming back. If so, he wanted to be on the highway in plenty of time to flag it down. He held his breath, straining to pick up the slightest of sounds, but if there was an engine roaring out there somewhere, he couldn't hear it.

Just the dream, then.

Disappointed, he settled back down.

Tomorrow I'll find a phone and call Dad. Tomorrow everything will be okay.

It took a while, but he finally fell back asleep, and when he did, the dream returned.

"Run!"

SIERRA NEVADA MOUNTAINS, CALIFORNIA
9:15 PM PACIFIC STANDARD TIME (PST)

MARTINA GABLE STARED up at the sky. Unlike the night before, there were no clouds, so the stars shined brightly over the cabin. Running in a thick band across the field of black was the Milky Way, the light from most of its stars generated long before mankind had taken its first step. She wondered if light that old would still be reaching Earth when man took his last.

She heard the door open behind her, but she didn't turn to see who it was.

"What are you looking at?" Riley Weber asked.

Martina watched the sky for a moment longer, then shook her head. "Nothing."

Riley hesitated before saying, "Sorry. I didn't mean to bother you."

Martina looked back. "You didn't. I was just…trying to think about nothing."

"I've been trying to think about nothing all evening."

Riley's chin shook as she bit her lip and started to cry. Martina put her arms around her friend. She wanted to say something like "We're going to be okay," but she couldn't bring herself to lie, so she kept silent as she stroked Riley's hair and let the girl sob.

Both Martina's family and Riley's family had escaped to the mountains in hopes of avoiding the Sage Flu. And while it had not touched them so far, they'd had their own near tragedy when Riley's twin sister Laurie wandered off the previous night and nearly died of exposure. That afternoon, Mr. Weber had decided to take her back down the mountain to get medical attention. Without any cell phone coverage or land line at the cabin, Mr. Weber and Laurie hadn't been heard from since.

Riley took a deep breath as her tears finally lost strength. She pulled out of Martina's arms, and said, "Thanks. I guess I just needed to let that out, huh?"

"We're all going to need to let it out at one point or another, I think."

Riley looked up at the stars. After a moment, she said, "Tell me about college."

"What do you want to know?" Martina asked. Riley was still a senior at Burroughs High School, while Martina was in her freshman year at Cal State University, Northridge.

"What's it like living on your own?"

Martina shrugged. "It's fun sometimes."

"Only sometimes?"

"Well, I still have to study. And Mom's not there to clean up for me or do the laundry."

"Still better than living at home, I bet," Riley said.

"They both have their ups and downs, but, yeah, it's pretty cool." Martina gave her friend a smile. "Come on. I'm getting cold."

Back in the house, they found Martina's parents in the kitchen making hot chocolate for Martina's brother Donny and Riley's younger sister Pamela, who were lying on the floor in front of the fireplace, playing games on their iPods.

"You two want any?" Martina's dad asked as he poured the brown liquid into mugs.

"Definitely," Martina said.

"Me, too," Riley chimed in.

"You want to see if your mom wants some?" he asked.

Riley looked around. "She still in her room?"

Martina's mom nodded, picked up one of mugs, and held it out. "Why don't you take one back? She's had a rough day. No reason to make her come out and deal with all of us."

"Thanks, Mrs. Gable," Riley said.

She took the mug and headed toward the back bedrooms.

"Here you go, honey." Mr. Gable handed Martina a mug. "It's hot, so be careful. Pamela, Donny, yours is ready."

Neither of the other two kids moved.

"Hey!" Mr. Gable yelled.

Martina walked over and kicked her brother's foot.

Donny pulled one of the earphones out of his ear. "What?"

She pointed at their dad.

"Hot chocolate," Mr. Gable said.

"Cool." Donny jumped up and motioned for Pamela to join him.

The girl looked over, saw the steaming mugs, and hopped up, too.

"Martina?"

Riley was standing in the hallway, motioning for Martina to join her.

"What's up?" Martina asked as she walked over.

"Mom…she…" Riley couldn't seem to finish, so instead she hurried over to the door of the bedroom her parents had been using.

As soon as Martina joined her, Riley pushed it open several inches.

The light was on inside so Martina didn't have any problem seeing Mrs. Weber lying on the bed. At first she thought the woman was asleep, but then she noticed the sweat along Mrs. Weber's hairline, and the look of pain on her face. Suddenly, Riley's mom twisted back and forth, and let out a low groan that turned into a cough.

Without even meaning to, Martina took a step backward. "Did you go inside?" she asked Riley, though she already knew the answer. She could see the mug of hot chocolate sitting on the nightstand.

"She's my mom," Riley said. "What am I going to do?"

"Stay here. I'll be right back." Martina dashed back to the living room. After catching her mother's eye, she said, "Can I see you for a minute?"

"Sure."

Once her mother had entered the hallway, Martina whispered, "It's Mrs. Weber. I think she's sick."

Her mother's eyes grew wide. "What?"

Martina led her over to the bedroom door so she could peek through. She watched as the blood drained from her mother's face.

Before either of them could say anything, Donny called out from the living room. "Hey, Mom. Can you bring me a tissue when you come back? I need to blow my nose."

4

GREAT FALLS, MONTANA
10:23 PM MST

DR. BRADLEY GARDINER sat on the couch in his living room, his wife Kathy on one side and their fourteen-year-old daughter Emily on the other. None of them had said anything for over an hour as they watched the news on TV.

Many cities were reporting minor instances of civil unrest, while others, such as St. Petersburg, Florida, were experiencing fires that were spreading faster than the areas depleted of emergency personnel could handle.

The most shocking images, though, were of the silent streets in New York, Los Angeles, Tokyo, Beijing, Moscow, London, and the other great cities of the world. Daytime, nighttime, evening, morning—it didn't matter. There wasn't a soul in sight for as far as the cameras could see.

"We are expecting more detailed information about food distribution sometime tomorrow. We're also anticipating more on when a Sage Flu vaccine will be ready. We've been told that the...oh, excuse me. We're going to cut to our colleagues at the BBC, where the British prime minister has just begun addressing Parliament."

The news anchor was replaced by an interior shot from the House of Commons. On either side of the chamber were rows of chairs, rising toward the walls like bleachers on opposite sides of a narrow basketball court. Only a handful of the seats were occupied, and everyone was wearing a mask.

Standing in front of a lectern was the prime minister, recognizable even behind his mask.

"…safety of all. This is not a time for debate or delay, for both will only result in more deaths. I have spoken to—"

There was a loud knock on the door. Gardiner's daughter jumped, while his wife jerked under his arm.

"Who could that be?" Emily asked.

"I don't know, sweetie," Gardiner said. He rose from the couch.

"Brad," his wife said, shaking her head. "Whoever it is, just ignore them."

A second knock was followed by a woman's voice. "Dr. Gardiner?"

Kathy shook her head again. "Don't," she mouthed.

"She knows we're here," he said.

"I don't care."

"Dr. Gardiner?" the woman said again. "I'm Captain Scott, US Air Force."

The air force had basically taken over the town when the national state of emergency was declared.

"I have to see what she wants," Gardiner said.

Kathy, not looking happy, said, "Wait for me."

Together they entered the foyer, and Gardiner flipped on the outside light. Looking through the spy hole in the door, the first thing he noted was that the porch was still dark. He flipped the switch off and back on again. The light remained off. There was enough illumination coming from the streetlamp that he could make out the shape of the woman on the other side of the door.

"Dr. Gardiner?" she said again.

"I'm here," Gardiner said. "What is it you need?"

"Sir, we've had an emergency over at the base that requires your assistance."

"You should contact the hospital if you need anyone. I'm not on call right now."

"We realize that. That's why I'm here. We need a surgeon, but decided it would be best not to disturb the rotation at Benefis."

Gardiner frowned. "What's the emergency?"

"Internal injuries. I have X-rays right here to show you."

"Don't you have your own surgeons?"

"We do, sir, but they are both currently occupied." The woman paused. "It was a helicopter crash, sir. Multiple injuries. We need your help."

Gardiner dipped his head and nodded to himself. "All right. Give me a minute."

"No problem."

"No!" Kathy said. "You can't go. Not tonight."

"People are hurt. It's my job to take care of them."

"Dad," Emily said. "You'll get sick if you go out there." She pointed back at the TV. "It's everywhere."

The doctor grabbed his coat from the closet. "I'm sure it won't take long, but don't wait up."

"Wait!" Kathy said. She hurried over to the entrance table. "You need a mask." She grabbed the box of paper masks Gardiner had brought home from the hospital, and pulled one out. "Here."

There was another knock on the door. "Dr. Gardiner, we need to hurry."

THE DOCTOR'S HOUSE sat on the north side of Young Street. A nice, multibedroom home with a big front yard and two-car garage. While large by Great Falls standards, it would have been considered moderate in most larger cities, given the owner's profession.

Chloe parked the motorcycle down the street and approached on foot.

Light from a television flickered through the windows at the front of the house. As she got closer, she could see at least two people sitting on a couch watching TV. It was tuned to the news, of course. She doubted there was anything else on.

She moved over to the front door, quietly worked the cover off the porch light, and unscrewed the bulb. Once the cover was back in place, she knocked.

When the doctor had finally responded, she used the

tactic she'd come up with on the drive over to convince him to open the door. While he said he was coming, the door was still shut, so she placed her ear against it, and heard two women arguing with the doctor to stay.

Chloe knocked again. "Dr. Gardiner, we need to hurry."

"I'll call you when I get there," she heard him say. "And I'll have them bring me home as soon as I'm done."

"Please, Dad. Please don't go."

"Sweetie, you know I have to. I'll be all right."

Chloe chewed on her lower lip, troubled by the conversation.

Crap.

Discarding her original idea, she retrieved her gun.

The deadbolt clunked open, and the doorknob began to turn.

"Put your mask on first," the older woman—probably his wife—said.

The doorknob recoiled to its original position as the doctor let go, but the door itself was now unlocked.

Chloe turned the knob and eased the door open. The wife was helping her husband put a paper mask over his head while the daughter watched from a few feet away. None of them showed any of the physical signs of being ill.

"Sorry," Chloe said as she stepped inside and closed the door behind her. "Change of plans."

The Gardiners turned in surprise. When they caught sight of her gun, they froze.

"Is there anyone else in the house?" Chloe asked.

The man shook his head. "No."

Had he answered too fast? She looked at the daughter. "Is he telling the truth?"

The girl's eyes were locked on the gun.

"Hey," Chloe said. "Is he telling the truth?"

The girl jerked her head up. "What? Yes. Just the three of us."

She seemed far too scared to lie.

"Okay," Chloe said. "This is your lucky day."

"What do you want?" Gardiner asked. "I don't have any

drugs here. But you're welcome to any money or food you want."

"I've already told you what I want, Doctor—you. I have an injured man who needs your help."

"Take him to the hospital."

"Not that easy," Chloe said.

She looked past them into the rest of the house. Beside the living room, there was a stairway leading up to the second story where the bedrooms probably were, and the open door to a bathroom. Along the back wall of the living room was a wide break, and on the other side was what looked like the dining room. She figured the kitchen had to be back there somewhere, too.

"Into the other room," she said.

"What are you going to do to us?" Gardiner's wife asked.

"Save your life."

Gardiner looked at her like she was crazy. "Please, just leave us alone."

"Move it!" Chloe barked.

The Gardiners backed into the living room.

"Keep going," Chloe told them, motioning to the dining area. After they passed into the back part of the house, she signaled for them to stop.

Another quick scan. To her left a family room, and to the right an open-plan kitchen.

"That door," she said, nodding past Gardiner toward the kitchen. "Where does it lead?"

Gardiner glanced over his shoulder. "That? The…the garage."

"What do you got parked in there?"

"Um…uh…"

Chloe turned to his daughter. "What kind of cars?"

"Mom's BMW. And the Yukon."

A Yukon SUV.

Perfect.

GETTING THE GARDINERS into the Yukon wasn't

particularly difficult. Despite the fact Chloe never directly pointed her gun at any of them, its mere presence was enough to ensure their cooperation.

She had the doctor take the driver's seat while she herded the two women into the back with her—the daughter, whose name was Emily, in the middle; and the wife, Kathy, behind her husband.

Gardiner turned on the headlights as they backed out of the garage and down the driveway.

"No," Chloe said. "Lights off."

He looked for a moment like he was going to argue, so she raised the gun a few inches and he flicked the lights off.

"Which way?" he asked.

"To the left. Keep it slow."

The Ranch was northwest of Great Falls. The main route out of town would have been via the interstate, the same way she'd come in, but the roadblock eliminated that option. Searching on her phone for a new route, she saw a pair of two-lane highways that led roughly in the right direction. She hoped the air force hadn't seen it necessary to block those off, too.

"As soon as you can, head down to Central, then go west," she told the doctor.

At the next corner, Gardiner turned the Yukon left.

"Where are you taking us?" Kathy asked.

"Someplace safe," Chloe said.

"Safe? We were safe in our home."

Chloe looked over at her. "No. Not even close."

"What do you mean?"

Chloe looked back at the road and ignored the question.

As they turned onto Central, she saw headlights several blocks away heading toward them. To the Yukon's right was a bank with a parking lot that went all the way back to the next street.

"Turn in here," Chloe ordered. "Now."

Gardiner hesitated.

"Do it!"

He turned the SUV into the parking lot.

"Pull around the back of the building, and stop," she said.

Once they were hidden from the main street, she rolled down the window a half inch. Cold air streamed in, threatening to undo the increase in cabin temperature the SUV's heater had achieved.

At first the sound of the other vehicle was only a low rumble in the distance, but it grew in intensity as it traveled in their direction.

A truck, she realized. A big one. Maybe even a couple of them.

"Don't be stupid," she said, flashing the gun at Gardiner and his wife, making sure they got the message. "You don't want to see me angry. I guarantee it."

They both nodded, the doctor going so far as to take his hands off the steering wheel and set them in his lap.

The noise was loud now. Definitely two trucks, diesel engines. The first reached the bank and drove past. But as the second was nearing, Chloe caught a flash of red behind the Yukon. She glanced over her shoulder, then whipped her head back around.

"Foot off the brake!" she yelled.

Their brake lights flashed again.

"Off the brake!"

She reached through the opening between the two front seats, grabbed the doctor by the arm, and shoved the end of her pistol into the side of his head. Gardiner's wife and daughter screamed.

"Off!" Chloe yelled.

"You won't hurt me. You need me," the doctor said.

Chloe glared at him for half a second, then let go. She reached across Emily and grabbed Kathy's arm. "You're right. But I don't need your wife."

Gardiner pulled his foot off, and the brake lights went out. "Don't hurt her. Please."

Without letting go of the woman, Chloe focused her attention on the trucks outside. The engine of the first one was fading as it continued down the road, but the second seemed to be slowing.

"Listen to me, very, very carefully," Chloe said. "Drive onto the back street, go five blocks, then take us back over to Central. Not once will you touch the brakes. Understood?"

Voice full of fear, Gardiner said, "Yes."

"Then move!"

The Yukon pulled away from the building and exited the parking lot at the back, getting onto the street that paralleled Central.

It wasn't going to be a perfect getaway, Chloe knew. With the snow, their tracks would be seen and easily followed. But the big truck would not be the right vehicle to do that in, so if the people in it thought the Yukon was worth checking out, they would have to radio it in and request another vehicle be dispatched.

She didn't let go of Kathy until they made the transition back over to Central. Behind them, she could see the lights of the second truck. As she'd suspected, it had stopped near the bank.

She looked out the front. No headlights coming toward them, only empty road.

As they passed a sign pointing toward the entrance to the interstate, she said, "Keep going straight."

It wasn't long before the unused space between buildings increased as the city thinned. At the Sun River, the road bent to the north, mirroring the contour of the waterway, then bent again before settling on a western direction once it finally crossed the water.

"Can I turn the lights on now?" Gardiner asked.

With the city truly behind them, there were no streetlamps to help with navigation.

Chloe thought for a moment, then shook her head. "Not yet. Stay in the middle. You'll be fine."

The decision turned out to be a good one. When the Yukon topped a slight rise, a lit-up barricade similar to the roadblock on the interstate came into view. It was about a half mile away.

"Foot off the gas," Chloe said. "But don't touch the

brake."

The doctor did as ordered, and the SUV slowed to a crawl.

Chloe brought up the map on her cell again, this time switching to satellite view. A glowing dot indicated their position on the map. Just ahead and on the right was what looked like a dirt road that ran up to a farm. It stopped there, but on either side were fields that ran along the highway for at least a mile.

"Okay, let's go, but keep your speed way down," she said. "We're looking for a road on our right."

The road was heralded by a large mailbox and an old sign that read FRESH EGGS. The ground was bumpy, so the doctor had to lower their speed even more. While the fields that surrounded the farmhouse were open, the home and the barn were fenced in on three sides. Unfortunately, the only way to get to the rear of the fields without being spotted from the road was through the farmhouse area.

"Keep to the right," Chloe directed as soon as they entered the property. "Past the barn."

The doctor followed Chloe's directions, slowing as they neared the fence again.

"Drive along it." Several seconds later, she pointed out the window. "There. Roll to a stop."

As she'd hoped, there was a gate in the fence, no doubt to allow farm equipment in and out of the field.

Once the car was stopped, Chloe said, "Mrs. Gardiner, you'll need to get out and open that for us. I know you might be tempted to run for help, but the moment you start doing anything other than what I've asked, we will leave you behind. If that happens, you will *never* see your family again. That's not a threat. It's simply a fact."

"I won't go anywhere," Kathy said.

Chloe put a hand on Emily's arm, just in case the woman had any plans to pull her daughter out with her. "Make it quick."

Kathy opened the door, shut it again, and ran over to the fence. It took her a moment, but finally the gate swung open, and she hurried back into the SUV.

"Good," Chloe said as the woman settled back in her seat. She let go of Emily and tapped the back of the doctor's seat. "Stay to the back of the field as far from the highway as you can. Keep your speed down, but keep it moving. Go."

She had not been willing to take the chance of letting the Gardiners grab their winter gear before they left, so it wasn't surprising that Kathy was now shivering. Using her free hand, Chloe removed the few items she'd been carrying in the pockets of her own jacket, took it off, and handed it to the woman. "Here. This will help."

"You should have given that to her before she went outside," the doctor said, a touch of anger in his voice.

"You're right. I should have. I'm sorry," she said, meaning it.

She kept an eye on the roadblock as the Yukon bounced and dipped its way across the field. There were no signs of anyone getting out of the truck, no sudden spotlight streaking across the field toward the SUV, no warning shots booming through the air.

When the roadblock had receded to a distant halo of light behind them, Chloe instructed the doctor to head back to the highway. Five minutes later, they were on the snow-covered blacktop again, and able to increase their speed to twenty miles an hour.

"How much farther?" Gardiner asked.

"A ways."

Silence.

"Is there really a sick man where you're taking us?"

"Yes."

"Then maybe we should let my wife drive. She grew up out here. She's better in these kinds of conditions than I am. And I'm guessing you probably don't want me to be dead tired when we arrive."

It was the last point that sold her.

They stopped in the middle of the road, and the two older Gardiners switched positions.

"Can I turn the lights on now?" Kathy asked as she

buckled in.

Chloe thought about it, then nodded. “Okay.”

Once they were moving again, the doctor said, “Mind if I try to get a little rest?”

“Go for it.”

“You look pretty tired, too. Maybe you should get some sleep.”

She gave him a humorless grin. “Nice try, Doc.”

December 25th

Christmas Day

World Population
7,165,618,453

Change Over Previous Day
- 11,274,398

5

THE RANCH, MONTANA
3:52 AM MST

IT WAS NEARLY four in the morning when they reached the turnoff for the Ranch. Trees grew right up to the edge of the long dirt road leading to the home of the Resistance, helping to limit the amount of accumulated snow so far. Still, it took them another fifty minutes before they reached the burnt hulk of the Lodge, which had been the Ranch's main building.

"What happened?" Emily asked, unable to contain her curiosity.

"We had some unwanted visitors," Chloe said. She leaned forward and pointed to where the road passed the Lodge and went back up a small hill into the trees. "Go up there, and stop right at the top."

Kathy steered the SUV around the grounds and up the slope.

As soon as they stopped moving, Chloe said, "Kill the engine."

Kathy did so.

Chloe held out her hand. "Keys."

Kathy pulled them out of the ignition, her hand shaking slightly.

"Don't be nervous. You're going to be thanking me soon enough." Once Chloe had the keys, she said, "We'll be outside for a few minutes. It's going to be cold, but it won't be for long."

"You want your coat back?" Kathy asked. She had taken it off once she warmed up, so it was sitting in the front passenger seat.

"No. You can use it."

Instead of donning it, Kathy handed it to her daughter. "Honey, put this on when we get out."

"Okay You all out first," Chloe told them. "You can run, but as you saw, we're not close to anything. You're going to want to stick with me."

After the Gardiners exited, Chloe opened her own door. She leaned into the front and engaged the door locks in case the others had plans of jumping right back in once she was out. A moment later, she came around the front of the car and found them huddled together.

"Wh-which way?" the doctor asked.

"Follow me."

She led them through the woods to the emergency tunnel entrance. The hatch opened right before they arrived and Miller stuck his head out. "Wondering when you'd come back. Success, I assume?"

"Yeah," Chloe said.

"Come on in and get warm," he said, giving them all a wave before he disappeared back down the hole.

The doctor and his family looked at each other, their expressions uncertain.

Finally Gardiner said, "I'll go first." He lowered himself through the opening. A moment later, he called up, "It's okay. Send Emily down."

The daughter passed through the opening, but before Kathy stepped into the hole, she looked at Chloe. "If anything happens to my family, *you* will be the one who pays," she said. She climbed down into the tunnel without waiting for a response.

As soon as Chloe was inside, Miller closed the hatch and led them down the tunnel.

"How is he?" Chloe asked, hoping they weren't too late.

"No change," Miller said.

She allowed herself a brief, relieved smile.

"What *is* this place?" the doctor asked.

"We call it the Bunker," Miller told him. "The whole property's known as the Ranch. We try to keep it simple around here."

At the end of the tunnel, they stepped around the large, thick, blast-like door into the true Bunker.

"What the hell?" the doctor said, as the Gardiners all stopped in the middle of the hall.

The Bunker was a labyrinth of well-lit corridors and rooms that served as the Resistance's underground control facility. Despite the lack of windows, its new, clean look made people quickly forget they were underground.

"Come on," Chloe said. "There's no time to waste."

The doctor and his family stayed where they were for another moment before they caught up.

"How big is this place?" he asked.

"Big," Chloe said. "You can take the tour later. Right now you need to help my friend."

They navigated to the medical area. Even at this early hour, there were over a dozen people moving around. The door to the patient room was closed. Through the window, Chloe could see Josie Ash sitting next to her father's bed, asleep.

Lily Franklin looked up from the desk where she was sitting. "A doctor?" she asked, hopeful. In the wake of Billy's death, her nurse's training made her the ranking medical officer.

Chloe pointed at Gardiner. "Him."

"The others?"

"His family."

Lily glanced at a woman across the room. "Vicky, we need three inoculations." She turned back to Chloe. "Unless you already took care of that."

"I didn't have any vaccine with me."

"Vaccine? What vaccine?" Gardiner said.

"The Sage Flu." She looked into Ash's room. "I'll get Josie out of the way."

"Hold on." Gardiner grabbed her arm. "You have a vaccine for the Sage Flu?"

"Remember when I said I was going to save your lives? I wasn't lying."

"No one has a vaccine."

"We do."

"How do you know it even works?"

"It works."

Vicky approached them, three syringes in her hand. "Which arm do you prefer?"

"No one is sticking anything into any of us until I know what's in there," Gardiner said. "Who knows what you might be putting into us."

Lily grabbed one of the syringes, stuck it in her own arm, and depressed the plunger. The whole time she kept her eyes locked on the doctor. "Worse case, it's not going to hurt you. Best, we're right, and we'll have saved you from being one of the billions who are about to die. Or would you rather take your chances outside?"

"How can you have a vaccine?"

"Because we knew it was coming," Chloe said.

"Then why didn't everyone else know?"

"People didn't want to listen."

"Brad," Kathy said. "Maybe we should take it, just in case."

"Either do it or don't," Chloe said. "I don't care. But you need to get in there and help my friend."

Gardiner looked into Ash's room, then at his wife. Finally he gave Vicky a nod. While she administered shots to the two women, a fourth syringe was retrieved and the doctor was inoculated.

"All right," he said. "Let's see what's wrong with the patient."

6

SIERRA NEVADA MOUNTAINS
7:17 AM PST

AT FIRST MRS. Weber was the only one showing signs of the flu. Then, around ten p.m., Donny began coughing. By one a.m., everyone in the house except Martina was sick.

The only sleep Martina had been able to get was half an hour sometime during the night when she'd sat down at the dining table, only meaning to rest her eyes. She had woken to the sound of Riley hacking on the couch.

Since then, she'd been moving from room to room, giving those who were still conscious water, and wiping everyone's face with a cool towel.

Memories of the outbreak the previous spring kept coming to her. As one of victims, she remembered what the illness had felt like. The pain in her chest from coughing, the weakness in her muscles, and the overwhelming sensation that all she wanted to do was sleep. But she and all her friends who got sick that day had lived.

That was the hope she was clinging to—that her family and the Webers would live, too.

As she walked back to the kitchen, she cut the corner coming out of the hallway too close and stubbed her toe against the wall.

"Ow! Dammit!"

Hopping on her other foot, she grabbed her injured toe and inspected the damage. The top half of the nail was bent back a quarter inch, and she could feel blood pooling where it had been. She closed her eyes and gritted her teeth, letting a wave of pain pass through her.

You're such an idiot. You need to pay attention!

She hopped into the kitchen and raised her foot into the sink. Repositioning the faucet, she let cold water flow over her toe. It was painful at first, but soon the wounded area grew numb. As carefully as she could, she bent the nail back into place, then got a dish towel and wrapped it around the injury.

"So stupid," she muttered. Lowering her foot to the floor, she found she could walk if she put most of her weight on her heel.

She thought about sitting down for a few minutes, but there had been something that needed doing. What was it? She racked her brain, and glanced back at the wall she'd hit her toe against.

Water! That was it. She needed to do another round for everyone. She filled a cup and stopped first at Riley and Donny, the two in the living room.

"Here you go," Martina said, lifting Donny's head so she could dribble some of the liquid into his mouth. He coughed, and everything she'd poured in came flying out. "Donny, come on!" She knew he couldn't help it, but it was so frustrating.

When he settled down, she tried again. This time, she was able to get about a quarter of a cup down without it spewing back out. She moved over to Riley.

"Have some water."

Riley opened her eyes halfway. She was the last to get sick, and wasn't quite as bad off as the others yet. "Not sure…I'm…thirsty."

"Just a little bit, okay? You need it."

Riley tried to nod. "Okay."

Martina tilted the cup to her friend's lips.

When she had at first started giving everyone drinks, she'd used separate cups for each person, but she soon gave that up. They all had the same thing, after all. It wasn't like they could make each other sicker.

"Thanks," Riley said when she'd had enough. "I'm…sorry you have…to…do this…by your…self."

"Don't have anything better to do."

As Martina stood up, Riley said, "Hey."

"Yeah?"

"Merry Christmas."

Martina had totally forgotten. "Yeah, merry Christmas."

She went to her parents' room next. They didn't open their eyes when she poured water into their mouths.

Pamela had moved into the other bedroom with Mrs. Weber. Martina gave some to the girl before circling the bed to Pamela and Riley's mom.

"Time for some water," she said. She didn't expect a response. Mrs. Weber hadn't been awake for hours.

She put a hand under the woman's neck to raise her head, but quickly dropped it. Mrs. Weber's skin was ice cold. Martina touched the woman's forehead. It was the same. Not wanting to do it, but knowing she had no choice, she felt Mrs. Weber's wrist for a pulse. When she let go, she started to cry.

"What?" Pamela asked, her voice weak.

"Nothing," Martina said, silencing her tears. How do you tell a young girl her mother had just died? "Go back to sleep."

Pamela mumbled something, then fell silent.

Martina limped her way out of the room, back into the main part of the cabin.

They're all going to die. All of them.

It suddenly felt as if the cabin were squeezing in on her, the air disappearing second by second.

She ran to the front door as fast as her stubbed toe would let her, wanting nothing more than to get out of the house. She grabbed her jacket off the hook, pulled it on, and started to don her boots but switched to her father's instead. They were big enough that she should be able to keep the towel wrapped around the top of her foot.

Outside, the air was crisp and clear. She took a deep breath. As she exhaled, a cloud of vapor momentarily obscured her vision. She repeated the process two more times, feeling a bit more in control with each clearing of her lungs.

When she felt panic would no longer overtake her, she wondered what she should do about Mrs. Weber. At some point she would have to move her out of the house, right?

Not if I get sick, too.

If? When, right? *When* she got sick?

Everyone else had come down with it. She was just the last. Someone had to be. But, with the exception of Mrs. Weber, they had all fallen sick within a couple hours of each other. Here it was, five hours since the last one—Riley—had fallen ill, and Martina still felt fine.

Well, exhausted and scared out of her mind, but not physically ill.

It hasn't hit you yet, that's all.

She walked over to the car and climbed into the passenger seat. The keys were still in the ignition. As she turned on the electrical system, the lights on the radio came on, and a voice came out of the speakers.

"…time. North Korea has released a statement claiming that their borders are free and clear of the disease, and that the North Korean people are unaffected and will remain so. It's important to note that this statement was sent in email form to all major media outlets, and was unsigned. North Korean state television has been showing a series of patriotic still images accompanied by music since right after—"

She turned the dial, hoping to find something else, anything but news. She discovered two other stations, but both were more of the same. At one point, she came across a quick hit of music, but then it was gone, and her attempts to get it back failed.

She switched the car off and stared out the window.

What am I going to do?

7

MONTANA
8:40 AM MST

FOR THE PAST few days, as Brandon had been on the run, his rest had been spotty at best. It was little wonder, then, that on Christmas Eve, with the snow outside his lean-to muffling all sound, he had fallen into a deep sleep for the first time since he'd left the Ranch.

On Christmas morning, he woke with the gradualness of a summer vacation day, slowly coming back to consciousness as his mind chased the wisp of a forgotten dream—not the running one this time, but something warm and inviting and happy.

It was the cold that finally reminded him where he was. At some point during the night, he'd slipped his head inside his sleeping bag, leaving only a small hole for air to pass through. It was more than enough, though, for the frigid tendrils of the winter morning to worm their way around his cheeks and across his nose.

He opened the hole wider and stuck his face out. For a second he couldn't breathe, the cold a stark contrast to the heat of his bag. Once the shock passed, he looked around. The lean-to had worked incredibly well. Snow was piled against it nearly halfway up, yet none of the dead branches that made up the structure had collapsed in on him during the night.

He twisted in the bag so he could see the open end of his temporary house. It appeared that a good foot and a half of snow had fallen during the night. Though it was still cloudy, it wasn't snowing now.

A white Christmas.

A year ago he would have gotten a thrill from that. Not today.

Keeping his legs within the warmth of his sleeping bag, he removed a package of trail mix from his backpack, and ate half of it before forcing himself to stop. He couldn't be sure when he would next find shelter and more food, so he had to conserve his supplies.

A fire would have been nice, but while he had the book of matches that he'd found in Mr. Hayes's pocket, no way could he find any wood to burn that wasn't wet from the snow. So, with reluctance, he extracted himself from his sleeping bag, pulled on his boots, and packed up.

When he reached the highway a few minutes later, he spotted two rutted tracks running down the middle that definitely had not been there before.

A car, he thought. Judging by the several inches of snow that had accumulated in each trench, he realized it had come by sometime in the early morning while he was sleeping.

He grimaced at the lost chance of hitching a ride. At least the passing vehicle had done him one favor. By walking in one of the depressions, he was able to make better time than he would have otherwise.

Like the day before, he was struck by the silence. Was this how it would be from now on? Had the world turned quiet? Not the kind of thoughts a kid his age should be having, but as much as he wanted to be home looking through his baseball card collection or reading the latest X-Men, he knew *that* Brandon was gone. He wasn't even a teenager yet, but at times he felt like he was already an adult.

Around noon, a noise in the distance momentarily cut through the silence. It was there for a second, then gone, not long enough to identify. Snow falling out of a tree, maybe? He'd seen that happen a couple of times already. There would be a crack of a branch as the weight of the snow became too much to bear, and snow and limb would come crashing down together.

Or maybe the sound had been nothing. Just his imagination.

He shook that thought away the moment he had it. *Not* nothing. He couldn't let himself think that way.

It's a truck, he decided. *And it's coming this way.*

He could envision a pickup truck with a heated cab slicing through the snow, obliterating the tracks left by the car. *No, no. A big rig.* One with a sleeping cabin in back, and a built-in refrigerator stocked with food. It would stop as soon as the driver saw him, and the man behind the wheel would offer him a ride to wherever he wanted to go.

The Ranch, if he wanted.

Except there was nothing at the Ranch anymore. He'd seen Project Eden's attack on the Resistance's headquarters, had seen the smoke rising in the air. He was sure anyone left alive in the Bunker had been taken away by the men in the helicopters.

No. There was no going back to the Ranch.

Thoughts of the attack darkened his mood. He tried to concentrate on the imaginary truck again. It was big and red and had a horn like a train whistle. It would be pulling a trailer full of—

The noise again.

Not an illusion.

A rumble, not quite as far away as before. But not the kind of rumble he associated with a truck.

An airplane?

He looked to the sky, but the clouds were still low and gray. If there were a plane up there, it wouldn't be able to see him.

It's gotta be a car. It has to be something on the road, right?

He heard it again, even closer. Whatever it was, it was coming fast, which meant it couldn't be a car or even a truck, not with the snow on the road.

His shoulders sagged. A plane, flying above the clouds.

"Keep walking," he said. "You'll find something soon."

He all but tuned the noise out as he continued down the road, but as the noise grew even closer, he couldn't help but notice the distinct sound it was making.

Whoop-whoop-whoop.

Not an airplane. A helicopter.

The helicopters that had flown over the Ranch during the attack flashed through his mind. He could almost see the one that had hovered outside the barn while he and Mr. Hayes had hidden in the horse stalls.

It had to be the Project Eden people. They were coming for him.

Just as the thought finished, the dark silhouette of a helicopter dipped below the clouds about a quarter mile away. Brandon whipped his head side to side, looking for someplace to hide, but over the last couple of miles the trees on the right had moved farther from the road, and on the left they had disappeared altogether.

He looked back the way he'd come. The road had been taking a gentle curve. About a hundred yards behind him, the ground to the east dipped several feet, creating a short drop-off. Along the wall of the drop there appeared to be some kind of opening that ran under the road. A storm drain? A pipe?

Whatever it was, it was better than standing out in the open.

He started to run, each step a struggle as he pulled a foot out of the snow and sank it back in again. Every few seconds, he glanced over his shoulder. Though he could hear the helicopter coming closer, it had disappeared into the clouds again.

It didn't see you, it didn't see you. It didn't.

A few seconds later, the helicopter suddenly broke through the clouds right above the culvert Brandon had been heading toward. He stumbled in surprise and fell to the ground.

Keep moving!

He rose unsteadily to his feet as the helicopter descended to the road. Any thin hope he still had that those on board hadn't seen him disappeared.

The culvert no longer an option, he turned south. He tried to run, but the snow was too high and he ended up more in a loping jog.

Someone shouted at him, but Brandon didn't stop. It wasn't long, though, before he heard the crush of snow under boots coming up fast behind him. He grabbed both straps of his pack and tried to increase his speed.

"Hey, stop!" one of the people pursuing him yelled.

There was something odd about the voice, something that triggered a memory. Brandon's family's house at Barker Flats. Josie sick in the bathroom, and his mother—though he didn't know it at the time—dead in his parents' bedroom. The paramedics who burst into the house had all been wearing protective clothing and hoods that enclosed their heads. When they talked, their voices sounded very much like the one yelling at him now. Muffled.

"Kid! We're not going to hurt you!"

Someone grabbed Brandon's backpack and jerked him to a stop. A hand gripped him by the shoulders and twisted him around. There were two men, both outfitted in dark green plastic-looking suits and hooded masks.

"Where do you think you're going?" the one who'd turned him asked.

Brandon tried to pull away from him.

"Relax, buddy. We're here to help you. Tell us your name."

Brandon tried to shrug off the man's grip, but he wasn't strong enough. "Please, let me go!"

The man glanced back at his partner. "Saunders, a little help."

Saunders took hold of Brandon's other arm.

"You can walk or we carry you. Either way, you're coming with us," the first man said.

Brandon knew there was nothing he could do. Even if he were able to break free of their grasps, he wouldn't get more than a few steps before they caught him again.

"I'll walk," he said.

He wondered where they were going to take him. Back

to the Ranch? Was that where they were keeping the others? Or someplace else?

At least he'd be with his sister.

Unless something had happened to her.

Don't even think that. Josie's fine. They're all fine. You'll see them soon.

As they neared the helicopter, he noticed something he hadn't seen earlier, something he knew wasn't on the helicopters that had attacked the Ranch. Painted in black along the tail were the words UNITED STATES ARMY.

THE BUNKER
12:21 PM MST

JOSIE PACED THE hallway right outside the alcove that served as the Bunker's dining area, too worked up to sit for even a moment.

Chloe had tried to get her to eat something, but Josie had only shaken her head. How could she eat when her father—her only living parent—was in surgery, and her brother was lost in the wilderness? If either of them didn't survive, she wasn't sure she'd ever be able to eat again. So back and forth she went, her mind both numb and hyper-alert.

She heard the footsteps before she saw the three women turn down the hallway in front of her—Rachel Hamilton with the woman and the girl Chloe had brought back with the doctor.

As they neared her, Rachel stopped, her eyes full of compassion. "I take it there hasn't been any news."

Josie shook her head. "No."

"I'm sure everything's going to be fine."

Josie nodded, but said nothing as she rocked from foot to foot.

"Have you met Emily and Kathy?" Rachel asked. "I believe you and Emily are the same age."

"Hey," Emily said, holding out her hand.

Josie hesitated a moment, then shook it. "Hey."

"My dad's a good doctor," Emily said. "If your dad can be fixed, he'll fix him."

"He can be fixed," Josie said quickly.

"I'm sure he can. I was just saying—"

"I know what you were saying."

After an awkward couple of seconds, Rachel donned a smile, and said to Emily and Kathy, "Who's hungry?"

Josie grimaced as the other three walked into the alcove. She shouldn't have snapped. Emily was only trying to be nice. Josie's father would not have been happy with her.

With a sigh, she turned and walked over to the table where the women had just sat down. "I'm sorry," she said. "That was…well…"

Rachel touched Josie on the arm. "It's okay. We all know you're worried about your dad." She patted the bench next to her. "I'm sure you could use something to eat. Why don't you join us?"

"I'm fine."

"At least have something to drink. Water?"

Josie had to admit she was thirsty, so she nodded and took the offered seat.

Raising her voice, Rachel said, "Bobbie?"

Bobbie, the Ranch's cook, stuck her head out the kitchen door. "Morning, Rachel."

"Morning. We have a couple of newcomers who could use some breakfast. This is Kathy Gardiner and her daughter, Emily."

Bobbie smiled. "Ladies. You came in with the doctor?"

Kathy nodded. "My husband."

"Welcome. It's good to have you, *and* your husband. How do eggs, bacon, and some hash browns sound?"

"Good," Kathy said. "Um, great, actually."

"Scrambled? Fried?"

"Fried," Kathy told her.

"Can I have mine sunny side up?" Emily asked.

"You can have them any way you want," Bobbie said. "That's what I'm here for."

"Can you send out four bottles of water when you get a chance?" Rachel asked.

"Will do." Bobbie disappeared back into the kitchen.

"Bobbie's a great cook," Rachel said. "You're in for a treat."

Kathy gave a halfhearted smile. It was clear she was still trying to process everything that had happened since Chloe took them from their home.

"How long have you lived here?" Emily asked Josie.

"I don't. I mean, *we* don't. My dad and my brother and me, we just visit sometimes."

"Oh. Well, where are you from, then?"

That was a good question. Their last home had been in Iowa, but they weren't there very long. Before that? "My dad was in the army. We traveled…"

Josie lost all train of thought as she spotted Matt and the doctor heading down the hallway toward the dining area.

She stared at them, unable to take another breath. She'd been desperately waiting for news about her father, but suddenly wasn't sure she wanted to know what the doctor had to say. What if the news was bad? What if her father hadn't made it? If the latter were the case, then every second she didn't know was another second her father would still be alive in her mind.

Emily twisted around, following Josie's gaze. As soon as she realized who was coming, she jumped out of her seat and ran to her father. Kathy was up a second later, following right behind her daughter. All three hugged as if they'd been separated for months.

"You're okay?" the doctor asked. "Any problems?"

Kathy shook her head, and Emily said, "They're making us breakfast."

"Now that sounds like a great idea," he said. As they turned toward the table, Matt whispered something to the man, and they both glanced at Josie. The doctor nodded and walked over to her. "You're my patient's daughter. Josie, right?"

Josie nodded, unable to speak.

"Then I guess you're the one I need to talk to."

This time her nod was so slight she almost didn't move her head.

"As I'm sure you were aware, your dad was pretty banged up."

This is it, she thought. *This is the part when he tells me he couldn't do anything.* She braced herself.

"Shrapnel cut through part of his intestines and destroyed one of his kidneys."

"Brad!" Kathy said. "She's just a girl. You can't tell her that."

"She deserves to know," he said, and looked at Josie again. "You want to know, right?"

Want? No. She didn't want to know anything. But she *had* to know, so she nodded again.

"Also, one of his ribs punctured a lung." The doctor paused. "But your dad is tough, a fighter. And thank God for the medical facility you have here. It's top-notch. If he'd been anywhere else short of a fully equipped hospital, I doubt he would have made it."

It took Josie a moment to process his words. "He…he's okay?"

"He's not okay. Not by a long shot. But he will be."

She shot to her feet and threw her arms around him. "Thank you," she said. "Thank you."

She gave him one last squeeze before sprinting out of the alcove and down the hall. When she reached the surgical room, she threw open the door and rushed in. But the room was unoccupied.

Of course he wouldn't be here, she chastised herself. He'd be back in the room they had him in before.

She raced out the door and down the hall again. Before she reached the medical suite, she nearly ran into Chloe, running out of another corridor.

"I just heard," Chloe said, falling in beside Josie. "He's going to be okay."

Josie glanced at her but made no reply, afraid that if she acknowledged it she might jinx everything and make it untrue. She needed to see her father first. She needed to see him alive and breathing.

They rushed through the open door of the medical suite, into the observation area. Behind the glass wall of patient room number one, they could see Lily in scrubs and a mask, checking the bag hanging from the IV stand. On the bed next to her lay Josie's father, an oxygen tube running under his nose. Josie watched his chest move up and down, and sighed in relief.

"He looks good," Chloe said.

She was right. He *did* look good, or at least better than before. There was color in his face now, and he seemed to be resting a lot more comfortably.

When Lily noticed them, she came out and pulled the mask off her face.

"He's going to be okay?" Josie asked, wanting the confirmation from someone she knew.

"We'll need a little more time before we know for sure."

"But it's looking good, right?"

Lily gave her a tired smile. "Yes. It's looking good."

Josie almost laughed as she hugged first Lily, then Chloe. "Can I go in and see him?"

"He's still unconscious, and probably will be for another day at least."

"I don't care."

Lily hesitated a second, then nodded. "Sure, but you need to wear a mask and gloves. And you have to scrub up first." She pointed toward the sink attached to the wall, and glanced at Chloe. "I suppose you want to go in, too."

"I'm fine out here," Chloe said. "Just glad to know he's going to live."

"We all are."

MATT WATCHED AS Josie raced away from the cafeteria, happy that the girl had finally received some good news.

"I really didn't think he was going to make it," Rachel

said, moving up next to him.

He glanced at his sister. "Neither did I."

"Any news on Brandon?"

He shook his head. "Christina's been trying to get us a good satellite image of the area, but nothing useful yet."

"He's a smart kid, and his dad prepared him well. He'll be okay." She paused. "I received confirmation that the package arrived in Atlanta."

"Good," he said, though he knew it wouldn't change anything. Still, they had to try every angle they could. "I'm going to head over to the comm room." He glanced at Dr. Gardiner and his family. "Do you mind staying with them? I'm sure they're going to have a lot of questions."

"Already been asking."

The communications room was a quick walk down the hall. As it seemed to always be now, the room was buzzing with activity. For the first few days after the virus was released, they had monitored the growing disaster, hoping that somehow, someway it would fail. Of course it hadn't.

As of that morning, Matt had ordered everyone to begin LIC—locate-inoculate-consolidate. Their task was to find pockets of uninfected survivors, get them vaccine, and bring everyone together before Project Eden could move in and eliminate them. The only ones excused from LIC were Christina and her small team. Their focus was on finding Brandon.

It was a massive undertaking, one destined to fail over and over again, but Matt knew they would have successes, too. That's what they had to focus on.

It had been long assumed that radio would be the main way they'd find survivors, so the Resistance had computers placed around the world that were now automatically monitoring as many frequencies as possible for signals that might indicate survivors.

Kenji Yamabe, LIC's project leader, had co-opted the largest monitor in the room to display a list of discovered survivor sites and their statuses.

"That's it?" Matt asked. The list was woefully short, no

more than three dozen locations.

“It’s still early,” Kenji said.

The Resistance had predicted that the first several days after the release of the virus would be quiet, as people who weren’t already infected hunkered down and did what they could to survive. At some point they would reach out for help. That’s when things would start getting really busy. Still, Matt didn’t have to like waiting for that point to be reached. He wanted their field teams to be actively distributing the vaccine now, not sitting around while more and more died.

It would have been great if they could have roamed the streets and inoculated everyone they saw, sick or not, but their supply of the vaccine derived from Daniel Ash’s immunity was limited. They couldn’t afford to waste a single dose on someone who was going to die of the flu anyway.

Matt stared at the screen.

Thirty-eight groups, representing a total of probably not more than a thousand people. Barely a drop in the ocean of humanity.

There will be more, he thought.

There has to be.

8

CENTERS FOR DISEASE CONTROL AND PREVENTION
ATLANTA, GEORGIA
2:38 PM EST

IMMEDIATELY FOLLOWING THE president's briefing the previous evening, Dr. Esposito had flown back to Atlanta and gone straight to his lab at the CDC, arriving shortly before one a.m.

As he'd requested, his whole team was waiting for him when he walked in. The first thing everyone wanted to know was why the president had said there would be a vaccine in no more than a year. Esposito let them voice their frustrations for a few minutes before holding up his hand to quiet them.

"The simple truth is that the vaccine will be done when it's done," he'd said.

"Then why didn't he say that?" one of the technicians asked.

"To save lives." He explained what the CDC director had told him, then said, "Our job is to create that vaccine as quickly as we can. If that takes more than a year, so be it. But the sooner we get it done, the more lives we save."

"What if we don't have a year?" another of his team members asked. "I mean, this thing is tearing through everyone. There might not even be anyone to vaccinate in a month, let alone a year."

A few others raised their voices in agreement.

Esposito held up his hand again. "Yes, many people are going to die, but at some point it's sure to level off. We've seen that before with other outbreaks. There will be *plenty* of people still around, people who will need our vaccine. We all have to believe that, otherwise there is no reason for us to even continue. If *any* of you are ready to give up, you need to leave now. We are at the front line of the fight for the very existence of our species, and it's up to us to ensure that we win. I don't need anyone on this team who isn't one hundred percent dedicated to that. So, does anyone want out?" He scanned the faces in front of him, but no one said a word. "Good. Then we need to get to work. Speed is paramount. I've never said this before, but this time cut corners if you have to. Just get us to a solution."

Despite the hour, they had all gone back to work. By the time morning arrived, a few had crawled off to catch a few hours of sleep, while most kept at the task of studying the virus's genetic makeup and coming up with potential ways to kill it.

Around nine a.m., a package arrived for Dr. Esposito. It was a square box, about six inches on each side. There were no postage stamps or labels from one of the overnight delivery companies, only what had been printed on top—his name and address at the CDC, the name DEARING LABORATORIES in the spot for the return address, and URGENT printed across the bottom. He had never heard of Dearing before, and had no idea what was inside.

"How did this arrive?" he asked the woman who'd brought it in. With the curfew, getting any package was a surprise.

"I don't know. Messenger, I guess. I wasn't there when it came in," she said, then left.

Esposito carried it over to his desk and set it down, intending to open it to see what was so urgent. But as he leaned over to grab his scissors, a drop of liquid hit the back of his hand. He jerked up in surprise, and felt another drop trickle onto his upper lip. He touched it. Mucus, draining from his right nostril.

He grabbed a tissue and wiped the discharge from his face, then said, "Everyone, stop what you're doing."

They all looked at him.

"How is everyone feeling?"

A few shrugs.

"Tired," someone said.

"Yeah. Definitely," another agreed.

"Anyone feel ill?" Esposito asked. "Like you have a cold, maybe?"

Surprise and concern spread across the faces of his team, no one missing the significance of the question.

"I feel okay," Paige said. She was the one closest to him.

"Me, too," Ralph added.

Others nodded and said words to the same effect.

Across the room, Carol Burton raised her hand. "I have a headache. Is that what you mean?"

Almost as one, everyone in the room turned toward her.

Esposito had a headache, too, but that wasn't unusual when he was working on a difficult problem, so it hadn't even registered until now. "Any other symptoms?"

She shook her head. "No."

Maybe he was overreacting. He just hadn't had any sleep, that's all. Plus the flight to DC probably hadn't helped. The air on planes was notoriously dry, so it would have been easy for his nose to become irritated.

He took in a breath to calm himself, but as the air passed into his lungs, he could feel the hint of a scratch in his throat. Without saying anything, he turned to his computer, brought up the security system for his lab, and entered the code activating a lockdown.

His lab was actually a series of connected rooms, some for delicate, hands-on work that required wearing special suits and passing through chambers designed to keep deadly bugs from escaping, and some, like the room they were now in, used for more theoretical work and not considered high risk. No virus or other harmful agent was ever present there, not on purpose, anyway. But the CDC was a cautious organization, and had built in the ability for Esposito's entire lab complex to be sealed off from the rest of the building.

The thud was loud and unmistakable as the isolation locks on the exits engaged.

"What the hell?" Ralph said, looking toward the door.

A few of the others jumped up.

"Why did that lock?"

"What's going on?"

The light on Esposito's phone started to blink. Security, no doubt, calling to find out what was going on.

"Everyone sit," Esposito said, ignoring the phone for a moment. "*I* engaged the lockdown."

"Why?" Ralph asked.

To answer, Esposito grabbed another tissue and blew his nose.

They all stared at him.

"That doesn't mean you have it," Ralph said.

"Let's hope you're right. But until we know for sure, those doors stay locked."

"Jesus," Tom Hauldon said.

"I want everyone to write down who you've been in contact with, so we can figure out how the virus might have gotten in here, and who outside needs to be quarantined."

Someone pounded on the door, and looked through the small window centered in the top half. It was Wayne Kovacs, the CDC's assistant director. He caught Esposito's eyes and raised his hand so Esposito could see the cell phone he was holding.

Esposito looked back at his desk phone. The line that had been blinking cut off for two seconds, then started to blink again. The doctor picked up the receiver and punched the button.

3:17 PM EST

"IT'S POSITIVE," MATTY said.

Esposito could almost see the hope drain from his

colleagues' faces. His own face, though, remained neutral, a part of him having accepted the fact he'd come down with SF-B.

"What about my test?" Carol asked.

Paige checked her results. "Also positive."

Carol collapsed into her chair. "Oh, God."

That seemed to be the trigger everyone was waiting for as panicked conversations broke out all over the room. Before Esposito could do anything about it, his phone rang.

He picked it up. "What?"

"The results?" Wayne Kovacs asked.

"Positive."

"Just you or both?"

"Both."

"Oh, shit."

"Would it have been better if it were just me?"

"That's not what I meant," the assistant director said. "Michael, we can't let you out of there."

"Don't you think I know that? Why do you think I locked us down?" He hung up.

For a few seconds, he seriously considered giving up and letting everyone do what they wanted. But he couldn't. This was bigger than the people gathered in the room with him, whether they were infected or not.

He raised his hands. "Everybody, quiet."

No one seemed to hear him.

"Hey!" he shouted, and let out a shrill whistle. "Quiet!"

That did the trick.

"We have two choices," he said.

"Die or die?" someone suggested.

"We don't know if we're all going to die."

"Ninety-nine percent mortality rate," Norman Chu shot back.

"That was the first wave of SF-A," Esposito said. "We don't know if SF-B will behave the same."

"So it could be even higher," Chu said.

"Or lower," Esposito said. "The thing is, there's a chance one or more of us will be able to walk out of this room when this is all over. But that's not what I'm talking about."

An uneasy quiet fell over the room, everyone staring at him.

"We can feel sorry for ourselves until this is over, or we could try to get some work done, and make some progress for those who'll be taking on the task after us. Maybe even take advantage of our situation. We're all test subjects now." He paused. "You can each choose what you want to do, but I'm going to work."

The silence that followed lasted only a few seconds. Then Ralph said, "We should run tests on everyone right away. Establish a baseline of those infected and not infected. Then we pull blood every half hour so we can chart progress."

"Excellent idea. So I take it you're with me."

Ralph looked around at his peers and nodded.

"I'm with you, too," Cindy said.

"Me, too," Paige announced.

By the time they finished going around the room, everyone, even Norman Chu, had agreed to continue.

"Keep detailed notes," Esposito said, once they'd divided up the work. "Clear, understandable notes. Assume you'll never be able to speak to whoever will use them. If any of you have something you want to run by the group, shout it out. Anything else?"

No one said anything.

"Let's get to work."

As he sat back down, he absently moved the box from Dearing Laboratories—a fictitious name used by the Resistance—onto the shelf behind his desk to get it out of his way, never knowing that three vials of the vaccine they were trying to create were inside.

SITUATION ROOM, THE WHITE HOUSE
3:22 PM EST

"THAT'S CONFIRMED?...THEN have them run it

again!...Yes, again...Call me as soon as you have the results." The director of the CDC hung up the phone.

The others gathered around the table—the president's chief of staff; his national security advisor; the attorney general; and the secretaries of Homeland Security, Defense, and Health and Human Services—were all staring at him, waiting. Like him, they were all wearing surgical masks.

"The preliminary test is positive," the director said.

The secretary of defense blanched. "Good God."

"I've ordered a second test to be sure. I'm told that only two people in the lab are experiencing symptoms, and even those are mild at this point."

"What's the chance the first test could be wrong?" Dale Gilford, the president's chief of staff, asked.

The director hesitated. "It's unclear. The test was developed based on the original strain of Sage Flu, and even then it would occasionally misidentify a case of everyday flu as Sage."

"Give me a number."

The director didn't answer right away. He looked uncomfortable, as if he'd been backed into a corner. Finally he shrugged. "Ten percent."

"Ten percent that it's wrong."

"Yes."

Gilford stood up. "I'm having the president moved to Camp David."

One of those who'd tested positive was Dr. Michael Esposito, who'd been sitting in this very room a little over twelve hours before. Even more troubling, he'd had an in-person briefing with the president. If Esposito was showing signs now, that must mean he'd already been infected or perhaps became infected while he was in Washington.

Which meant the virus had entered the White House.

"Maybe he should be flown directly to Lark River," the secretary of Homeland Security suggested.

Lark River was the code name for a secret underground facility not far outside the capital where the president could stay for months, protected from the world outside.

"I'll suggest it," Gilford said. "But he won't go for it. Not unless there's no choice."

"Gil," the national security advisor said. "There may be no choice. This thing is spreading. Fast."

Gilford acknowledged the advisor with a solemn nod and walked out of the room. While the head of the NSA was right, Gilford knew his boss. The president would feel like he was running away if he went to Lark River. He would want to stay someplace more visible to the American public. Even Camp David was going to be a fight.

As he walked through the West Wing, he saw a group of staffers huddled together, talking. When they spotted him, their conversation ceased, and all eyes turned to the chief of staff. He passed by, grim-faced, but said nothing.

Eva Bennett, the president's secretary, looked up as Gilford approached her desk. Standing beside the doorway to the Oval Office was one of the president's secret service agents.

"He's talking to the British PM right now," Ms. Bennett said. "He should be off in a minute or two."

"He needs to be off now," Gilford said. "We need to initiate Rollout."

Immediately, the secret service agent raised his cuff to his mouth and relayed the order. Within seconds, his associates would be preparing for the president's departure.

Ms. Bennett had always been a rock, no matter what crisis they'd faced in the past. But for the first time ever, Gilford saw fear in her eyes.

"We'll leave as soon as he's ready," he said as he opened the door to the Oval Office.

The president was sitting behind the *Resolute* desk, his chair swiveled so that his back was to the door. Holding the phone to his ear, he looked over his shoulder and gave Gilford a nod of acknowledgment.

"We need to talk. Now," Gilford said, keeping his voice low so that the prime minister wouldn't hear him.

"That's right," the president said into the phone. "Absolutely agree."

Gilford walked all the way to the desk. "Mr. President, we don't have time to wait."

The president turned to Gilford, then said, "Prime Minister, I apologize, but I have a briefing I need to attend. Let's plan on reconnecting in a couple of hours...Yes, very important...okay." He hung up and looked at Gilford. "What is it?"

"It's time to get you out of here, sir. The staff is preparing Rollout right now."

"Call it off," the president said.

"Sir, it's not safe here anymore. We've confirmed there's been at least one infected person in the White House within the last day. It'll be safer to get you out of here."

"No, it won't."

The president's stubbornness was admirable, but this wasn't a budget fight on Capitol Hill. "Lark River would be best," Gilford said, "but, at the very least, Camp David would—"

"I'm not leaving."

"But, sir, if you stay, there's an excellent chance you'll be infected."

The president stared at him for a moment, his eyes looking more tired than Gilford had ever seen them. "Gil, I'm already infected."

It took Gilford a moment to register what the president had said. "Sir?"

"My eyes hurt. My throat's tender. And my sinuses are throbbing. I already have it."

Gilford froze, unable to speak.

"Let everyone leave who wants to," the president said. "In fact, you should encourage them to do so. I'm staying."

"The first lady? Your son?"

"Already on the way to Camp David. But I was with them this morning. Given the rate of transmission of this thing, they're most likely infected, too."

"Dear God."

"Go on, Gil. Let the staff go home to their families, then check the line of succession. Find out who's uninfected, get *them* to Lark River. Whoever's highest among them, tell them I'll be handing over my job soon."

Gilford walked out of the Oval Office, numb.

"When do we leave, sir?" the secret service agent asked.

Gilford blinked twice. "We don't," he said. He looked at Ms. Bennett. "Can you have everyone gather in the conference room? I'll be there in a few minutes."

"Of course," she said. "Gil, what's going on?"

Not even realizing she'd asked a question, Chief of Staff Gilford walked out of the room and down the hall to the private restroom just off his office, where he kneeled in front of the toilet and threw up.

9

MALMSTROM AIR FORCE BASE, MONTANA
1:57 PM MST

DESPITE THE BEST efforts of the men on the helicopter, Brandon remained silent. Though the markings on the outside of the craft claimed it belonged to the US Army, he was reluctant to believe it. The Project Eden people could have easily painted the same markings on *their* helicopters, he thought.

It wasn't until the craft touched down at a military base that he had to admit maybe the markings were genuine. There were several other aircraft around, though most seemed to belong to the air force, not the army.

Brandon was hustled across the tarmac into a warm, nearby building.

"Who we got here?" a man in uniform, also wearing a mask that covered his whole face, asked one of Brandon's escorts.

"Don't know. He's not talking. Found him walking down the middle of a road north of here. As far as we could tell, there was nothing else around him."

"All right, I'll take him."

One of the two escorts set Brandon's pack on the floor, while the other gave Brandon a pat on the back before they left.

"So, you going to tell us your name?" the new man said.

Brandon hesitated, but finally decided it might be okay.

"Brandon. Brandon Ash."

"Okay, Brandon Ash. Where are you from?"

"Um, Iowa."

"Iowa? I'm guessing you didn't walk from there. Where's your family?"

"I don't know," Brandon said.

"You got separated?"

Brandon wasn't sure how he should handle things. If he told the man the truth, it would lead to other questions that he didn't know the answers to. And, knowing adults, he didn't think the man and his friends would believe him anyway.

He decided to answer the man's question with a nod.

"So what happened?"

Brandon thought quickly. "We…we went out for a drive and got stuck in the snow. My dad went out to try and find help. When he didn't come back, I went to look for him."

"When was this?"

"Yesterday."

"You've been wandering around on your own since yesterday?"

A nod, though it had actually been longer than that.

"I imagine you're probably pretty hungry."

"Yes, sir."

"We'll get you some chow in a second. A couple more questions, all right?"

"Sure."

"How you feeling? Any fever? Sniffles? Sore throat?"

"No, sir."

"Headaches? Muscle ache?"

While his muscles did ache from his prolonged hike, he knew that wasn't what the man was concerned about, so he shook his head.

"Okay, good. I need to take a blood sample. You're not going to get all squeamish on me, are you?"

"No. I'm not scared of needles."

"Glad to hear it. Can you take off your jacket?"

Brandon pulled the zipper down and removed his right arm, but left his left in its sleeve. He then pulled the shirt and sweater he was wearing up past his elbow and held out his arm.

"You've done this before," the man said.

"A couple times."

"Come on over here."

The man led him to a table that had a kit on top containing syringes and other medical supplies.

"What you got in there?" the man asked, nodding at the pack Brandon had carried over with him.

Brandon shrugged. "Some food, camping stuff."

"Were you guys going out for a hike?"

Brandon went back to simply nodding.

"Kind of a bad time of year for hiking."

"Christmas hike," Brandon said, hoping that would be enough of an answer.

It seemed to do the trick. "I get it. Tradition, right?"

"Yeah."

The man took two vials of blood from Brandon's arm, then said, "We have just enough time to get you something hot to eat before your plane leaves. Sound good to you?"

"Plane?"

"Can't keep you here, little man. Not enough room or staff."

"Where am I going?"

"Colorado."

THERE WERE FIVE other passengers on the airplane—three more children and two men. All of them, including Brandon, had been issued full facial masks like the soldiers had been wearing, and were assigned seats in separate rows. The other children looked scared, while the men looked pissed off.

Seven soldiers were also scattered throughout the cabin. Unlike the one who'd questioned Brandon, they were hard-faced and said very little.

The plane was in the air for over an hour and a half. As they came in for a landing, Brandon looked out the window.

Not too far away was a tall mountain range, similar to the mountains in Montana, and between it and where they were landing, rolling hills. There was snow on the ground surrounding the runway, though not nearly as much as he'd experienced farther north. Two or three inches at most.

As they rolled down the taxiway, Brandon saw many more military planes and trucks and helicopters parked off to the side, and figured this must be another base. Once the plane finally stopped, the soldier in the front stood up.

"When the door opens, you will get out one by one as we point to you," he said. "Outside will be two transport vehicles. You four kids will get into the one on the left." He looked at the two men. "Gentlemen, yours will be the one on the right. Everyone understand?"

"Where are you taking us?" one of the kids asked, a girl, maybe a year or so younger than Brandon.

"Someplace safe."

"That's not really an answer," one of the men said.

"That's the answer you're getting right now, sir."

"Well, I'm not getting into *anything* until I know where I'm going. In fact..." The man stood up. "I want to talk to whoever's in charge right now."

"Sir, please be seated."

The man scooted into the aisle and started walking toward the front.

"Sir, I'm warning you. Return to your seat now."

The man kept coming.

"Sir, I will not say it again."

"I don't give a damn about your warnings. I want you to get—"

The man had been so focused on the soldier at the front that he hadn't heard the one who moved in quickly behind him. With blinding speed, the protesting man was shoved to the ground, wrenched back to his feet, and forcibly marched to a seat in the very last row.

This wasn't the first time Brandon had seen violence, so it didn't shock him. The other kids, though, stared at the soldiers, looking scared out of their minds.

A moment later, the door swung open, and another soldier—a woman this time—stepped on board. She was a captain, the insignia on her uniform the same as Brandon's father's had been when he was in the army.

"Are we ready here?" she asked.

"One of our passengers isn't being as cooperative as we would have liked, but everyone else is set."

She turned to the cabin and said in a loud voice, "Good afternoon. I am Captain Valverde, and I am here to make sure you all get to your destinations. We'll start with the children."

Brandon was the last one the male soldier pointed at. He grabbed his pack, scooted into the aisle behind the two girls and the other boy, and headed for the door.

The air outside was brisk, but not as cold as Montana had been. As promised, there were two vehicles waiting. They were like a combo between a bus and a van, and reminded Brandon of a vehicle his family had ridden in when they'd gone to pick up a rental car at an airport once.

The door opened in the middle as they reached their vehicle.

"Please sit in separate rows," Captain Valverde said.

Brandon took a seat near the back, then looked out the window in time to see the two male adult passengers coming down the stairs. The first was walking on his own, while the second—the protestor—was being half carried down. When they reached the tarmac, the second passenger tried to squirm away from the soldier holding him, but the only thing he got out of it was a fist in his gut and a punch to the jaw.

One of the girls let out a gasp.

The driver of their van, wearing a full containment suit, looked into the rearview mirror, stared at the girl for a moment, and dropped his gaze back to the front window.

Though Brandon didn't have a view of the girl's face, he could see she was shaking and thought she might start crying. The row across the aisle from her was empty. He gave it only a moment's thought before he moved up next to her.

This drew another look from the man at the wheel, but Brandon ignored him.

"Hey, it's going to be all right," he said to the girl.

She looked at him, tears running down her cheeks. "I want to go home."

"We all do," he told her. "But we can't right now."

"I want to go home."

"When this is over, they'll take you home."

"Really?"

"They're not going to hurt us. They're just trying to keep us safe from, you know, what's happening out there." He pointed out the window. "The flu."

He could see she wanted to believe him. He reached across the aisle and took her hand. "Don't worry. I'll make sure everything's okay."

"Hey! What's going on?" The voice came from the front of the van.

Brandon immediately dropped the girl's hand and turned forward. Captain Valverde was staring at him from near the front row.

"I was helping her calm down, that's all," Brandon said.

The captain considered him for another moment, then said, "You're sitting too close. You need to move to another row."

As he stood up, he whispered to the girl, "What's your name?"

"Loni."

He smiled. "I'm Brandon."

"Thank you, Brandon."

THE VAN TOOK them across the base, out a main gate, and toward the mountains. For the first few minutes, Brandon watched the other van follow them, but before they left the base, it turned right and moved out of sight. He never saw it again.

For thirty minutes, they wound their way higher and higher in the mountains before turning down a narrower road. On the whole trip up, Brandon saw only two other vehicles, both military. With the roads here clear of snow, it felt even odder than when he'd been walking down the deserted highway in Montana.

Another turn took them onto a narrow, one-lane road with a sign arcing over the entrance that read:

CAMP KILEY

The road twisted through the trees for nearly ten minutes before they reached a clearing with eight identical rectangular buildings in two rows of four to the left, and three larger buildings to the right. Straight ahead was a covered picnic area that went right down to the edge of a small, frozen lake.

The van pulled to a stop in front of one of the larger buildings. There were lights on inside, and steam covering the windows.

"All right. This is our stop," Captain Valverde said. "But I need to check one thing first."

"What is this place?" asked the girl Brandon hadn't talked to yet.

"Camp Kiley. Didn't you read the sign?" the boy said.

"Yeah, I read the sign, but that's not what I meant."

"Hold it down," the captain said. "This is a temporary resident facility for unaccompanied minors."

"Unaccompanied minors?" Loni said.

"Means kids who are alone," the boy announced as if she were stupid.

"How long do we have to stay here?" the first girl asked.

"Until we know the flu has run its course, and it's safe for you to return home."

"What if it's never safe?"

Captain Valverde smiled compassionately. "That won't happen. Don't worry."

A soldier exited the building and walked over to the van. When the door opened, he stuck his head in and said, "You're all clear."

"Excellent," the captain said. She turned to the kids and pulled her mask off her face. "Good news. You've all passed your blood tests, and none of you have the virus."

Brandon wasn't surprised by his results. His father had passed down the gene that made him immune. Unless the others also had the immunity, they were just lucky.

"Leave your masks in the van," the captain instructed them, "and follow me."

She escorted them into the building, which turned out to be a cafeteria. There were close to fifty people present. Only half a dozen were adults. The kids were anywhere from kindergarten age to almost old enough to be done with high school.

Two soldiers were standing by the door as they walked in. One of them pointed at Brandon's backpack. "Need to search that. Can't have any weapons or things like that here."

"Oh…um, sure." Brandon handed over his pack.

The other kids also had their bags searched. Once everyone was cleared, Captain Valverde took them to the front of the room.

"Good afternoon, everyone," she said in a voice loud enough for the whole room to hear.

Everyone hushed.

"I've brought four new children to join us." She turned to Brandon and his travel mates. "This is Marisa, Loni, Eddie, and Brandon. Please introduce yourselves to them when you have a moment." She looked at the new arrivals. "If you have any questions, you can ask one of the adult supervisors—Miss Collins, Mrs. Trieb, Mr. Munson, Mr. Whitney, Sergeant Lukes, and Specialist Granter."

Specialist Granter was the one who'd checked Brandon's bag.

"Where do we sleep?" Marisa asked.

"You will each be assigned a bed in one of the dormitories. I know it's not like home, but it's not bad."

A few of the kids who'd been there laughed.

"All right, you can all go back to what you were doing," the captain said. "And don't forget to welcome your new friends."

10

PALO ALTO, CALIFORNIA
8:14 PM PST

JAMES SUMNER, CEO of Yeti Pepper—a highly successful mobile application developer—had over six hundred bottles of wine in his private collection. Each bottle was carefully chosen not only for its taste, but also for its reputation. The majority was housed in a climate-controlled facility up the road in San Francisco, while he kept nearly one hundred at home in case a special occasion arose.

This night was one such occasion. In fact, it was probably the biggest occasion of all. It was Christmas evening, but that wasn't why he was standing in his well-designed wine closet.

Though only in his early fifties, this would be his last night alive. He'd hoped that wouldn't be the case. He had always dreamt of passing away at ninety while drifting off to sleep at a café in Loire Valley in France. But ninety was not to be, nor eighty, nor seventy, nor even sixty.

That morning, not long after breakfast, he had coughed for the first time. As the afternoon had progressed, his symptoms had worsened. He was now drained and congested and sore from coughing, but he had not yet given up the ghost.

What he was trying to decide was which wine would be his last.

In no particular hurry, he pulled bottle after bottle from

the exquisitely handcrafted rack, read each label, and put it back if he thought it unworthy. So far, there were only two bottles he hadn't returned to their place—the 1945 Pétrus Bordeaux, and the 1982 Château Haut-Brion, a first-growth Bordeaux.

He slid another from its slot. A 2005 Romanée-Conti Burgundy. He had bought three bottles at auction for over twenty-three thousand dollars each. He rubbed his thumb lightly across the label, but, in the end, he returned it to the rack. It was good—excellent, in fact—just not…right.

When he reached the end, he moved to the next rack. As he did, he noticed something on the floor, tucked into the back corner of the room, almost out of sight. It was a simple, brown paper bag, bottle-size, sitting upright and full. He had forgotten all about it.

As he picked it up, a cough exploded from his chest, and he had to grab one of the racks to keep from falling down.

When the fit passed, he set the bag on the table next to the Pétrus and Haut-Brion, then carefully opened the top and pulled the bottle out.

He couldn't help but smile as he set it down.

Boone's Farm Tickle Pink.

Not only was there no date, there was no cork, just a screw top.

When his sister had given it to him, he had rolled his eyes and grimaced.

"I just thought, you know…" Lauraine had said.

He had played dumb at the time, but of course he did know.

That had been, what? Three years ago? He hadn't seen her since. She'd emailed him once, saying she was going to be in town and wanted to have dinner with him, but he had claimed another commitment. Now he couldn't even remember if he'd really had one.

The bottle had made him angry at the time. It had evoked memories he had long buried and never wanted to think about again. When he arrived home that night, he fully intended to throw the low-rent wine in the trash, but found himself unable to do it. Instead, he hid the Tickle Pink in his wine vault, thinking that in a few days he'd get around to disposing it.

Apparently, he never did.

He'd been eighteen and in the final semester of his senior year of high school. Lauraine, a year and a half younger, was a sophomore. That afternoon, their father had informed him there was no way his parents could afford to send him to the university in the fall, and that he'd be better off getting a job and learning a skill. It had come as a shock. His mother had promised him they'd pay for college. He'd been counting on it. It was how he would avoid following in his father's footsteps.

Lauraine, his biggest supporter and best friend back then, had found him outside of town along the trail by the river they used to hike together. She'd come prepared with two bottles of Tickle Pink. They passed them back and forth, drinking straight out of the top. She let him vent his anger, nodding in encouragement. At some point, they had started laughing as more of the horrible wine flowed.

It was the first time he'd ever been drunk, and he'd never had a headache as bad as the one he had the next morning—before or since.

It was funny, though. His father's refusal to live up to his mother's promise had been the push Sumner needed. The day after he graduated, he packed the few things he wanted to take with him into his crappy little car and headed west, not stopping until he reached the ocean.

He looked at the three bottles on the table. People would pay seven hundred dollars for one glass of the Haut-Brion. *He* had paid that much. And for the Pétrus—if you could buy only a glass—eight grand. The Boone's Farm? When he was younger, he could get the whole bottle for a few bucks. He doubted the price had come up much.

He thought about Lauraine. She had always treated him with love and kindness, something he couldn't say he'd done in return.

The Pétrus. The Haut-Brion. The Tickle Pink.

It wasn't even a contest.

He grabbed the Boone's Farm by the neck, and closed the door to his wine closet for the last time.

MADISON, WISCONSIN
10:20 PM CENTRAL STANDARD TIME (CST)

IT WAS WEIRD being one of only a few people in the dorm, but Belinda Ramsey had no place else to go for the holidays. Home was out of the question. Her mother, a professional drunk, had kicked Belinda out of the house when the girl had still been in high school. She'd gone to live with her grandmother, but Grams had died last summer.

That was the extent of her family, and hence the reason she had opted to stay at school while everyone else had rushed away.

She had counted a total of three others who seemed to be doing the same thing she was, all on lower floors than hers. Of course, they had all needed special permission to stay at the dorms because technically they were closed. When Belinda received her approval, she was told she would have to provide her own meals, as the cafeteria would not be open again until just before the new term began.

That was fine. There was a microwave oven on her floor, so she had stocked up on Top Ramen and frozen pizzas. Her plan was to spend the first part of the break working on her book. She was an English major with dreams of being an author. The story she was writing was a thinly veiled version of her own life. It was a bit painful to put on the page at times, but nowhere near as bad as she'd expected.

For the week leading up to Christmas Day, she had decided to seclude herself on her floor and do nothing but write, sleep, and, occasionally, eat. That way, she could avoid all the "Christmas cheer" that would remind her she had no one to share the holidays with. She disconnected the Internet and unplugged the TV. She even turned off her phone, though she didn't think anyone would be calling her, her college friends undoubtedly busy at home.

It was amazing how well it was going. The first couple of days, she was able to write over two thousand words each. The third day dipped a little, only eighteen hundred, but day four was amazing. Three thousand, six hundred, and seventy-eight. She had never written that many words in one day before. The writer's high she had when she finally removed her fingers from the keyboard was the purest combination of euphoria and serenity she had ever felt.

The rest of the week had gone so well that she had lost track of the days and actually worked through Christmas, the day she had originally planned as a break. It was after ten p.m. when she finally realized it. She laughed at herself for getting so lost in her work.

She had been planning on calling her friend Patty to wish her a merry Christmas, but Patty's home was in Delaware, so it was nearly eleven thirty there. Probably too late.

Belinda decided to text her instead. She could give Patty a call tomorrow. She dug her phone out of the dresser where she'd stuffed it, and turned it on. As it went through warming up and connecting to the network, she walked down the hall to the common area, grabbed the frozen mini-supreme pizza she'd been saving for this day out of the refrigerator, and popped it into the microwave.

Four minutes later she returned to her room with her gourmet meal on an elegant paper plate. From her smaller dorm-room fridge, she grabbed a Diet Coke and plopped down on her bed. The pizza was still a bit too hot, so she picked up her phone to text Patty, but paused, surprised, as she looked at the screen.

She had over two dozen text messages, and nearly as many voicemails. Most were from Patty, while the rest were from her other two close friends, Josh and Kaylee.

Patty:

where r u? r u okay?

Patty:

r there any containers there?

Patty:

why rn't u answering ur phone?

Kaylee:

B, you ok? You're all alone. You should come here.

Patty:

answer ur phone!

Josh:

Are you watching this? PCN...crazy!

Patty:

Belinda, please PLEASE answer!!!

Belinda stopped reading and listened to the first of Patty's voicemails. "God, I hope you're okay. You're probably watching TV, right? This is insane. Please tell me there are none of these things in Madison. Call me back as soon as you get this, okay?"

Ignoring the rest of the messages, she called Patty.

Two rings. Three. Four.

"Hi, it's Patty. Leave me a message and I'll get back to you."

Beep.

"Patty? It's Belinda. What's going on? I just got your messages. Call me."

She tried Kaylee next. This time it didn't even ring before going to voicemail. Belinda left a similar message for her.

She called Josh.

Two rings. "Hello?"

"Josh?"

There was a pause, a sniffle, then a stuttering voice, "Josh isn't with us anymore."

Her brow furrowed. "I'm sorry. What does that mean?"

"Please don't call again."

The line went dead.

Despite the request, she did call again, but went straight to voicemail this time.

She stared at her phone. What the hell was going on?

Are you watching this?

Josh's message.

She rushed across the room, plugged in her TV, and turned it on.

Though the television was tuned to what normally would be the Glitz Network, the logo in the corner belonged to Prime Cable News.

She watched for five minutes, but nearly nothing the news anchors said made sense. It was as if they were speaking another language, or, probably closer to the truth, working off a set of known facts Belinda was unaware of. What was clear was that something horrible either had happened or was happening.

She grabbed her computer and switched on the Wi-Fi for the first time in over a week. As soon as she had the signal, she opened her email program. While the messages started to download, she launched her web browser and went to the PCN website. There, she devoured story after unbelievable story, her shock growing with every paragraph.

When she read everything she could, she searched for news more specific to Madison.

TEN SHIPPING CONTAINERS LOCATED AROUND CITY

A later story talked of finding five more boxes. In the most recent article, posted that morning, she read about the sick showing up in large numbers at local hospitals, and that at least seven hundred people had already died. The reporter speculated that the total was far greater than that, as there were likely many more who had been too sick to seek medical help and passed away in their homes. The death toll was probably in the thousands, the reporter said.

Thousands? That was just here in Madison. If this was truly as spread out as the other reports suggested, then…

Oh, my God.

Unable to focus on the words anymore, Belinda walked over to her window and looked outside. Six floors below was the park that surrounded the dorm. Sometime in the past few days it must have snowed. The last time she'd checked, the ground had been bare, but now there was a layer of white at least a few inches thick.

The only way she could pick out the pathways was by the lights that lined them. Usually the grounds crew kept the paths clear to prevent the buildup of ice. But there wasn't even so much as a footprint in the snow. Anywhere.

She looked back at the door to her room. When the break had begun, someone from the cleaning staff had come up to her floor every other day to do a light dusting, and see if the trash needed removing. Belinda couldn't remember the last time she'd seen or heard one of them.

With a sense of dread, she reentered the hallway and made her way back to the common room. The trash can had one of those flopping panels to push rubbish through. She pulled the entire top off and looked inside the barrel. She could see the discarded containers and wrappers from her meals stretching back at least five days. Someone should have dumped it out already.

She ran to the stairwell door and pulled it open, thinking she could find one of the other students who'd stayed. But before she took the first step down, a voice in her head screamed, *Wait!*

The virus. The highly *contagious* virus. If anyone below had it, they'd give it to her. At the moment she felt okay. Actually, she felt good, never healthier. If she wanted to stay that way, she needed to avoid everyone at all costs.

She backed away from the stairs and slowly closed the

door.

Using an extra bedsheet she had, she tied off the staircase door's handle, making it harder for someone on the other side to open it. She dragged her roommate's dresser out of their room and leaned it against the door. It might not have stopped anyone, but at the very least, it would crash down when the door opened, alerting her that someone was coming.

A bigger problem was the elevator. She could call it up and pull the stop button, but she had no idea who might have been inside in the past several days. Perhaps the virus was waiting for her on the control panel.

The thought made her pause. An hour before, she'd only been worried about where she should break the next paragraph of her story, and now she was living in fear of killer microbes.

The best she could do with the elevator was to tie her roommate's mattress in front of the opening. She wasn't satisfied with it at all, but she didn't know what else to do.

For the next ninety minutes, she sat on the floor watching the news, her pizza forgotten. When she finally turned it off, she didn't go to bed. Instead, she sat down with her laptop, opened a new file, and began to type.

She knew she would never finish the story she'd been working on. She had something different to write now.

Something that would consume her.

11

ISABELLA ISLAND, COSTA RICA
11:27 PM CENTRAL STANDARD TIME

"ANYTHING?" ROBERT ASKED.

A second of static, then Enrique's voice came over the radio. "No. Nothing."

"What about you, Evan?"

"Still clear over here, too," Evan reported.

Thankfully the moon had come up an hour earlier, giving the spotters plenty of light to see most vessels that might approach the island.

"Great. I'll check back in a bit."

It had been a wild, unreal few days.

Isabella Island was a small private bump of land, sticking out of the ocean thirty-five miles off the Caribbean coast of Costa Rica. It had been purchased several years earlier by the Albino Entertainment Group—owners of hotels in Las Vegas, Macau, Greece, and the French Riviera—and turned into an island-wide resort that shared the island's name. Twice a day, a private ferry would shuttle new guests to Isabella, and take those who had checked out back to the mainland.

The island was far enough offshore that Costa Rica was below the horizon, and, if guests wanted to, they could pretend they had found a bit of paradise in the middle of nowhere. Every Christmas, the resort ran a special deal aimed directly at singles who were looking for alternatives to spending the holidays with relatives they'd rather avoid. In fact, the humorous ad campaign they ran each year had won numerous Clio Awards, and was the main reason the island was always at full capacity during the holidays.

The management had expected to have every room occupied by Christmas Eve. What they hadn't counted on was a worldwide terror attack.

On Thursday, December 22nd, the resort had been running at sixty percent capacity, with the bulk of guests due to arrive the morning of Christmas Eve. As usual, most of those already on the island spent their day by the water—sunbathing, jet skiing, swimming, and surfing.

One of the appealing features of the hotel was that none of the rooms had televisions. In fact, there were only five on the entire island. One in the manager's office, one in the lobby that normally played a feed from a computer that listed the day's available activities, and the other three in the open-air bar on the veranda overlooking the ocean.

On that Thursday, instead of being tuned to sporting events, the bar's TVs were playing a marathon of Christmas movies off Blu-ray discs, so news of what was happening in the rest of the world didn't reach anyone on the island until Dominic Ray, the manager, received a call from his brother over the satellite phone at a quarter to five in the afternoon. Before he'd hung up, Dominic had turned on the television in his office, and watched in stunned silence at the unfolding drama surrounding the mysterious shipping containers.

The businessman in him wanted to keep the news to himself, and let his guests continue to enjoy their stay. But he was, at heart, a man of good conscience, so there was no way he could keep this quiet.

He picked up the hotel phone and called Renee, his assistant manager.

"In five minutes, I want you to sound the tsunami alarm."

"The alarm? Why?"

"I want to do a drill."

"We never do drills this late in the day. We haven't even briefed the new guests." The last ferry of the day had made its stop fifteen minutes early, leaving eleven new guests while taking away seventeen.

"I don't care. Just do it."

Because of the tsunami that had struck the Indian Ocean back in 2004, the resort's owners had been required to install an alarm and conduct weekly drills. After each group of guests finished checking in, they were given a briefing and a pamphlet that explained what was to be done if the alarm went off—make their way as quickly as possible to the hotel restaurant. The hotel itself was built in tiers up the side of the island's only hill, with the restaurant at the top where the view was best.

Dominic reached the restaurant just as the alarm went off.

There was minor confusion at first, not only with the unprepared guests, but also with the staff who had not expected a test. Most of the employees, after a few seconds of surprise, decided it must be real, and started directing the guests where to go.

As people began streaming into the restaurant, Renee, who arrived right after the alarm was activated, counted them off. Since the island was private, management knew the exact number of visitors.

The guests were a mix of the winded, the scared, the confused, and the annoyed. Those closest to Dominic asked him what was going on, but all he said was, "In a minute."

Finally, Renee worked her way through the crowd to where he was standing. "I think that's it."

"Everyone?"

"No. We're missing five guests. Apparently there was a small group that went around to the far side."

Dominic frowned. He had hoped everyone would be there, but it wasn't surprising. "Thanks, Renee."

He pulled out a chair from a nearby table, and climbed onto it so he was high enough for all to see him.

"Everyone! Everyone, if I could have your attention."

The noise in the room lowered but didn't die.

"Please," he said. "This is important."

It took another moment, but finally they all quieted down.

"First of all, there is no tsunami."

Voices again, most relieved, but a few angry.

"So this was just a drill?" someone shouted.

"It's not a drill, either."

That garnered him several curious looks. He waited until he had everyone's attention again, then said, "There's something you need to know."

It wasn't exactly a mad rush down to the bar after the meeting, but close to it. Once everyone was reassembled there, Robert, the bartender and Dominic's best friend, switched off *Miracle on 34th Street* and turned on CNN International.

Though the crowd numbered nearly two hundred, for the first ninety minutes there weren't more than a dozen words spoken. The only reason that changed later was because Dominic told Robert that for the rest of the night, it would be an open bar. Surprisingly, only a handful of people drank more than they should have. The rest nursed their booze while they digested the unbelievable news.

It wasn't until late that night before people started returning to their rooms. Eventually, only Dominic, Robert, and Renee remained. They sat together at a table, a bottle of barely touched Johnnie Walker Blue Label whiskey in front of them.

"So I've been thinking," Robert said.

"What?" Dominic asked.

"The ferry. What happens when it comes in the morning?"

"You're thinking a lot of people will want to go home?" Renee said.

"Well, yeah."

"Anyone who wants to go should be able to," Dominic said. "The boat can hold up to a hundred, if need be."

Robert nodded, and was quiet for a moment. "Good, but that's not really what I'm concerned about."

"Okay," Dominic said. "What, then?"

"What if there are new guests on the boat?"

Dominic shrugged. "We give them rooms."

Again, Robert took a second before he spoke. "I don't think anyone on that boat, guest *or* crew, should get off."

"What are you talking about?"

"Dominic, there's none of those containers here on the island." Though there had been no search done since they'd heard the news, the staff knew the island well. If there had been a container there, it would have been spotted already. "Costa Rica, on the other hand, *is* one of the places that's reported having them. What if that woman in that video they've been playing is right, and the containers have been spitting out the Sage Flu? Right now, we're all safe. But if someone on the boat tomorrow morning came in contact with that stuff, then…"

Renee stared at him. "What if the *boat*'s tainted?"

"Right, of course," Robert said. "We can't even let it dock."

"That video might be a crock. Even CNN hasn't been able to confirm it," Dominic argued. "It could be nothing."

"I hope it *is* nothing," Robert said. "But why take the chance? If we're wrong, no harm."

"If we're wrong, we'll get fired."

"Better fired than letting something on this island that might harm us."

"Or kill us," Renee added.

Dominic looked at her. "You agree with him?"

"Dominic, you're the one who told us about it in the first place," she said. "You know this isn't nothing."

Dominic looked back at the monitor. CNN was showing a montage of the found boxes. Each time another came up, a graphic identified the new location. New York, Mexico City, Madrid, Cairo, Hong Kong, Lima. The list of locations went on and on.

He looked back at Robert and Renee. "What do we do about the people who want to leave?"

EARLY THE NEXT morning, all one hundred and ninety-three people on the island gathered once more in the restaurant. Taking turns, Dominic, Renee, and Robert explained the situation as they saw it, then Dominic presented the options.

"You can either stay or leave, that's up to you, but if you do leave, you cannot come back. The boat should be here at 8:30. If you want to be on it, you need to be down at the dock no later than 8:10. That's in thirty-five minutes. Questions?"

There were plenty, but most were from people needing to hear again what Dominic and the others had already said, so they cut off the questions after ten minutes.

Isabella Island was graced with a magnificent sheltered bay. The ferry's route took it between the two offset arms of land jutting out from either side of the bay that created a natural channel between the Caribbean and the bay itself. The dock was located across the bay from the channel exit. At the moment, one of the resort's speedboats and all three of its scuba boats were tied to the pier, waiting.

One hundred feet to the west was the swimming platform—a wooden deck built on top of two dozen airtight drums. Or at least that's where it had been until shortly after the sun had come up, when Robert and two of the guys who helped maintain the water sports equipment had cut it from the ties that held it in place, and towed it out closer to the passageway. There, they used a couple of anchors to hold it down. Robert had tested it. He reported it was a bit wobbly, but it would do.

The first of those wanting to leave arrived at the dock a few minutes before eight.

"You can get on Scuba One," Dominic told them.

After Scuba One was filled, Dominic and Robert directed new arrivals to Scuba Two, then Scuba Three. When the last boat was nearing capacity, Dominic worried that a second trip might be needed, but they were able to squeeze everyone on. All told, there were sixty-three who wanted off—fifty-seven guests and six staff.

Robert looked at his watch, then back at the sea. "We

should be able to see them by now."

Dominic put a hand over his eyes to cut the glare. The bay was on the east side, facing away from Costa Rica, so the boat had to come all the way around the calmer end of the island on the right. There was no sign of it yet.

When the ferry still hadn't shown up ten minutes later, Dominic had one of the employees hand out bottles of soda to those waiting on the boats. Water would have been better, but as Renee had pointed out, it would be smart to hold on to the water they had for now.

"Maybe they're not coming," one of the staff members standing on the beach with them said.

It was a definite possibility, Dominic thought. Who knew how crazy things had gotten on the mainland?

But a few minutes later, Robert said, "There it is."

The medium-sized, two-deck passenger ferry had just peeked around the corner of the island. They watched it until it was almost to the seaside mouth of the passage.

"You'd better go," Robert said.

Dominic hesitated for a second, then nodded and jogged out to the speedboat where Jalen Dunn, the speedboat pilot and water-ski instructor, was waiting. As soon as he was on board, the boat pulled away from the dock and raced across the bay.

Dominic glanced at the repositioned swimming platform as they passed by. Was that really all that would be standing between them and potential death? He didn't have time to ponder it, though, as the speedboat suddenly entered the choppier water of the passage.

Ahead, he could see the ferry entering the other end.

"How far do you want to go?" Jalen yelled.

"This is probably good," Dominic hollered back. "We want to make sure they get in far enough that they don't just turn around and leave."

Jalen throttled the boat down to a point where the motor held them in place with the moving current. Picking up the electronic megaphone Robert had put in the boat earlier, Dominic nervously played with the switch.

The wait seemed to take forever. When the ferry was about two hundred feet away, he could stand it no more. "Now," he said.

Jalen revved up the engine, and drove the speedboat all the way around the ferry and back up the other side, slowing and matching the bigger boat's pace as it came abreast with the bridge.

As they'd circled around, Dominic had tried to determine how many people were on board. He saw a handful at most, which made him feel better. They had been expecting at least fifty people on this trip alone.

On the bridge, he could see one of the ferry's crew glancing over at their boat. He raised the megaphone.

"Attention, *Albino Mer*," he said, using the ferry's name. His voice echoed across the water, just above the sounds of the engines. "Attention, *Albino Mer*."

This time the door at the side of the bridge opened, and Carlos Guzman, the boat's captain, looked out.

"Good morning, Carlos. It's Dominic."

Carlos put his hands around his mouth and shouted back, "What's going on?"

"There's a problem with our dock," Dominic said, using the story he, Robert, and Renee had worked up. They worried if they went with the truth, the *Albino Mer* would leave without taking those who wanted to go home with them. "One of the pillars has rotted through. Stable enough for our smaller boats, but didn't think we should chance it with you."

"So what are we supposed to do?"

"Already got it worked out," Dominic said.

A few minutes later, as the two boats cleared the end of the passage, the floating platform came into view. Scuba One was already pulled up next to it, with the other two boats approaching quickly.

"We're going to use the platform to transfer everyone," Dominic said through the megaphone.

"Would be easier if the boats just tie up to our ramp in back."

Of course the captain was right. "Pull up beside the

platform," Dominic said as if he hadn't heard the other man. He glanced at Jalen. "Take us over there."

Jalen increased their speed, taking them toward the platform and cutting off any further conversation. By the time the *Albino Mer* completely cleared the channel, the speedboat was tucking in behind Scuba One.

"Get them out there," Dominic yelled across to Robert. He didn't want to give Carlos any excuse to try anything other than using the platform.

The *Albino Mer* slowed as it approached the other side of the platform. For a moment, it looked as though it might even stop before it got there, but it continued to slide forward through the water.

"Once it gets here, start boarding right away," Robert said loudly enough for the passengers who were already on the platform to hear. To those still on his boat, he said, "Off. Everyone off."

The moment the last guest left Scuba One, Robert pulled away, and Scuba Two moved into its place.

As soon as the *Albino Mer* stopped, Dominic caught a glance of three people who were definitely not crew members looking like they intended to get off. But as planned, those waiting on the platform rushed on to the ferry the moment a crew member removed the chain from the boarding gate, preventing anyone from disembarking.

Passengers from Scuba Two immediately took the platform space vacated by the passengers from Scuba One. Once they were all off their ship, it moved to the side, and Scuba Three moved in, unloaded, and pulled away.

In this manner, there was a continuous stream of passengers right up until the end.

Dominic tensed as the last five people climbed on board the ferry. As he'd expected, the three he'd seen earlier approached the now freed-up gate. He raised the megaphone again.

"I'm sorry," he said. "The resort is currently closed. You will need to stay on the ship."

The one in the lead, a blond and burly guy of maybe

twenty-five, shouted, "What are you talking about? I've got a reservation. I've already paid for this. I'm coming off."

"I'm sorry," Dominic repeated. "But we're not taking any guests right now. We'll get you a refund or you can reschedule in the future."

"I'm not rescheduling. I planned to be here now, so I'm coming."

One of the resort staffers on Scuba Three pulled out the gun Dominic had given him from the safe that morning, and pointed it at the guy.

"Holy fuck." The blond man jumped back, hiding behind an interior partition.

"I told you. The resort's closed," Dominic said. He pointed the megaphone toward the front of the *Albino Mer*. "Carlos, take the ferry out. And don't come back tonight."

Quickly, Scuba One moved in next to the swimming dock. When he was close enough, Robert jumped off, holding a gas can, and started dousing the timbers. When the crewman at the back of the ferry saw what he was doing, he shouted toward the pilothouse.

Someone up front must have seen what Robert was doing, too, because the *Albino Mer*'s engines suddenly revved up, and the boat pulled away.

Once Robert was done and back on Scuba One, the staffer who was with him pulled the boat back several feet. Robert threw a lit book of matches across the growing water gap. With a *whoosh*, the swimming platform turned into a blazing beacon in the middle of the bay.

The *Albino Mer* made a big circle around the burning structure as it cut through the water back toward the passage to the sea. All its new passengers were pressed against the cabin windows, staring at the burning wood that moments before had been their bridge to the ferry.

Without being told, Jalen guided the speedboat behind the ferry, and he and Dominic followed the *Albino Mer* all the way back to the open sea. When they reached the end of the passage, they stopped and watched the ferry until it passed out of sight.

"All right," Dominic said. "Take us back home."

IT WAS ROBERT'S idea to post sentries. He argued that others might flee the mainland and try for the safety of Isabella Island. Dominic hoped he was wrong, but it was a good idea, so a schedule was drawn up from the names of those who remained. The first watchers were given walkie-talkies and positioned around the central hill so that all directions could be seen.

Those who weren't on watch gathered in the terrace bar where the TVs continued to paint a darker and darker picture of the rest of the world. Then, in the middle of the afternoon, CNN carried a live speech from the president of the United States. He confirmed their worst fears, that the substance being pumped out of the shipping containers indeed appeared to be the deadly Sage Flu. He also put his entire country on a twenty-four-hour curfew. Many other nations quickly followed suit, including Costa Rica. For a good thirty minutes, no one in the bar said a word.

When the time for the arrival of the afternoon ferry approached, Dominic was sure it wouldn't come. But he and Jalen went out to the passage in the speedboat again, this time with Robert and Evan—one of the resort's guests—in the second speedboat.

Every few minutes they'd check in with the spotters to see if the *Albino Mer* had appeared on the horizon, but there continued to be no sign of the ship, so they returned to the resort.

Sleep that night was something that came only in short chunks of twenty or thirty minutes at most. Around four a.m. Dominic gave up and went down to the bar. He wasn't surprised to see that nearly half the other residents were there.

The news on CNN that Christmas Eve morning brought more of the same. If any of them had been hoping for something that looked like it might turn the situation around, they were disappointed.

It was around ten thirty when the radio crackled.

"There's a couple of white spots on the horizon," the voice said.

Robert, who was sitting next to Dominic, picked up the walkie-talkie. "Who is this?"

"Clint Lee."

They checked the handwritten duty sheet. Lee was positioned facing west toward Costa Rica.

Robert pushed the SEND button on his radio. "Which way are they headed?"

"Can't tell yet," Lee said.

A few minutes later he reported back.

"They're getting bigger."

Robert looked at Dominic, concerned.

"They could be headed out into the Gulf," Dominic said. "Might miss us by miles."

"Or they could be headed here. If they are, we need to be ready."

"What if we can't scare them off?"

"Did you guys hear me?" Lee asked. "They're getting closer."

Robert picked up the radio. "Heard you, Clint. Hold on, okay?" He looked at Dominic. "We have to keep them off the island. There's no way we can know if they've been exposed or not."

"How are we supposed to do that?" Dominic asked, feeling like Robert hadn't answered his first question.

"We can't let them on."

Dominic stared at his friend, suddenly realizing that Robert *had* answered his question. "You mean kill them?"

Robert was quiet for a second. "Only if we have to."

"I don't know if I could do that. I don't know if any of these people here can do that."

"Dominic, stop thinking like you're still running a resort. The resort's gone. This place, this is our survival. Anything out there beyond the beach..." He pointed toward the ocean. "Is death. If we let *anyone* in, it's the same as putting a gun to each of our heads."

Intellectually, Dominic could grasp that, but in practice?

"Hopefully they'll just pass by," he said.

They didn't.

Forty minutes later, it was clear the two boats were headed for Isabella Island.

With Robert taking charge, they set out in the two speedboats with four volunteers and the full complement of the resort's weapons—three handguns, a shotgun, and all four scuba spearguns.

Robert was at the wheel of the first speedboat, with Dominic sitting nervously in the seat beside him. Between Dominic's feet was the megaphone. He hoped that was all they were going to need.

They sped across the bay, through the passage, and into the open waters of the Gulf. The sea was rougher than it had been yesterday, perhaps matching the mood that had engulfed the planet. The speedboat jerked up and down as it plowed through the choppy swells.

Taking the same path the ferry had when it left the morning before, they raced around the end of the island so that they could reach the west side. The other ships were clearly visible now about half a mile offshore, two cruisers with awning-covered cockpits and probably small cabins below. Nothing fancy—fishing boats for the tourists. Something they might go out on for the day, but probably not spend the night on. Boats like those seldom came anywhere near the island, usually sticking closer to the Costa Rican coastline.

Robert picked up the walkie-talkie. "Enrique, stay right with him."

Enrique, driving the other boat, tucked in ten yards behind them as Robert put them on an intercept course. Two hundred feet before they reached the other boats, they turned sharply to the right, cutting across the cruisers' path. They circled around and did it again, making it clear they wanted the other boats to stop.

It took a third pass to get the cruisers to idle down their engines.

"Stay in front of them," Robert ordered Enrique. He

moved his boat in closer, and glanced at Dominic. "Give it a shot."

Dominic could see at least a dozen people on each cruiser—men, women, children, with none looking over forty. They were a mix of Hispanic, Caucasian, and African-American.

He raised the bullhorn to his mouth. "Turn your boats around. The Isabella Island Resort is closed." He repeated the message in Spanish.

Robert circled them on the other side.

"The island is closed," Dominic repeated. "You cannot go there."

Someone shouted, "You can't do that! We have to land. We're trying to save our families."

Dominic tensed. How would they turn these people...the *children* away?

"Tell them again," Robert said. "Tell them we'll be forced to take action if they don't leave."

"You need to leave now," Dominic said into the megaphone. "If you don't…" He paused, an idea forming in his mind. "If you don't, you're going to get sick. The virus is on the island. We have too many people to take care of already."

Robert looked over at him, surprised.

"You've been hit, too?"

"Yes." Dominic was tempted to embellish the story, but held his tongue.

The group on the first cruiser huddled together. After several minutes, the sister boat moved in so that the two were almost touching.

"That was quick thinking," Robert said in a low voice.

"I hope it works," Dominic replied.

They could hear raised voices coming from the conference.

Robert slipped out of the pilot's seat. "Maybe they need a little extra motivation."

He retrieved a pistol from the front storage locker.

"What are you doing?" Dominic asked, eyes widening.

"Bring a little reality to their discussion."

Robert aimed the gun's barrel just in front of the two boats, and pulled the trigger. The *boom* echoed across the water. Everyone froze for a moment, then looked over at the speedboat.

"Give me that," Robert said as he took the megaphone from Dominic. He raised it to his lips. "You've already been told the island is closed. Now turn your boats around."

"There's nowhere else to go!" a woman screamed. "Nowhere safe!"

"It's not safe here, either."

"But our children!"

Dominic could see Robert close his eyes for a second. "We're sorry. We wish we could help," Robert said. "We don't have the resources. We can't let you on the island, and we *will* stop you if you try."

To emphasize the point, one of the men on Enrique's boat held the shotgun out to his side so it could be seen.

"You have three minutes," Robert said, "or we will assume you are trying to stay."

"Then what? You'll shoot us?" another woman yelled.

"We'd rather not, but none of you is getting on the island. So the choice is yours."

"Here," Dominic said, holding out his hand.

"What are you going to say?" Robert asked.

"Just give it to me."

Robert reluctantly handed back the megaphone.

Dominic spoke into it. "How much fuel do you have left?"

A quick conversation, then a man called out, "Why?"

"Do you have enough to go fifty kilometers?"

"Maybe. Not much more than that."

Robert whispered, "What are you thinking?"

Dominic answered him by saying into the megaphone, "Santa Teresa Island is about forty-five or so kilometers due south of here. It's about half the size of Isabella, but is uninhabited. You'll be safe there."

"We don't have enough supplies," one of the men said.

"We can spare you some rice, and maybe a few other things."

Robert pushed the megaphone away from Dominic's mouth. "What are you talking about? We need everything we've got."

"We have plenty," Dominic said. The resort was well stocked for the holidays. "Would you rather shoot them? Shoot those kids?"

Robert looked conflicted, but he dropped his hand to his side.

The people on the cruiser were talking together again. When they finished, one of the men yelled, "You're sure about Santa Teresa?"

"One hundred percent. If you don't have charts, we can get you one."

For a few minutes, the only sound was the low gurgle of the boats' engines.

"Okay," the man said. "We'd appreciate whatever you can give us."

Relieved, Dominic switched places with the man with the shotgun on the other speedboat. He and Enrique headed back into the bay.

They ended up giving the refugees a map, two bags of rice, a few cases of canned vegetables, some fruit and dried goods, and two fishing poles with extra tackle. They transferred them via an unmanned rubber boat, which they also let the others keep.

Once the food was on board, the cruisers headed south away from Isabella Island. The speedboats stayed where they were until the two other vessels disappeared over the horizon, then they headed back to the resort.

"Would you really have shot them?" Dominic asked Robert when they were back in the bar, glasses of beer in front of them.

"I don't know. But would we really have had a choice?"

Dominic didn't know the answer to that.

There were no more sightings the rest of Christmas Eve.

On Christmas, as they were having a solemn dinner,

another ship was seen. A freighter this time, large on the horizon. But it never came within twenty miles of the island as it kept on a southwesterly course.

Later that night, after Robert checked in with the spotters again and received the all clear, Dominic said, “Maybe we’ve made it through the worst of it.”

“Maybe,” Robert agreed. “But we shouldn’t let our guard down. There’re still going to be people who might see coming out here as a good idea.”

Dominic nodded, knowing his friend was right. But he also knew, if things kept going the way they seemed to be going elsewhere in the world, the chance of another boat showing up was going to decrease rapidly as each new day came.

There would be no one left to make the trip.

December 26th

World Population
5,844,029,917

Change Over Previous Day
- 1,321,588,536

12

LAS CRUCES, NEW MEXICO
5:45 AM MST

SO FAR, ESTIMATES indicated that at least two and a half billion people had been infected with the KV-27a virus, with a substantial proportion already having succumbed. Since that was a bit ahead of schedule, Perez had been concerned that the virus might burn itself out before the desired level of elimination had occurred, but the lead Project Eden scientists assured him that humanity had already reached a tipping point, and there would be no turning back. By the time the plague had run its course, over ninety-nine percent of the human race would be gone.

That's when Project Eden's real work would begin, implementing plans for a reborn human civilization that would benefit from all the existing knowledge and technology without the pressures of an overpopulated world.

Project Eden would lead this new society.

And Perez would lead Project Eden.

Claudia, sitting at her desk at the other end of the converted conference room, said, "Forwarding you a new report from Choi in North Korea."

Even before she finished speaking, Perez's computer bonged with the incoming email. He read the report and smiled.

Getting shipping containers into North Korea had not been feasible, so, as with a few other places, one of the

Project's alternative methods had been employed. In this case, several airplanes had been painted to look like they were part of the Air China fleet. On the morning of Implementation Day, after the real Air China planes had been removed from the equation, these new aircraft took over the routes into North Korea, and began spraying the virus as soon as they crossed the border. It wasn't quite the saturation level the containers could achieve, but, according to Choi's report, it seemed to have done the job.

The planes had been sure to hit places where military and government officials would be. With the current Great Leader and all his colleagues falling ill or already dead, the country had become rudderless. If it weren't for the fact that the disease had also taken hold among the general population, the people might have risen up and finally taken back their nation.

"Anything new on Russia?" Perez asked.

"Not since the last check-in."

The outbreak in Russia had triggered a minor civil war, as several opposing factions saw it as their chance to seize control of the country. In the end, of course, they would all lose.

The phone rang and Claudia answered it. After a moment, she put her hand over the receiver and said, "Hendricks in Switzerland. He'd like to talk to you."

Perez nodded and picked up the phone. "Yes?"

"Director Perez, I'm a bit worried. We've compiled the latest data here, and our infection rates are a good fifteen percent below those elsewhere."

"You've double-checked the numbers?"

"Yes, sir. I'm afraid we were right about that storm."

There had been a snowstorm covering most of Switzerland and part of northern Italy on Implementation Day. Hendricks and those he worked with had been concerned it would prevent the virus from gaining proper traction in the area.

Small setbacks like this were to be expected, though, and there were contingencies to deal with them.

“All right. What’s your weather like now?” Perez asked.

“Clear,” Hendricks reported. “But another storm is due in two days.”

Perez looked over at Claudia. “Inform Manfred he is a go for the flyover mission of sections seven and eight.”

“Yes, sir.” She picked up her phone and made the call.

To Hendricks, Perez said, “The dousing will begin as soon as it’s dark. Your levels should come up in another thirty-six hours. If they don’t, we’ll go again. Keep a close watch.”

“I will.”

The phone rang again.

“Philippe Soto,” Claudia announced after answering it. “Rio.”

Perez picked up his receiver. “Yes?”

“Director, we’ve had some problems at Angra.”

“What problems?”

Angra was the nuclear power plant outside Rio de Janeiro. It was Soto’s job to make sure all South American utility plants—such as hydroelectric and nuclear—were secure. There were similar missions on the other continents. The hope, which so far had proved to be true, was that most of these types of facilities would be either shut down or reduced to self-sustaining levels by the operators as it became clear their staffs were quickly dwindling. The Project Eden teams were supposed to jump in when that didn’t happen. The last thing they wanted was an infrastructure in chaos.

“The government dispatched an army unit to guard the reactors,” Soto said. “They’re entrenched inside the buildings surrounding both Angra 1 and 2, and don’t appear to have been infected.”

“There’s been no order to shut the reactors down?”

“No.”

“Can we make that happen?”

“Um, I don’t think there’s anyone in charge down here anymore.”

“What about facility personnel? How many do they still have on site?”

"That's our biggest concern. We think only two. They might be able to keep things going, but if anything happens to them, the reactors will be on autopilot."

An annoyance, but with the safety features built into nuclear facilities, there wasn't likely to be any kind of disaster. So Perez knew Soto's men could wait until the soldiers ran out of supplies and had to leave, but that would require the team to remain on site.

"I take it your men are needed elsewhere," Perez said.

"They should be in Buenos Aires already," Soto admitted.

"All right. You have my permission to leave Angra and come back later."

"Thank you," Soto said. "I'll have them return as soon as possible."

Perez hung up and turned his attention to other matters, not knowing that Mata had been in error. There were no facility personnel still in the Angra facility, and while the reactors did have all the standard safety protocols and equipment in place, not everything always worked as planned. Especially when the only people in the building were young soldiers whose level of fear was only going to increase when the alarms started sounding, prompting them to try to shut the reactor down themselves.

In forty-two hours, Angra 1 would go critical, rendering the entire area unapproachable. Three weeks later, Angra 2 would follow, and the coastline south of Rio de Janeiro would become uninhabitable for thousands of years.

13

BOULDER, COLORADO
7:25 AM MST

THERE WERE TWO reasons why Nolan Gaines didn't want to get up that morning. The first and most painful was that he'd watched his wife Wendy take her last breath the evening before.

It had been not long after eight. He had just put Ellie to bed. She was so exhausted from the excitement of the day, she had fallen asleep sitting up while playing with her new stuffed bear. After he tucked her in, he went into the bedroom to check on Wendy. One touch of her cheek was enough to send him into panic. Her skin was freezing. He was sure she was already dead, but soon realized her chest was still moving up and down. For about the millionth time that day, he called 911, and for the millionth time he received the same "all circuits are busy" message.

He crawled into bed behind her and hugged her tightly, hoping to pass on some of his warmth, but her temperature continued to plummet. He was stroking her face when he realized she had stopped breathing. He searched frantically for a pulse, but found none.

He'd never been trained in CPR, but that didn't stop him from trying. He pumped her chest, willing her heart to beat again. It was no use. She was gone.

Instead of calling 911 this time, he called the main police number. No busy-circuits message, but no live operator either.

Only voicemail.

He left a message with his name, address, the news that his wife had died, and that he didn't know what to do. Drained of energy and with his head pounding, he dropped onto the living room couch and was soon asleep.

The second reason he wished he could stay asleep was that the illness he now realized had been coming on the night before had taken full control of his body. His throat, his chest, his head—they all screamed at him for attention. Even his skin hurt.

"Daddy?"

He forced his eyelids open.

"Daddy, where are you?" Ellie's voice drifted into the living room from the back of the house. "Mommy doesn't want to wake up."

Oh, Jesus!

Despite the pain, he pushed himself to his feet and staggered into the hallway. His daughter wasn't there.

"Baby, where are you?"

"Daddy?" She was in the master bedroom.

No, no, no!

When he reached the door to the room he'd shared with Wendy, he saw Ellie sitting on the bed where he normally slept, his wife lying still beside her.

"Hi, sweetie," he said. He tried to smile as he walked over to the bed.

"Mommy's still asleep," Ellie whispered.

"Mommy's not feeling very well."

"Like last night?"

"Yes, like last night." He wanted to pick her up but didn't think he had the energy, so he held out his hand instead. "Come on. I'll make you some breakfast."

After she ate, he put *Elf* on TV, and let her play with her new toys by the Christmas tree. He then sat down on the couch and promptly fell back to sleep.

Several tugs on his arm woke him. His eyes hurt even worse than before—*everything* hurt worse.

"Movie's over, Daddy," she said. She studied him, her

face pinched. "Are you okay?"

"Think I'm a little sick, too, sweetie."

Her eyes softened dramatically. "Oh, no. You want me to make you some soup?"

Despite his condition, he laughed, or tried to, anyway, as it quickly became a cough.

When the spasm passed, he sat up. "What would you like to watch now?"

"Rudolph?"

"Good choice."

Once he got the program going, he asked Ellie, "You feel okay?"

She nodded without taking her eyes from the TV.

"You don't have to cough? No runny nose?"

"Uh-uh."

"What about your head?"

"My head?"

"Does it hurt?"

She put a hand on top of her head and said, as if it were a silly question, "My head doesn't hurt."

"Of course not," he said. He pushed himself unsteadily to his feet. "You watch your show. I'll be right back."

As she picked up her bear and started dancing him to the music, Nolan staggered out of the room. Using the hallway wall to keep his balance, he returned to the master bedroom. There was no denying his condition was mirroring that of his wife's the day before. He knew that meant his life could be measured in nothing more than hours. It wasn't the thought of dying that scared him. It was Ellie.

She wasn't sick, not yet, anyway. Perhaps she would wake up tomorrow feeling like he did now, but there would be no one here to take care of her. And what if she was still well? Maybe she'd be alive for days without anyone to help her. A horrifying image of Ellie sitting on his bed, trying in vain to wake both him and Wendy, flashed through his mind.

He grabbed his cell phone from his nightstand, and started working his way through his contact list, calling everyone he knew living in the Boulder area. But the few who actually answered sounded as sick as he was. When he reached the end of the list, he dropped the phone on the floor and buried his face in his hands.

What was he going to do? He couldn't leave Ellie alone. She was barely five, for God's sake.

Wendy's phone, he thought. She would have the numbers for people he didn't.

He found her purse on the kitchen table. After pulling out her cell, he took a quick peek in at Ellie. She seemed to be doing fine, so he returned to the rear of the house where she wouldn't hear him. But what had started off with hope ended in the same despair he'd experienced with his own contact list. No one could help.

Out of options, he tried 911 again. Busy. So once more he dialed the general number.

"Please, I need help," he said as soon as the voicemail beep sounded. "My name is Nolan Gaines. I'm ill and don't think I'll make it through the day, but I have a daughter here. She's only five. Her name is Ellie. She's not sick yet. She'll be all alone once I'm gone. Please. Please send someone to help her."

He hung up without realizing he hadn't left an address.

"Doing okay?" he asked as he walked back into the living room.

Without looking up, Ellie said, "They shouldn't be so mean to him just because he has a red nose."

"No, they shouldn't." He sat on the couch. "Hey, come back here and sit with me." When she was on the couch beside him, he put his arm around her and kissed her on top of her head. "I love you, Ellie. I love you so much."

"I love you, too, Daddy."

The words were like a tonic, easing his concern for a moment, but not taking it completely away.

"I love you, baby," he whispered.

14

SIERRA NEVADA MOUNTAINS, CALIFORNIA
6:58 AM PST

IT WAS EXHAUSTION that had finally caused Martina to fall asleep in the early hours of the morning, but her bone-weary coma was only able to mask her anxiety for so long, and four hours after her eyes had shut, her sense of dread opened them again.

She shuffled into the bathroom and forced herself to take a shower. As the hot water poured down her back, she rolled her head around and around, working the kinks out of her neck. Finally, she started to feel human again. She paused.

She *was* feeling human again.

What she was not feeling was sick.

Was it just taking longer to grab hold of her system? Or had she somehow managed to not catch it yet?

After she dried off and dressed, she went into the kitchen, wet a rag, filled a glass with water, and once more started her rounds. Her first stop was the room Mrs. Weber had died in. Martina had moved the woman outside the previous afternoon, so Pamela now had the room to herself.

Martina sat on the bed and slipped a hand under Pamela's head to lift it, but quickly realized the girl didn't need any water. Like Mrs. Weber, Pamela was dead.

Martina found it hard to breathe as she backed out of the room. She had planned on checking her parents next, but changed her mind and headed to the living room first. There, she found her brother dead, too, and though Riley was still breathing, Martina thought it wouldn't be long before she joined Donny and Pamela.

Steeling herself, she reentered the hallway and walked up to the door of her parents' room. For a moment, she just stood there, unable to open it.

Finally she forced herself to turn the knob.

Her mother and father lay side by side, pretty much in the same position they'd been in when she last checked on them. The one big difference was that the pain that had been etched on their faces was gone.

She had braced herself for this. She had known deep down what she was going to find, but actually standing there and seeing her parents like this, realizing she could never talk to them again, was beyond devastating. A part of her wanted to lie down between them, to take her parents' hands in hers as she waited for her own death to come, but her feet wouldn't move.

It was noise in the other room that finally stirred her—a thump, and a groan, then something falling on the floor. Martina returned to the living room, and stopped abruptly. Riley was sitting on the couch, her elbows propped on her knees, her head in her hands.

"Riley?" Martina said, hardly believing her eyes.

Her friend's head jerked back in surprise. When her eyes focused on Martina, she said, "Water?"

"What? Oh, sure. No problem." Martina was still carrying the glass she'd been taking to her parents' room. She rushed it over, and raised it to her friend's lips. "Here."

Riley took a few sips, then coughed. Martina yanked the glass away.

"No," Riley said. "More."

By the time she had enough, the glass was half empty.

Martina grabbed the blanket off the couch and draped it around Riley's shoulders.

"How are you feeling?" she asked.

"Like crap."

Riley may have felt like crap, but Martina could see that

it was several levels above the point of no return she'd been hovering around most of the night.

"Maybe you should lie back down," Martina suggested.

"Need to go to the bathroom."

"You have to throw up?"

Riley looked annoyed. "No. I didn't say that."

Putting an arm around her friend's waist, Martina helped Riley walk to the bathroom.

"You need help?" she asked once she got her inside.

"I think I'm okay."

Martina closed the door partway and waited nearby. After a while, the toilet flushed and water began running into the sink. When she heard the unmistakable yet surprising sound of Riley brushing her teeth, Martina pushed the door open again.

Riley looked over, the brush still in her mouth. "What?" she said, toothpaste foaming on her lips.

"Nothing. I…uh, I thought you were almost done."

"I am." Riley spit into the sink. "My mouth just felt like…*yuck.*"

If possible, Riley seemed even better than she had been a few minutes before.

When she was seated back on the couch, she asked, "How's everyone else?"

"Asleep," Martina said. She was afraid if she told her friend the truth, it might have an adverse effect on her recovery. "You want something to eat?"

"No. Maybe just a…maybe a nap."

"Sure."

Riley, moving slowly, stretched out once more on the sofa. Within moments, she was asleep.

For ten minutes, Martina sat on the floor next to her, worried that Riley would slip back to the near-death state she'd been in earlier, but her breathing remained strong, and the color that had returned to her cheeks was showing no signs of retreating. When Riley started snoring, Martina began to think her friend might actually live.

This realization caused her to wonder about something

she thought she'd never think about again—the future. What should they do now? She decided to check the radio again to find out what was happening in the rest of the world.

As she walked to the car, she saw dark clouds beginning to gather over the mountains again, and knew more snow would soon be on the way. Since they had no tire chains for the Webers' car, even just a few more inches would be enough to snow them in until the roads cleared again. How long would that be? A week? A month? All winter?

She climbed into the car and flipped the key. When the radio came on, all she heard was static. That was odd. When she'd last turned it off, she'd made sure to leave it tuned to a station out of Bakersfield. It was the strongest signal she'd found.

She scanned the AM band, slowing in the areas she'd found stations before, but she didn't even pick up the hint of a voice. She tried FM, but there was nothing there, either.

Worried, she got out of the car and looked at the sky again. The clouds now covered three quarters of the sky and had grown even darker. Snow coming for sure, in the next hour or two at most.

Even though it was only the two of them now, Martina was sure they didn't have enough food to last an entire winter. If they were snowed in and the flu didn't kill them, starvation would do the trick.

Riley and I are alive, she told herself. *It's my job to keep us that way.*

With a renewed sense of purpose, Martina ran back into the house. She spent three minutes in the kitchen throwing food into two bags, then grabbed a case of water and carried everything out to the car.

As she went back inside, she knew there was one other thing she should take. With reluctance, she reentered her parents' room, and retrieved her father's rifle and the two boxes of extra shells he'd kept in his bag. She hoped she didn't need the weapon, but she had no idea what they would find once they were off the mountains.

She kissed her father's forehead, and then her mother's.

"I'm sorry I can't stay," she said, sure they would understand. "I'll come back as soon as I can. I love you."

Wiping tears from her eyes, she returned to the living room and knelt down next her brother. She kissed him on the cheek, said, "I need to borrow this," and grabbed his backpack.

She removed the contents, set them next to Donny, and put the gun and ammunition into the bag.

"Riley, get up," she said, moving over to the couch. She gave her friend's shoulder a shake. "Riley, come on."

The girl stirred and opened her eyes only wide enough to see. "What is it?"

"We need to go."

Martina slipped an arm under her friend and started to lift her up.

"Go where?"

"Don't worry about it. You can sleep in the car."

"The car? The others are there?"

Martina forced a smile. "No. It's just you and me."

"What about them?"

"Come on." Martina pulled Riley to her feet and walked her to the front door.

"I don't…understand," Riley said as they stepped outside.

"I'll explain later. Right now we've got to go."

She helped Riley into the back and told her to lie down. Her friend still looked confused, but stretched out across the seat. Martina ran back into the house, grabbed a couple blankets, two pillows, and their sleeping bags, just in case.

At the car, she slipped one of the pillows under Riley's head, covered her with the blankets, stuffed everything else into the front passenger seat, and climbed in behind the wheel.

The engine, not happy with the cold, ran rough for nearly a minute before it warmed up. As Martina shifted into Reverse, she took one last look at the house.

"I'll be back," she whispered. "I promise."

She took her foot off the brake, backed up a dozen feet, and dropped the car into Drive.

Right before they reached the main road, a snowflake hit the windshield.

15

THE BUNKER, MONTANA
8:37 AM MST

JOSIE WAS WAITING by the large door to the Bunker's emergency tunnel as the latest search party returned.

She had spent the entire night in the chair next to her father's bed, sleeping, her hand on his. When she woke that morning, he was still unconscious, but Dr. Gardiner had told her his vital signs were continuing to improve.

She hadn't wanted to leave, but the doctor needed to examine her dad's wounds, and said it would be easier if she wasn't there. He'd suggested she go get something to eat. Though she still wasn't hungry, she went down to the kitchen anyway. A man was having breakfast at one of the tables, a walkie-talkie sitting near his plate. As Josie was asking Bobbie for a glass of orange juice, the radio had squawked to life, announcing that Brandon's search party was on its way back inside. That sent her racing down the hall to the tunnel.

She shifted from one foot to the other as she waited, hopeful. But when the searchers finally appeared, she could see from the looks on their faces that they had once again been unsuccessful.

She heard Matt Hamilton's distinctive limp coming down the hall behind her. "Any luck?" he asked as he reached them.

A man from the search party said, "We didn't see him, but there was—"

"You still have people out there looking for him, right?"

Josie asked Matt.

"Of course," Matt said. "We're searching around the clock now. I told you we would." He focused back on the man he'd been talking to. "There was what?"

"Tracks," the man said. "Out on the highway."

"Brandon's?" Josie asked.

"Hard to say."

"Maybe we should go down to my office," Matt suggested.

Josie instantly knew he was trying to cut her out of the conversation. "No!" she told him. "I want to hear what he has to say."

Matt looked as though he were going to fight her on it, but then he sighed in resignation. "Okay, okay. But don't interrupt him again."

"I won't." She looked at the searcher. "Go ahead. What about the tracks?"

The man looked at Matt, who nodded. "There were several of them. Some big. Boots, probably men. One set smaller. Could be a woman." He inclined his head toward Josie. "Could be your brother. They were on the highway a good thirty miles from here. Whoever made the smaller tracks looked like they'd been traveling alone for a while. The larger arrived by helicopter."

"Helicopter?" Matt said, concerned.

Josie was worried, too. Helicopters had attacked the Ranch.

"Two skid prints," the man said. "Looked like they all got on and flew away."

"How long ago, do you think?" Matt asked.

"Had to have been within twenty-four hours, between that last snowstorm and this morning."

Matt pulled out his walkie-talkie. "Christina?"

Static. "Go for Christina."

"Check the local radar archives, and see if you can find a helicopter that landed on the highway about thirty miles southeast of here in the last…" He paused. "Let's say thirty-six hours."

"On it."

As he put the radio away, Josie said, "Do you think they have Brandon? It's them, isn't it?"

"We don't know anything yet," Matt said. "Let's see if we can ID the helicopter first." He looked over at the search team. "You all get some rest. I need you back out there in six hours."

"Yes, sir."

As the team left for their quarters, Josie matched Matt stride for stride as he headed toward the communications room.

"If they took him, what are we going to do?" she asked.

"We'll deal with that when we know more. There's a very good chance those prints aren't even Brandon's."

"They could be. I mean, don't you need to have a plan just in case?"

They turned onto a new hallway.

"Josie, I promised you that we'll find him. I don't plan on breaking that."

"I didn't say anything about breaking your promise. I just want to know if there's a plan for what to do if he was on that helicopter."

Stopping in the middle of the corridor, he turned to her. "No, there's no plan. Not yet. But if we think he was on that helicopter, we'll come up with one based on what we learn."

Logically, she could understand it, but it wasn't the answer she wanted to hear. "You *will* go after him, right? No matter where he is."

"Yes. We will. Now, please, let me go help them figure this out. I'll let you know as soon as we know anything."

She studied him for a moment, wanting to stay with him so she could be there the moment new information came in, but realizing she'd probably pushed her luck as far as she could for now. "The *second* you know something."

"I give you my word."

THERE WAS A knock on Josie's door.

She opened it to find Chloe standing on the other side.

"Matt sent me to get you," the woman said.

Josie immediately stepped into the hallway and closed the door. "They found him, didn't they? Was he on that helicopter?"

"Matt's got the details."

"Just tell me. Was he on it?"

Chloe hesitated, then nodded. "We think so."

Together they walked quickly through the Bunker to the communications room, where they found Matt leaning over the shoulder of another man sitting at a computer terminal. There was a map of a small city on the screen.

"Is that where he is?" Josie asked.

"We think it's possible," Matt said.

"Where is that?"

"Great Falls, Montana. It's southeast of us." He pointed at an airport at the east end of town. "Malmstrom Air Force Base. This is where the helicopter landed after it left the highway."

"And you're sure Brandon was on it?"

Matt nodded. "I had the search team out there right now follow the set of smaller footprints back as far as they could. They discovered the person had built a shelter to hide from the storm the previous night. Inside was a wrapper from a granola bar, same brand we stock in our emergency dumps. So, the same kind Brandon would have had with him. It's not definite proof, but it seems pretty likely."

"I want to go," she said.

"Hold on."

"You're sending people out, right? I want to be one of them."

"You're not going anywhere. Your dad would never allow that."

"My dad's still recovering from surgery. Until he gets better, *I* represent our family, and one of us has to go. I'm the only choice."

"No. That's not going to happen."

Josie glared at him. "Then I'll go on my own."

"No, you won't. You couldn't get out without someone stopping you."

"I'll keep trying. I *will* get out. I promise you."

Matt scoffed and shook his head. Before he could say anything else, Chloe said, "I'll be responsible for her."

He spun around. "What?"

"She can ride with me."

"No one even said you're going."

"I'm saying it, and I'm saying Josie can come along. I'll make sure nothing happens to her."

"You can't promise that."

"This isn't the same world anymore," Chloe said. "You know that as well as any of us. You've been preparing us for it." She paused. "Kids can't afford to be kids now. She's going. If you want to send anyone with us, I suggest you pick them out now because we're leaving."

ONE OF THE motorbikes was out with the search party, meaning there were only two available to the rescue team. Since they would need seat space for Brandon, there was only room for one other on their expedition. Miller, the man who'd been with Josie's father when he was hurt in the explosion, was the first to volunteer.

As soon as the bikes were gassed up, and Josie and her two companions were outfitted for the trip, they took off.

The ride over the snow-covered roads was cold and treacherous, but Josie barely noticed. She hugged tight to Chloe's back and peered over the woman's shoulder at the road ahead, sure that they would find her brother.

When they reached the spot where the helicopter had landed, they stopped only long enough for a quick look before continuing south. After a while, the road veered to the east and met the interstate. Though it also had been covered with snow, they were able to increase their speed as they drove down the wider and better maintained I-15.

About five miles before they reached Great Falls, Chloe signaled for Miller to follow her off the road.

"Where are we going?" Josie asked.

Chloe turned her head a few inches and yelled, "When I came through before, there was a roadblock not far from here. Would rather go around it this time."

The new route was bumpy, but no military personnel tried to stop them.

It was midafternoon when they finally crossed into the city limits. The pale light of the low winter sun made the quiet town look stark and empty. Josie glanced at the houses they were passing. Though she was sure there were people inside, they all looked deserted.

About a mile from the base, they slowed to a stop.

"Was that here last time?" Miller asked.

"I didn't get this far east," Chloe said. "But I doubt it."

Stopped at an angle partway into the intersection just ahead was a military truck. The disturbing part, though, wasn't the truck itself, but the man lying motionless on the ground below the open driver's door.

"You okay?" Chloe asked Josie.

"I'm fine," Josie said. This wasn't her first body.

Chloe took them forward slowly, keeping tight to the left side of the road so they were as far from the man and the truck as possible.

"Kind of looks like the vehicle that was manning the roadblock," Chloe said.

"Well, he *is* wearing a uniform," Miller said.

A nod from Chloe.

Now that they were closer, they could see the man's open eyes staring at the sky, and under each, the dark circles that were one of the signs of Sage Flu.

"He must have been here at least half a day," Miller said.

"Why hasn't anyone moved him?" Josie asked.

Chloe looked around. "I'm not sure there's anyone who could."

They approached Malmstrom Air Force Base from 2nd Avenue. As soon as the main gate came into view, Chloe and Miller pulled to the side of the road.

"Hop off," Chloe said to Josie.

“Why?”

“I want to check something. I’ll be right back.”

Though she didn’t want to, Josie dismounted the bike.

“Stay with her,” Chloe said. She then gunned her engine and continued down the road.

Josie stepped out into the street so she could see where Chloe was going. As Chloe neared the gate, Josie expected someone to step out of the building to greet her, but even when Chloe stopped right at the entrance, the door to the building remained closed. She waited there for a moment, then got off her bike and went inside. Two minutes later, she reappeared, hopped on her motorcycle, and raced back to Josie and Miller.

“So?” Miller asked.

“One guard. Dead. At least as long as the guy we passed.”

Josie climbed back onto the bike and they drove unhindered onto the base.

Malmstrom was a military base, so someone should have been chasing them down to find out who they were, but there was no one else on the roads, and no sign of anyone in the buildings they passed. The place had turned into a ghost town.

“Are they all dead?” Josie asked.

“If not yet,” Chloe said, “soon enough.”

They headed to the airfield where the archived radar information indicated the helicopter had landed. It was clear that a big operation, or perhaps even several, had been underway. Trucks and cars were parked in front of most of the buildings, with dozens of planes and helicopters lined up not far away, some of which looked like they were in the process of being loaded with cargo.

Chloe led them over to the nearest cluster of helicopters and parked.

The moment the motorcycle’s engines cut off, they were plunged into a chilling silence. There was nothing. No wind. No mechanical sounds. No voices.

Not.

A.

Thing.

"Check the helicopters," Chloe said to Miller. "See if there are any logs or something like that." She motioned at the closest building. "Josie and I will check in there."

The inside of the building was a big, open office that had dozens of desks covered with folders and clipboards and papers. None, unfortunately, seemed to have anything to do with Brandon. Miller had similar luck with his search.

"Let's try that next group of helicopters," Chloe said.

They drove down to where the three aircraft were parked. These were smaller than the ones they'd just checked, and unlikely to have been the type of vehicle Brandon had been picked up in. Predictably, they came up dry again. Another building had four helicopters out front, but still no information about Brandon.

There were only two helicopters at their next stop, but their skids were about the right size to have made the indentations in the snow back on the highway where Brandon had been taken. While Miller once more checked for flight logs, Chloe and Josie searched inside the building they were next to.

"What's this?" Josie said, carrying over to Chloe a clipboard she'd found on one of the desks.

The header on the top sheet read:

OPERATION PIPER

Below were several names, followed by numbers that ranged between five and sixteen. Some had addresses, some didn't. But none had any of the typical identifiers seen on other documents that indicated the names belonged to Air Force personnel.

Chloe looked it over and frowned. "I don't know. Where did you find it?"

Josie led her back to the desk. It was Chloe who found the folder. She read through a few of the sheets inside, then said, "He *was* here."

"What do you mean, 'was'?" Josie asked.

"They airlifted him out. Apparently they were gathering up kids who didn't have guardians."

"Why would they do that?"

"Probably thinking they were protecting them." Chloe looked at the file again. "It says here they were taken to Colorado Springs, Colorado."

Josie's heart sank. "How are we supposed to get there?"

"Getting there isn't going to be the problem." Chloe pulled out her phone.

"Who are you calling?"

Chloe hesitated before punching in a number. Instead of raising it to her ear, she hit the speaker button so Josie could hear, too. After two rings, Matt answered. She quickly filled him in on what they'd found, and said, "We need the jet. How soon can Harlan and Barry get it here?"

"I'm not sure that's such a—"

"Don't," Chloe warned him as she shot a reassuring glance at Josie. "We're going. So how long do we have to wait?"

A pause, then, "They can be there within an hour."

"Good. Tell them to land right at Malmstrom. No one's here but us."

"All right, but the minute I need them anywhere else, they're out of there. Understand?"

"I understand." After she hung up, she smiled at Josie. "See? No problem."

"HOW SOON CAN Harlan and Barry get it here?"

Matt frowned. "I'm not sure that's such a—"

"Don't," Chloe said sharply over the phone. "We're going. So how long do we have to wait?"

Matt thought for a second. He was loath to take the jet out of circulation, in case it was needed to ferry vaccine to any survivors they might find, but he also couldn't justify having it sit on the runway while Brandon was taken farther and farther away from his family. "They can be there within an hour."

"Good. Tell them to land right at Malmstrom. No one's here but us."

"All right, but the minute I need them anywhere else, they're out of there. Understand?"

"I understand."

He hung up and looked across the room. "Kenji!"

The LIC leader glanced over.

"Have a load of vaccine taken to the plane right away. Say, enough for two hundred."

Kenji looked confused. "Is there a group out there I don't know about?"

Matt shook his head. "I need to send Harlan on a side trip, and I want him to be ready if he needs to go somewhere else later."

"Got it."

Matt had Christina call Harlan with instructions, then pulled his tin of ibuprofen out of his pocket and popped four pills into his mouth. His leg was really killing him today, and the stress wasn't helping things.

"Harlan can be in the air in ten minutes," Christina announced.

With a nod, he walked over to Kenji.

"The vaccine will be there in a few minutes," Kenji said.

"Thanks," Matt told him. "If something comes up, tell me right away, and we'll redirect the plane the moment we can."

"Nothing in our coverage area here yet, but we have identified four more groups."

"Where?" Matt asked, anxious for some good news.

Kenji led him to the computer station a woman named Terri Wright was manning. "Can you bring up the map?" he asked her.

"Two seconds," she said.

With a few clicks of the keys, a map of North America appeared, zooming in on a small town along the coast of Baja California.

Kenji glanced at Matt. "Santa Blanca. A little fishing village. Only ways in and out are by water and a twenty-mile dirt road. We picked up a call for help fifteen minutes ago."

"How many?" Matt asked.

"The guy we talked to said there are fifty-seven."

"Vaccine en route?"

Kenji nodded. "Out of San Diego. Should be there within ninety minutes." He touched Terri on the shoulder. "Next one."

The map shifted to a farm in Louisiana, where a family of twelve had gathered for Christmas and barricaded themselves in an old farmhouse. The closest vaccine to them was with the Resistance's contingent in Atlanta, and would take three hours to get there.

The third location was across the Atlantic in the town of Luleå in northern Sweden. A group of students and teachers who'd been involved in a research project during the winter break had taken refuge in one of the science buildings and been able to keep all others out. Their problem now was not only trying to avoid the flu, but it had been over twenty-four hours since they'd eaten the last of their food. Unfortunately, the closest vaccine to them was outside Amsterdam, and the nearest plane that could fly it up was currently on a mission in Macedonia. The survivors were told to hang tight and someone would get to them by tomorrow.

"And the fourth?" Matt asked.

"Bring it up," Kenji said.

When the final map location appeared, the image was all white—no roads, no town name, no anything.

"Where the hell is this?" Matt asked.

"Pull back," Kenji said.

The view zoomed out. It was an island, just off the coast of…

"Antarctica," Matt said.

"Uh-huh. King Sejong Station. It's Korean." He looked at Matt. "They have seventy-five people there."

"What about other facilities? There are dozens down there. Have we reached any of them?"

"Not yet. Sejong, however, says they'd talked to several other bases a couple days ago, and at least four had reported outbreaks."

"But *they're* okay?"

"Apparently. The station is closest to South America. I can send one of the teams but the problem is, that'll tie our people up for nearly twenty-four hours."

Which would leave a hole in their coverage. "I assume supplies aren't a problem for them," Matt said.

"They could go six months if they needed to without a new shipment."

Their isolation was a big plus, too, Matt knew. "Tell them…" He paused, hoping he was making the right decision. "Tell them we'll get to them as soon as possible. When you feel confident you can free up a team, send it."

It would have to do for now.

"Anything else?" Matt asked.

"We've picked up a few other faint signals that we've been trying to home in on, but no real info yet."

"Okay, let me know the moment that changes."

16

BOULDER, COLORADO
11:12 AM MST

JACK CUTROY'S HEAD was beginning to pound. And no wonder—it had been almost three days since he'd had any real sleep. Such was the life of an EMT in a world that was falling apart.

He and his partner Allen Descantes had spent the first few days decked out in biohazard suits, trying to save lives. That hadn't worked out so well. While they were still wearing the suits every day, their mission had changed.

Allen's phone rang again as they pulled up to the next address on their list. He checked the display and sent the call to voicemail.

"Sheila again?" Jack asked.

A nod.

"Dude, go home. I can handle this."

"That's not the job."

"Screw the job."

Allen's situation made Jack's headache seem trivial. Allen's wife Sheila had taken to calling him nearly every thirty minutes to plead with him to come home to her and their two kids. That was one problem Jack didn't have. He hadn't been in a relationship in nearly four months, and had never been married.

Jack knew his partner was being pulled by his conscience

in both directions—a duty to a job he swore to undertake no matter what, and a duty to his family that he'd vowed to protect at all costs.

Allen stared at the floor, then looked out the window. "Which house is it?"

Jack looked at the list. "Uh, 4324. That brown one there."

As they climbed out of the truck and headed to the house, Jack said, "I'm serious. Go home. If I can't handle this on my own, then I'm useless."

A frown from Allen. "I don't know. I can't just leave you alone."

"Yeah, you can. And you can do it without feeling guilty. All we're doing now is a glorified body check. It's not what we were trained to do." He paused. "Be with your family."

More silence. "You sure?"

"Absolutely."

They turned down the path that led to the front door.

"All right," Allen said, looking relieved. "After we drop off this one."

"Good. Then let's get this over with, huh?" Jack knocked on the door. "Boulder Fire Department!"

Dead silence from the other side.

He knocked again. "Boulder Fire Department. We're responding to your call."

Nothing.

He glanced at the list and read through the details of this particular stop. "All right," he said. "Let's try around back."

There was no lock on the gate, so they were able to get into the backyard without climbing the fence.

It was a nice place. Not a huge yard, but not too small. No pool, but there was a Jacuzzi, though there was no water in it at the moment. A pair of French doors along the back opened into what looked like a family room. Jack tried both handles. They were locked, so he peered through the window, but detected no movement.

Like pretty much everywhere else they'd been in the last day, they were probably too late.

He tapped on the glass. “Boulder Fire Department!”

Was that a noise? He cocked his head and listened, but decided it must have come from outside somewhere.

“You want this one?” he asked Allen.

“Sure.”

Once Jack was out of the way, Allen picked up a small potted plant from the patio, and struck it against the glass of the French door near the handle. Cracks rippled, but the window stayed intact. He hit harder on his second try, and this time the window shattered. After he knocked out the pieces stuck in the frame, he reached in and unlocked the door.

“Hello?” he called as they moved inside. “Hello. Anyone here? Boulder Fire Department.”

There was a Christmas tree all lit up in the living room, surrounded by wrapping paper and ribbons and boxes and toys.

“I don’t think I’m going to like this,” Allen said.

They checked the kitchen and dining room. Both were clear. With a sense of foreboding, Jack led them to the hallway entrance and flipped on the light. Before heading down it, he checked the seals around his wrists and neck, making sure everything was secured. The first room they came to was dark. He reached inside and turned on the light. Bathroom. Empty.

The next room appeared to be some kind of home office. The room opposite it was a child’s bedroom. The bed was short and unoccupied. He motioned to the closet, and Allen slid the doors back. No one there.

The master bedroom was the only place left. Jack sent up a silent prayer, hoping that the residents had abandoned the place, and he could strike this address from their list.

No such luck.

There was a body on the bed. A woman, young, maybe late twenties at most. Even with the marks on her face, Jack could tell she’d been pretty.

“Dead at least a day,” Allen said, leaning over the body.

There was a doorless walk-in closet along the wall on their right. Jack looked inside. Clothes and shoes, both women's and men's.

He eyed the door to the en suite bathroom. Not wanting to, but knowing they needed to be thorough, he forced himself over to the opening.

From there he could see it was a good-sized room. Comfortable. Dual sinks, a linen closet, separate shower and bath. The only thing out of place was the body lying in the tub.

It took all of his will to step over the threshold and walk across the tile floor for a better look.

Not just one body, but two.

The man, presumably husband to the woman lying on the bed, took up a majority of the space. Curled across his chest was a little girl.

Jesus, maybe I should go home, too.

There was something in the guy's right hand, shiny and metallic. Jack only needed to take another step closer to see it was a gun.

Oh, God. Had the guy killed his little girl then himself?

The message the man had left on police voicemail had been transcribed and included in the notes they were given. Even in print, the man had sounded desperate—a father scared of what would happen to his daughter after he died. Having not received an immediate response, had the guy decided he had no options left?

Wait, wait. Where's the blood? There's no blood.

Perhaps the man had been unable to follow through. Or maybe he'd succumbed to the flu before he could. Whatever the case, Jack was thankful the trigger hadn't been pulled. That was one sight he didn't think he would be able to stomach.

Still, they were both dead, which meant he and Allen had to—

He froze.

The girl was looking at him. Her eyes were only slits, but she was *definitely* looking at him.

He dropped to a knee. "Hey, there. Are you okay?"

Her eyes squeezed shut and she turned her face against

her father's chest.

Jack looked back at the clipboard and skimmed through the man's message again. "Are you Ellie?"

He could tell this surprised her. After a moment, her head twisted enough so that she could look at him with one eye.

"Don't be afraid, Ellie. I'm a fireman. I'm here to help you."

"Fireman?" she whispered.

"Uh-huh. Your daddy called us to come get you."

"Daddy won't wake up. Mommy, too."

"Yeah, they're in a deep sleep right now. That's why your daddy wanted you to come with us."

"He did?"

"He sure did."

"No," she said, shaking her head. "I stay with them."

"Hey, Allen," Jack called out. "I found the girl."

When Allen entered the bathroom, Ellie pulled tighter to her father.

"It's okay," Jack said. "He's my friend. Another fireman."

"She's alive?" Allen said, surprised.

"Yeah."

"Sick?"

"I don't know. Can't tell yet." To the girl he said, "It's okay. Can you tell me how you are feeling?"

It took a bit more coaxing before she finally said, "Scared."

"Of us?"

She nodded.

"Don't be scared of us. We're only here to help."

"Okay," she said, less than convinced.

"Can you tell me if you're feeling sick? Headache? Sore throat? Have you been coughing?"

She shook her head. "No. Just…just hungry."

"I think we can do something about that. What's your favorite thing to eat?"

She thought for a moment. "Peanut butter and jelly

sandwich."

"Why don't I go make you one?" Allen suggested.

"Okay. Grape jelly. Not Mommy's strawberry."

"Grape. Got it," Allen said, then left.

Jack held out his arms. "Let's go into the living room and let your father rest."

She hesitated.

"It's okay," he said. "I'm not going to hurt you."

She held on to her father a few seconds longer, then reached up. Jack picked her up and carried her out of the room.

"Why do you have that on your head?" she asked, touching his hood as they headed for the living room. "Makes your voice sound funny."

"It does, doesn't it?"

"Uh-huh."

"It's one of our uniforms," he told her. "For special days like today."

"Because it's Christmas time?"

"No, no," he said quickly. "Not Christmas. I just meant some days we wear them."

"Oh."

Allen appeared a short time later with a peanut butter and jelly sandwich wrapped in a paper towel. "Here you go," he said, handing it to her.

She took a big bite, and stopped mid-chew. Through a stuffed mouth, she said, "Tanks."

"Ellie, how about you eat that in our truck?" Jack asked.

Her head moved rapidly from side to side. "No. Have to stay here with Mommy and Daddy."

"Remember what I told you? Your daddy asked us to come and get you?"

"Stay here."

"Someone will come to take care of your parents," Allen said. "We need to take you someplace else…someplace where you can have more peanut butter and grape jelly sandwiches."

Looking skeptical, she said, "But Mommy and Daddy."

"Your mommy and daddy wanted you to come with us,"

Jack said. "Okay?"

She looked like she might cry, but she said, "Okay."

As Jack carried her toward the door, she suddenly stiffened and looked over his shoulder. "Bear!"

"What?"

"Santa brought me a bear. I need it!"

He looked at the toys around the Christmas tree but didn't see any bear. "Where is it?"

She began squirming in his arms. "I'll get it."

Not sure if he should take the chance, he set her down. The moment her feet touched the floor, she bolted across the room and into the hallway.

"Do you want to draw her blood or do you want me to do it?" Jack asked Allen as soon as she was gone.

"She's gotta have it already," Allen said. "She'd been breathing the same air as her parents. God only knows how long she was lying there with her dad."

"We still have to check."

Allen frowned. "Yeah. I guess. All right. I'll do it."

A few seconds later, Ellie ran back into the room, a black, curly-haired bear hugged to her side. Jack lifted her up.

"Ready?" he asked.

She nodded.

"All right. Let's go."

17

THE BUNKER, MONTANA
2:17 PM MST

THE FIRST THING Ash felt was the IV needle in his hand. Of course, he didn't know it was a needle at the time. To him, it just felt odd. Next came the pain in his ribs, tight and throbbing. His knee was sore, too. And there was an especially sharp pain along his abdomen.

What the hell's going on?

He blinked.

A white room, and some noise off to his side.

He closed his eyes again and tried to recall the last thing that had happened.

Night. The forest. No, a house in the forest. He'd been at a…a door. He'd been trying to talk to the…woman inside. What then? The window, right. He'd moved over to it and…and…and the current pulled back and she was there, looking startled. And then…?

There was no "and then." This was the "and then," this room. He'd been standing on the woman's porch, and now he was lying in this room, apparently injured.

Why had he been out at her house in the first place? Why had he wanted to talk to her?

He tried to remember the reason, but his mind was still mush.

He heard a door open. When his eyelids parted again, a man in a white jacket with a stethoscope around his neck was standing next to his bed. A doctor, Ash guessed. That would make sense, wouldn't it? But Ash had never seen him before.

The doctor was taking Ash's pulse. As he finished, he noticed that Ash's eyes were open.

"Welcome back," the man said.

Ash licked his lips. "Where am I?"

"That's a good question," the man said. "Not really sure I know the answer."

"I…don't understand."

"Hold on."

The doctor disappeared from view. There was the sound of the door opening again, and then the doctor's voice saying, "He's awake."

There were more voices, far away and not easy to understand. When the doctor finally came back to the bed, a familiar woman was with him.

"Captain Ash," she said, smiling. "How are you feeling?"

"I know you," he said.

"Lily," she told him.

Right. Lily. Nurse at the Ranch. Then this must be…

"The Bunker?" he asked.

"That's right."

He looked over at the doctor, confused.

Lily said, "That's Dr. Gardiner. He saved your life."

"Thank you."

"Apparently we're even," the doctor said as he pulled back the sheet and looked at the wounds on Ash's torso.

"Even?"

The doctor answered with only a smile. When he finished his examination, he pulled the sheet back into place. "I'll check back in a little while."

Once he was gone, Lily said, "Chloe kind of, well, kidnapped him and his family from Great Falls. If she hadn't, they would've died there. Coming here to save you meant they got inoculated."

The door burst open, and Matt and Rachel rushed in.

"Thank God," Rachel said, grabbing Ash's hand and

smiling. "How are you feeling?"

"He still needs a lot of rest," Lily told them.

"Of course, of course," Matt said.

It seemed to Ash as if they were all going to leave again. "Hold on. I…I…"

"What is it?" Lily asked.

He gave himself a moment to get his words in order. "Why am I here? What happened?"

"You don't remember?" Matt asked.

"I remember standing in front of a house. That's it."

"The house exploded," Matt said. "Knocked you into the yard. Thankfully Miller was with you, or you'd have died out there."

"But why were we there?"

Matt's brow furrowed, surprised. "You were looking for Brandon."

Brandon! It all came back in a rush.

He tried to sit up, but his torso screamed in pain.

"You just had surgery yesterday," Lily said. "You need to conserve your strength."

Ash grabbed Matt's wrist. "He wasn't in the house, was he?"

"No."

"You're sure?"

"Absolutely."

"You found him?" Ash asked, hoping that's what Matt had meant.

"Not quite. But we've found his trail, and think we know where he is."

Ash put his palms on the mattress, intending to try to sit up again, but Lily held him down.

"Let me go," he said. "I have to find him."

"You're not going anywhere," she said.

"You need to rest," Matt told him. "Don't worry. Chloe went to get him."

"Chloe?"

"She'll bring him back."

Ash relaxed. Though he'd rather be getting Brandon

himself, he trusted Chloe to handle it.

He could feel his eyelids growing heavy again. Forcing them to stay open, he said, “Josie, how is she?”

“She’s fine,” Matt said after a brief pause.

Good, Ash thought. This time he didn’t fight it as his eyes closed. Brandon on the verge of being found, Josie safe—that was as much as he could ask for at the moment.

18

UPPER MOJAVE DESERT, CALIFORNIA
12:44 PM PST

MARTINA'S HANDS ACHED from gripping the steering wheel of the Webers' car so tightly. The drive off the mountain had been the most nerve-wracking experience of her life.

While there had been areas where the snow barely covered the road, in other parts, the swirling winds had piled up drifts two—and even three—feet high. Every time she encountered one of these, she had to slow the car to a near standstill and find a way around it.

Then there was the ice. More than once, the car skidded on an unseen patch, threatening to slide off the road. She was pretty sure there was at least one time the tires on the passenger side had moved off the asphalt, edging dangerously close to the ditch that paralleled the road.

The scariest part by far, though, was when she reached the section of road that led down the canyon to the desert. Two lanes, barely any shoulder, no guardrails, and a seventy-degree downward slope on her right that promised a plummet to the rocky chasm floor several hundred feet below if she made even the slightest error.

Since there didn't appear to be any other vehicles using the road, she stuck to the middle of the asphalt and kept her speed low and steady. About the only good thing was that the snow was only at the very top, and it wasn't long before her worries simply consisted of taking a turn too wide and driving off the cliff.

When they finally reached the bottom, Martina stopped the car at the side of the road and climbed out. Leaning against the fender, she took several deep breaths until her body stopped shaking, and her heart rate slowed enough for her to concentrate on what to do next.

They were near the north end of Indian Wells Valley. Along the west side were the towering Sierra Nevada Mountains that she and Riley had just descended. Across the north was the smaller yet still imposing Coso Range. Hills in the south, and the gradual rise of the valley in the east served as the last two boundaries. In the distance on the east side, she could see the hump that was B Mountain. It was a big hill, really, located on the China Lake naval base. Its name was courtesy of the giant B the students at Burroughs High School—her alma mater—repainted on its rocks each year.

Home.

She looked toward the highway about a mile away. Usually during the week between Christmas and New Year's, US 395 was packed with skiers from LA headed to Mammoth Mountain three more hours to the north, but today there wasn't a car in sight.

She climbed back into the sedan and settled into her seat, her gaze pausing on the gas gauge. It had been at a little more than a quarter tank when they'd set out, but now it was nearly empty. Having never driven the Webers' car, she had no idea how far it could go on fumes. Ridgecrest was at least twenty miles away. And while the much smaller Inyokern was closer, it was still a good ten miles. What if they ran out of gas before then? Riley was in no condition for any kind of long hike.

Wasn't there something to the north? The last time she'd gone any farther in that direction had been a couple years earlier when the Burroughs softball team went to a tournament up in Bishop. She closed her eyes and tried to remember.

Yes. There had been something. A few stores and…a gas station, right?

She started the car, drove to the intersection with the highway, and looked left. She could make out a few buildings in the distance, maybe three or four miles away.

God, I hope I'm right, she thought, then turned north on 395.

About a quarter mile before she reached the buildings, a sign along the road read: PEARSONVILLE.

The town wasn't a thriving metropolis by any means, more a wide spot on the highway. Like everywhere else since they'd left the cabin, it was devoid of activity. It did have a gas station, though.

She pulled up to pump number one and hopped out. While the station still had power, the pump needed a credit card to activate it. Martina's ATM card would have worked, but it was buried in the sedan's trunk under the water and bags of food. Instead of digging it out, she decided to go inside the attached minimart to see if she could turn the pump on.

The door whooshed open, and a bong announced her arrival, but there was no one else there to hear it. The cash register and pump controller was in an area sealed off from the rest of the store by a Plexiglas partition. She tried the door that led into it, but it was locked.

Food's free today,but not the gas, apparently, she thought.

She frowned and took a look around. Near the back was a short hallway with one door to a bathroom, and a second that was unmarked. She opened the unmarked door.

Maintenance room—mops, buckets, cleaning supplies. On the floor under a shelf was a toolbox. She opened it up and found a hammer.

She knew the Plexiglas wouldn't give way, but the handle on the door was no match for her softball-enhanced swing. It broke off quickly, but the latch remained in place. Using a flathead screwdriver from the same toolkit, she inched the latch back until it finally popped free. With a simple push, the door opened.

Would have been easier to just use your card, she

thought. But the truth was, she didn't know what the future held, and the few hundred dollars still in her account might be needed for something else. It was better not to use it if she didn't need to.

The next trick was figuring out how to turn on the pump. It took a few tries before she let out a whoop of triumph as the light next to pump number one turned green.

"What are you doing?" The voice was muffled but still made her jump.

Riley was standing outside the store, looking through the window.

"You almost gave me a heart attack," Martina said.

"Why are you in there?"

"We need gas. Had to turn on the pump."

Riley looked around. "Where's the attendant who works here?"

"They're all gone."

For a second it was as if Riley had forgotten all about what was happening. Then it seemed to click.

"Right," Riley said. "Oh, shit." She grabbed the wall as if she'd suddenly lost all her strength.

Martina rushed from the booth and out of the store, the door bonging again as she left. When she reached Riley, she grabbed hold of her friend to steady her. "Look. You're alive. I'm alive. That's all that's important right now."

Riley stared at her for a second, then looked back at the car. "Where are the others?"

Martina hesitated. "There are no others. Only you and me."

"But…but my mom. Pamela."

"And Donny and my dad and my mom."

Riley gaped at her. "All of them?"

"Yes. All of them."

This time, Riley did lose the strength to stand, and almost took Martina down with her as she dropped onto the ground.

Martina wanted nothing more than to slump down next to Riley, but she knew one of them had to keep her head.

"Stay here. I'm going to get the gas started."

The pump worked flawlessly. As it filled the sedan's tank, Martina kept an eye on Riley, deciding it best to let her friend have a few minutes alone. The girl stared at the ground the entire time, unmoving. When the pump clicked off, Martina replaced the nozzle in its holder and walked back over.

"You going to be okay?"

For a second, Riley's expression didn't change. Then she looked up. "What?"

"Are you going to be all right?"

"All right? No. No, I'm not."

That's when the tears started.

Martina knelt in front of her. "I didn't mean it like that. I know we can't be all right. I just meant..." She stopped, thought about it. "Hell, I don't know what."

She started to cry, too.

How long it lasted, she didn't know—ten minutes, fifteen—but at some point the tide receded, and she was able to get control of herself again.

"I think M&Ms are in order," she said as she wiped her face and rose to her feet.

"Skittles," Riley blurted out. "I'd like Skittles."

It was tempting to clear the shelves and take as much as they could fit in the car, but neither girl could bring herself to do that yet. Deep down, they were both hoping that everything would go back to...if not normal then something close. Martina didn't let herself think about it too much, though, because deep down, she knew normal would never return.

Riley switched to the front passenger seat for the final leg of their drive. Her flu symptoms had been replaced by a general weakness one would expect after such an illness, similar to how Martina had felt after the spring outbreak.

That got Martina thinking again about her own condition. She still had no symptoms. It was like the virus had passed her by completely. It reminded her of something her mother had told her about chicken pox. Though Martina had received the vaccine when she was young and had never had the disease, her mom had said that wasn't always the case, and that everyone used to get it as a child.

"Your grandma made me go play with the neighbors' kids when they had it so that I'd catch it, too," her mom had said.

"Why would she do that?" Martina asked.

"So I'd get it over with and wouldn't have to worry about it anymore."

Martina still hadn't understood, so her mother explained, "Usually you only get chicken pox once. After that, your system builds up an immunity and you never get it again."

Could it be that after surviving her first brush with Sage Flu, Martina's system had built up immunity? If that were true, then…

She stopped herself, not wanting to hope too much. She could test the theory soon enough.

They saw their first body as they drove through Inyokern. Two bodies, actually. Both were sitting in a car parked on the other side of the road. Though they may have just been sleeping, neither girl believed that. The tiny town itself seemed otherwise deserted.

Once they passed the bed where the old railroad tracks had been, Martina increased their speed and raced down Inyokern Road toward Ridgecrest.

In disaster movies, when the world seemed to be coming to an end, streets would always be packed with abandoned cars. That wasn't what they found. The streets were completely empty. It was clear that the president's order for a nationwide curfew had been heeded and people had stayed home, where they had probably become too sick to venture out again.

At least it gave Martina and Riley clear sailing into town.

Though it was evident Riley no longer needed to see a doctor, she still wanted to go to the hospital. That would be where her father had taken her sister on Christmas Eve, and she hoped that would be where the girls would find them.

Like the roads, most of the parking lots they passed were

empty. But that wasn't true of the lot surrounding the hospital. It was jam-packed. There were even cars along China Lake Boulevard, where neither girl had ever seen any parked before.

Martina pulled into the lot, and stopped the sedan in the middle of the road near the main entrance. Given the lack of people, she was pretty sure what they would find inside, so blocking the way wouldn't be an issue.

Riley was out of the car first, moving surprisingly fast given her condition. Martina caught up to her just inside the hospital lobby, where her friend had come to a sudden stop.

The reason was immediately clear. Here was where the dead had taken up residence. There were over two dozen bodies in the lobby, sitting in chairs, lying on the floor, propped against the wall.

"Hello?" Riley called out, her voice weak.

"Anyone here?" Martina shouted. When no one responded, she looked at her friend. "If your sister was admitted, she'd be in one of the rooms, not out here."

"Right. Sure."

Behind the reception counter, Martina brought up the patient database on one of the computers, and searched for Laurie Weber.

"Her name's not here," she said.

"Maybe…maybe they got too busy to input everything. This place looks like it got crazy."

"Maybe," Martina said, not adding, "If she *is* here, she's probably dead."

It took them an hour to do a room-by-room search. What they found was a mix of the dead and the almost. The vast majority of the latter was unconscious, but a few moaned as Martina and Riley passed. It was a real-life house of horrors. Martina lost track of how many times she nearly screamed.

"She's not here," she said after they checked the last room on the top floor of the tower section.

Riley looked one way down the hall, then the other. "But this is where my dad would have taken her."

"Maybe they went home," Martina suggested, hoping it

would prod Riley into movement. The sooner they got out of the hospital, the sooner she'd stop feeling like there was something crawling under her skin.

"Home?" Riley said as if she didn't understand. Then her face brightened. "Yeah, they didn't have any room here. After Laurie was treated, Dad probably took her to the house."

They headed for the stairwell, walking at first, but running within the first couple of steps, both anxious to leave. Martina reached the bottom of the stairs first, threw the door open, and screamed.

"Help me. Please."

A man stood teetering a few feet on the other side of the door, facing her. He was wearing green scrubs, and looked about the same age as Martina's parents. There was no question he was sick—his watery eyes rimmed by blackened skin, snot running out of his nose.

He tried to raise his hand as if he wanted to reach out to her, but his arms only moved a few inches.

"Please," he repeated. "Someone has to take care of him."

The words seemed to knock the wind out of him. He fell back against the wall, panting.

"T…t…take care of who?" Martina asked from just inside the stairwell.

"Come on," Riley whispered. "We need to go."

Whether it was guilt for having screamed at the man, or compassion for his request, Martina couldn't bring herself to move. "Are you talking about a patient?"

A nod.

"Where is he?" she asked.

The man's lips parted, but no words came out.

"Where is he?" she repeated.

"Post…Op." The man's legs began to shake, and he slid down the wall until he was sitting on the floor. "Please."

As if in slow motion, his eyes closed and he tilted to the side, falling the rest of the way onto the hallway tiles. If he wasn't dead, he would be soon. Martina thought he'd probably been hanging on by sheer force of will, and now that someone had shown up, he could let go.

"Let's get out of here," Riley said. She stepped into the hallway and turned for the main exit. When she realized Martina wasn't following, she looked back. "Come on!"

"We need to check," Martina said.

"Why?"

"He asked us. We need to check."

"Are you kidding? His patient is probably dead." She paused, then added, "We've checked all the rooms already. There was nobody we could help."

"We didn't think about Post-Op."

Instead of waiting for Riley to come up with another argument, Martina headed to the right, looking for a map of the hospital.

"Martina, come on! Please!"

"Wait for me at the car. I won't take long," Martina shouted.

She found a map pinned to a bulletin board. Though Post-Op was not listed, Surgery was, so she figured it had to be in the same general area.

She located the surgical rooms first, then found Post-Op down the hall. It was a big room with several beds, most empty. Those that weren't were occupied by the dead. All except the bed at the back of the room.

Unlike the other beds, it was surrounded by a see-through plastic wall, and on it lay an older man. The heart monitor beside the bed beeped a steady, rhythmic beat.

Martina examined the plastic wall. Someone had duct-taped the top and bottom to the ceiling and floor. On her side of the wall were two big oxygen tanks, each with plastic piping running from their nozzles under the duct tape into the enclosed space.

"Hello?" she said.

The man on the bed stirred and opened his eyes.

"Who are you?" he asked, weary.

"Martina," she said. "Martina Gable."

He looked at the room beyond her. "Where's Frank?"

"You mean your doctor?"

"My son. He's taking care of me."

"Your son's your doctor?"

"Yes. Where is he?"

Just to be sure, she described the man she'd met in the hallway.

"That's him. Why isn't he here?"

She bit the inside of her lip, unable to tell the man what she'd seen.

He seemed to realize it on his own. "He's dead, isn't he?"

Martina still couldn't bring herself to speak.

"I knew he was sick," the man said. A tear slid down his cheeks. "He was pretending he wasn't, but I knew."

"How long have you been in there?" she asked.

"Since those damn containers opened up. Frank picked me up at home and put me in here."

"What…what can I do for you?"

"Nothing."

He turned away.

She looked around, unsure what to say or do. The man was trapped inside. Once he stepped out, he'd catch the flu. Her gaze fell on the air tanks. The gauge on one was completely empty, and the other was heading in that direction.

"You know where they store the air tanks?" she asked. "You're almost out. I'll get you another one."

"No. Please don't."

"But you'll suffocate in there."

"Please. Leave it. It would just be putting off the inevitable." He paused. "Frank only put me in here because it made him feel like he was doing something." He looked at her again and stared for a moment. "Why aren't you sick?"

"I don't know." She paused. "How about food? Do you need any?" She wasn't sure how she could get anything to him without letting some of the virus through.

He nodded at the cabinet next to his bed. "I have more than I need."

Frank had apparently set him up well.

She turned for the door. "I'm going to get you a new

tank."

"No! Please don't! What happens when that one runs low? Are you going to come back? And what about when there are no more tanks? I appreciate the offer, but you're only trying to make yourself feel better. If you hook up another tank, I'll rip down the wall and die that way. If you don't, at least I'll have a different option."

For several seconds, Martina didn't move. Finally she headed for the door.

"Please!" he yelled. "Let me be!"

Entering the hallway, she figured the storage room would probably be to the left since she didn't remember seeing anything like it in the other direction. But was the man right? Would she only be changing the tank for her own peace of mind?

As much as she wanted to deny it, she knew the answer to the question.

She found Riley waiting outside a minute later.

"Finally!" Riley said. "Did you find anyone?"

Martina shook her head. "You were right. We were too late."

THE WEBERS' PLACE was located in a small housing tract off Ridgecrest Boulevard, almost due south of the high school. Riley was leaning forward, nearly touching the dashboard as they rounded the corner onto her street.

Her house was near the middle of the block.

"I don't see our car," Martina said. Mr. Weber had used Martina's parents' car to bring Laurie back to Ridgecrest.

"Dad probably parked it in the garage," Riley said.

Martina didn't saying anything.

As the car rolled to a stop in the driveway, Riley threw her door open and jumped out.

"Hey, wait!" Martina yelled before hopping out after her. "Wait!"

Riley stopped and looked back.

"Maybe I should go in first," Martina suggested.

"Why?"

Did Martina really have to explain it? She stared at her friend, hoping to silently convey what she meant.

"I'm fine," Riley said. "Whatever we find, I'll deal with it. But I'm not waiting out here."

She tried the front door but it was locked. Before Martina could ask if she had a key, Riley sprinted toward the corner of the house.

"We can get in through my window," she yelled.

Her bedroom window was located along the side, right before the point where the backyard fence met the wall. With practiced ease, she popped the screen out, and pushed in on her window so that even though it was locked, the latch cleared the frame.

"I take it you've done this before," Martina said as they climbed inside.

With a quick nod, Riley moved to her bedroom door. "Dad? Laurie?" she called as she raced into the hallway.

The search was quick and unsatisfying. No one was home.

"Where are they?" Riley asked. She paused mid-step and whipped her head around. "We didn't check the garage." She ran through the kitchen, opened the garage door, and disappeared inside.

When Martina entered the garage a moment later, she found Riley standing in the empty space.

"Why aren't they here?" Riley asked. "If they're not at the hospital and not home, where…where…"

Martina thought her friend might start crying again, but Riley's eyes remained dry.

"Maybe he saw that the hospital was too busy," Martina said, "and took her to Bakersfield, or even Palmdale."

She didn't actually believe that, but she felt compelled to give her friend some hope. What she really thought was that they probably would never know.

Riley didn't seem to hear her, though, as she continued to stand in the middle of the room.

Martina gave her another moment, then walked over and

put an arm around Riley's shoulder. Slowly she guided her friend back into the house and sat her on the couch.

"Let me get you some water," she said, heading into the kitchen.

She opened a cabinet looking for a glass, but instead found bottles of tequila and rum and whiskey. Though she had never really taken to alcohol herself, she knew it had a way of relaxing people. Not knowing if one type would be better than another, she pulled down the closest bottle, Absolut Vodka, found a glass, and poured a healthy dose into it.

Back in the living room, Riley was still catatonic. Martina raised the glass to the girl's lips and dribbled a little into her friend's mouth. Riley sputtered, pulled away, and looked at Martina.

"What the hell is that?" she asked.

"Vodka." Martina lifted the glass again. "Come on, another sip. It'll make you feel better."

Riley scrunched up her face as Martina helped her take another sip, then she took control of the glass and tipped it all the way up so everything poured in quickly. When she was done, she squeezed her eyes shut for a second, her body tensing.

"That was *not* pleasant," she said.

"You want another?" Martina asked.

"No way."

Martina scrutinized her. "How do you feel?"

Riley considered the question. "Better, I guess." She paused, her eyes widening a bit. "Yeah, definitely better."

Martina stood up. "I'll get you some water now."

"Thanks."

When Martina returned, she found Riley lolled back against the couch, asleep. She repositioned her so that Riley was lying on the couch, and then draped a blanket over her. Finding a piece of paper in the kitchen, she wrote a note and put it on the coffee table so that Riley would find it if she woke up.

Running out for a bit. Won't be long.

Martina

She wanted to check out the hunch she'd had on the highway, and hoped to God she was right.

A few minutes later, she was heading west on Ridgecrest Boulevard, and not long after that, she passed the city limits into an area where the houses were more spread out, with acres of desert land between them. When she reached Jack's Ranch Road, she turned north, then east again at Horseshoe Lane. The house she was looking for was on the right side, about a quarter mile from the intersection. Like many of the homes in the area, it was two stories and surrounded by trees planted when the house had been built.

She tried not to get her hopes up as she turned onto the dirt driveway, but she couldn't help herself.

Please let me be right.

Nearing the house, she noticed something odd along the side that hadn't been there last time she visited. It looked like someone had been digging.

She stopped, turned off the engine, and climbed out of the car. The stillness of the house made her realize she was probably in for a disappointment. A part of her wanted to get back in the car and drive away. At least that way, the possibility of being right still existed.

Just check, she told herself.

The desert sand crunched under her feet as she approached the house. Her plan was to go right up to the front door and check if it was open, but she was pulled off course as she got a better look at the disturbed ground she'd noticed while driving up.

There were five roughly rectangular mounds of dirt, side by side.

Graves, she realized. They couldn't be anything else.

Five graves, not six. Of course, the last to die wouldn't be able to dig his own. Still…

"Noreen?" she called. "Noreen, are you here?"

She jogged to the small covered stoop at the front door and tried the handle. It was locked, so she pounded on the door.

"Noreen! Are you home?"

As she was about to knock again, there was an explosion above her and several dozen *thud-thud-thud*s on the grass behind her.

"Whoever you are, get the hell out of here!" The familiar voice came from above.

"Noreen! What are you doing?"

"Get out of here!" The gun blasted again.

"It's me, you idiot! Martina! Stop shooting at me!"

A pause. "Martina?"

"Yes! Why are you shooting?"

"You're…you're not sick?"

"No!"

Martina decided to chance looking out from under the porch's roof. Her friend was leaning out of a second-story window, a double-barreled shotgun pointed at the ground.

"Martina!"

"Who the hell did you think I was? A zombie or something?"

"Well…I, um…"

Martina realized that was *exactly* what her friend had been thinking. "For God's sake, put that thing away! There's no reason to shoot anybody! This isn't a video game!"

Noreen sheepishly pulled the gun inside.

"Get down here!" Martina told her.

When the door opened a few seconds later, the girls hesitated for a moment, and then threw their arms around each other.

"Oh, God. I thought I was the only one," Noreen said. "I thought I was all alone."

"You mean you and zombies," Martina told her.

"You, uh, could have been one."

Martina pulled back from the embrace, but kept her hands on her friend's arms. "No, I couldn't have been. There's no such thing. There's the dead, the dying, and us. No walking corpse that wants to eat you."

"They only eat brains."

"Noreen!"

"Okay, okay. Sorry. But what was I supposed to think? I'm sleeping on my bed, and suddenly someone's knocking on my door."

Martina smiled as she shook her head and pulled her friend into another embrace. Noreen had always had a vivid imagination, fed by a steady diet of horror films, manga comics, and time on her Xbox.

When they pulled apart again, Martina said, "Have you checked on the others?"

"What others?"

"From the team."

Noreen looked like she didn't understand. "The softball team?"

"Yeah."

"Why would I do that?"

"Don't you get it? It's why you and I are alive." Martina could tell it still wasn't sinking in. "The flu last spring. It's the same thing killing everyone now. We lived through it, and it made us immune."

It took a moment before hope dawned on Noreen's face. "You think so?"

"I'm not a scientist or anything, but you're alive and I'm alive. Don't you think we should check and see if the others are, too?"

AT FIRST, THE search was as fruitless as the one for Riley's father and sister. Some of their friends' homes were completely unoccupied, while others were serving as the final resting place for one or more bodies. None of the dead, however, were their old teammates.

Once they finished the east side of town, they headed across town on China Lake Boulevard toward Valerie Bechtel's house, up the hill near the college. As they passed the intersection with Ridgecrest Boulevard, Martina considered checking on Riley, but decided it would be better to let her sleep.

"Hey," Noreen said, looking out the front window. "Isn't that Jilly's car?"

Martina followed her friend's gaze. It *did* look like Jilly's car. It was parked in a lot between Wienerschnitzel and Carl's Jr.

"And that's Amanda's next to it," Noreen said. Amanda was another from the team. "And Martha's, and…and I think that's Valerie's."

Martina pulled into the lot and parked in an empty spot next to Carl's.

"Of course, this is where we'd find them," Noreen said, almost giddy.

Carl's had been one of the team's favorite hangouts.

As they climbed out of the car, they could hear loud music blasting from inside the restaurant but couldn't see anyone, as most of the dining area was tucked around the side of the kitchen, out of sight.

With a shared grin, they jogged over to the entrance and pulled the doors open.

The music wasn't just loud. It was blaring.

Katy Perry, "Last Friday Night."

Martina and Noreen peeked into the dining area. In the back corner, crowded around the table the team always claimed whenever possible, were eight girls with food and drinks spread out in front of them.

Martina held Noreen back until the song was finished, then gave her a tap on the back. They stepped out where they could be seen.

"You should be careful," Martina said loudly enough for everyone to hear. "The manager will kick you out for playing the music that loud."

Head twists and shocked stares.

"Holy shit," someone said.

The words broke the trance and suddenly the girls were up and rushing toward Martina and Noreen.

At some point as Martina passed from one embrace to

another, she began to laugh. It wasn't that she could forget her family was dead, or all the other things she had seen.

But for this moment, this one precious moment, she was happy again.

19

NEAR CAMP KILEY, COLORADO
3:41 PM MST

JACK CUTROY HAD gladly taken his reassignment. Anything would be a relief after days of finding only the dying and the dead. What had surprised him, though, was that the call with his new orders came from William Ownby, chief of the entire Boulder Fire Department. It turned out there was only a handful of personnel still on the job. From the sound of Ownby's voice, Jack had guessed it wouldn't be long before the chief went home, too.

"Need you to gas up your vehicle, then get over to the C&M Clinic," Ownby instructed. "You're on escort duty."

"What kind of escort duty?"

"That girl you picked up, Ellie Gaines. She passed her test."

"Test?"

"She's negative for the Sage Flu."

"You've got to be kidding. She was stuck in there with her parents for who knows how long."

"Well, she's clean," his boss said, sniffling. "There's a place near Colorado Springs called Camp Kiley. They're taking in kids who test negative but have nowhere to go. Need you to take her there."

Jack and the girl had now been on the road for nearly three hours. With the roads all but deserted, they were making great time, and were only about half an hour away from the camp.

He glanced over at Ellie, strapped into a car seat on the passenger side of the cab. “You doing all right?”

She nodded. “Uh-huh.”

“Need to go to the bathroom?”

A shake this time. “Uh-uh.”

“Thirsty? Hungry?”

More shakes.

Through the whole exchange she never once looked at him. Not surprising. She had to be scared out of her mind.

Jack focused back on the road and winced, his head hurting again. He’d taken a couple aspirin in Boulder before he’d donned his biosuit again, and it had helped for a while, but now the headache was back with a vengeance. Once he dropped the girl off, he could take a few more and maybe even find someplace he could sleep for a while. That would make him feel better for sure.

He really wished he could take off the hood. He knew keeping it on wasn’t helping his head at all, but keeping the suit was an order from on high, this time to protect the girl in case *he* was carrying the virus.

Of course, he wasn’t; he knew that. He still felt great. Well, he did have the headache, sure, but that was from overwork and lack of sleep. Still, orders were orders, and he’d been trained well enough to stick to them even if he didn’t think they were necessary.

He checked the GPS, ten curving-up miles left.

“Won’t be long now,” he said.

FROM THE TIME Brandon had arrived at Camp Kiley the day before, through the middle of the morning that day, cars and vans had come pretty much every few hours with new kids, sometimes just one, sometimes more.

The last had dropped off its passengers around ten thirty, but since then there had been no more deliveries. That was why the sound of an approaching vehicle made everyone perk up.

The truck that appeared out of the forest looked to Brandon like the kind EMTs used.

Loni, who had taken to staying close to him, asked, "How many?"

"Can't tell," Brandon said, only able to make out a man in protective gear behind the wheel.

As soon as the truck stopped, Sergeant Lukes jogged out and motioned for the driver to roll down the window. The two talked for several minutes, with the driver handing out a piece of paper at one point.

While all this was going on, Brandon, with Loni silently tagging along, worked his way close to where the other supervisors were waiting. Right after he got there, Sergeant Lukes finished his conversation and walked over to his colleagues.

"A girl," he said. "Five years old. Goes by the name Ellie."

"Just the one?" Mrs. Trieb asked.

"That's it."

"Where from?"

"Boulder."

"Blood test?" Mr. Munson asked.

The sergeant handed over the piece of paper he'd been given. Several of the supervisors looked it over. When they were through, Mrs. Trieb nodded. "All right. Looks good."

The sergeant moved back to the truck, this time heading for the passenger side, and opened the door. He leaned in for a few seconds. When he backed out, the girl was in his arms. She looked frightened.

The sergeant grabbed the door with his free hand and started to close it, but stopped when the driver said something. A big ball of fluff gently sailed out the door and into the sergeant's hand. A stuffed bear. He gave it to the girl, and it seemed to calm her down.

There was more conversation. At one point, the sergeant pointed down the road, twisting his hand one way and then the other as if giving directions. When he finally shut the door, the truck took off.

"This is Ellie," the sergeant said when he returned.

"Hi, Ellie," Miss Collins said. "Is it okay if I hold you?"

The girl hesitated for only a moment before letting Miss Collins take her.

"Let's go inside and get you something to eat, huh?" Miss Collins said.

As she turned, the stuffed bear Ellie was holding knocked against one of the other supervisors and fell to the ground. She didn't realize it until they were almost at the cafeteria door, when she suddenly looked around and started to hyperventilate.

"Bear! Bear!"

"What, sweetie?" Miss Collins asked.

"Bear!" The girl motioned with her hand back the way they'd come.

Brandon scooped it up and hurried over as Miss Collins was turning to see what the girl was talking about. "Here you go," he said, handing Ellie her stuffed animal.

She immediately hugged it to her chest.

"Thank you," Miss Collins said.

"No problem."

The girl gave him a smile.

"Make sure to hold on tight," he said.

She hugged the bear to her chest and smiled again. "Never let go."

"That's right," he said. "Never let go."

WHAT A DICK.

Jack couldn't believe the nerve of the guy. Come on. He'd been on the road for more than three hours, and had been awake for…well, he couldn't remember exactly how long now, but a *long* time. And on top of that, his headache wasn't going away.

All he'd asked the guy at Camp Kiley was if he could park his truck off to the side, and sleep in the cab for a little while before he headed back out.

"I'm sorry, sir. I can't allow you to do that," the man had

said.

Sure, he sounded polite, but he was being an asshole. He'd then gone so far as to give Jack directions to some lodge about ten miles away.

Up here? On the mountain? On these roads? That was too far. Jack was exhausted *and* hungry, but when he asked for some food? Forget it.

"I'm sure you can get something to eat at the lodge," the man had said.

How hard would it have been to just give him a sandwich or a piece of fruit, even. *A piece of goddamn fruit?* They wouldn't have had to do anything but throw it through the window.

If Jack hadn't reined himself in, he would have gunned the engine and spun the tires on the way out to show his anger. But an idea had come to him, and if he was going to follow up on it, any show of aggression would've put them on alert.

The road between the camp and the highway curved around a hill not long after he left. As soon as he was out of sight of the asshole and his friends, Jack pulled the truck to the side of the road and killed the engine. Before he could open the door, though, he tensed, his eyes squeezing shut.

It felt like a nuclear explosion had just gone off in his head.

Once it eased enough so he could function again, he removed his thick plastic hood with its built-in mask and stumbled out the door. From one of the truck's exterior compartments, he removed the kit with the aspirin and tried to dry swallow three pills. It was harder than he expected. His throat felt tight, constricted.

The headache. It's messing up my whole system.

He grabbed a half-empty bottle of water from up front, and used what was left to wash the aspirin down. He leaned against the truck, his eyes closed, and willed the pills to take effect. No such luck.

In fact, the only response he received was a growl from his stomach, notifying him that the aspirin was a poor substitute for food.

He looked across the road. Out there, through the trees, was Camp Kiley, and all the food his stomach could hold. Beds, too. Dammit, they'd have to let him use one.

Stepping away from the truck, he had the fleeting thought that there was some reason he should stay away from the camp. But it was in and out of his mind so fast that by the time he reached the trees, he had forgotten all about it.

THAT BIG BUILDING—that had to be the one, Jack thought.

The only problem was, most of the people at the camp were inside it. If they spotted him, especially that asshole who'd sent him away, they would probably chase him off again without giving him anything. Easier to sneak in and take what he wanted, but that probably meant waiting longer than his empty stomach could stand.

After scanning the rest of the camp, his gaze settled on the two rows of rectangular buildings. They were obviously dormitories. Maybe he couldn't get to the main food supply just yet, but if the residents of Camp Kiley were anything like how he was back when he'd gone to camp, some of them would have a little food stashed away in their bags. More than enough, he thought, to tide him over until the kitchen cleared out.

He started with the dorms along the back row since they were hidden from the building the others were in. Moving from bed to bed, he rummaged through each bag he found, but netted only a single candy bar in the first building he checked.

What was wrong with these kids? Hadn't they ever been to camp before?

Once more, he had the sensation he was missing something, that this situation was different than normal camp. And once more it faded away.

As he entered the second dorm, he felt something in his throat, like maybe he'd swallowed wrong when he'd chomped into the chocolate. He tried to clear it, and ended up coughing for several seconds. Ironically, it actually did the trick, though it left him with a tingling sensation in his chest, like he might have to cough again before long.

Whatever. Just find the food!

The new building proved to be a bit more lucrative. A bag of Doritos, two bottles of water, and a large, half-eaten chocolate chip cookie.

Nothing of note in the third dorm. In the fourth, three sticks of string cheese and another bottle of water.

As he moved toward the front row of four buildings, he heard the crunch of snow not far away. He pressed himself against the side of the nearest dorm, thinking he'd been seen. But the steps continued moving at a steady, unhurried pace, and a few seconds later the door of one of the buildings in the back row opened.

Jack decided then and there that maybe he had enough food to hold him over. As quietly as he could, he snuck back into cover of the woods, and found a downed tree to sit on while he enjoyed his stolen meal.

Surprisingly, he only got a few bites into the chocolate chip cookie before he found that he wasn't all that hungry anymore. He tried to set the cookie on the log beside him but somehow missed, and the cookie fell onto the thin layer of snow that covered the ground.

He closed his eyes. His headache was worse than ever now.

The next thing he knew, he found himself on his feet. He looked around for the log, but it was gone. Confused, he searched for something familiar. Trees and more trees and…

The dorms. He could just see them between the pines off to the left.

How the hell did he get here?

He tried to remember, but nothing came to him. *I need someplace to lie down for a bit, that's all.* He looked at the dorms again, and recalled the warm beds he'd seen inside. *I'll just stretch out on one for a little while.*

He staggered forward, his hands grabbing at the trees to

help keep him upright.

He was ten feet from the edge of the woods when his hand missed the trunk it was aiming for and he tumbled to the ground.

He made an effort to get back on his feet, but was barely able to raise his head off the snow.

This is all right, he thought. *Rest for a few minutes, then you can…*

Sleep came first, but Jack never rose to his feet again.

MASON LEWIS HAD been one of the first kids to arrive at Camp Kiley. Being older—he was fifteen—he had a better understanding of what was going on, but that didn't make it any easier. His nights had been spent mostly awake, and his days in shock.

Being basically a good kid, he appreciated the fact that Mrs. Trieb and the other supervisors were doing their best to keep everyone distracted. But their latest effort, organizing a game of Bingo in the cafeteria, wasn't working for him. So he'd excused himself, saying he needed some fresh air, and went back to his bunk in cabin seven.

Mason had been on a cross-country flight from his mom's place in Boston to his dad's in San Diego for the holidays, when his plane had made an emergency landing in Denver due to the imminent closing of airports across the country. He and one other kid had been jammed into a car and driven to the camp.

When he reached his cabin, he went straight to his bed, intending to stretch out for a little while, but as he sat down he noticed that his suitcase was unzipped. He had definitely not left it that way.

Angry, he pulled it open and hunted through his things to see what was missing, but everything seemed to be there. *What the hell?*

As he zipped up his bag, he caught sight of the suitcase belonging to the guy in the bunk next to him. It was open, too. Looking around, he saw that all the bags were open.

There was a thief among them. What else could it be?

He needed to tell Mrs. Trieb and Sergeant Lukes right away, as much to find out who did it, as to make sure *he* wasn't the one accused of stealing.

But when he returned to the cafeteria, news about someone searching through the dorms wasn't the only thing he brought back with him.

MUTATIONS OF THE KV-27a virus were bound to happen. Its creators at Project Eden had known this, and, from a strictly academic point of view, were curious to see how these would manifest. They had neither resources nor time to conduct a thorough study, however, so they would never know that one such occurrence happened in Boulder, Colorado.

There, a young emergency medical technician was infected by a strain of the virus that not only caused severe headaches, but also clouded the victim's mind and greatly impacted his sense of judgment.

The technician would not be the last to contract this variation, as his diminished sense of right and wrong allowed him to pass it along. An unfortunate occurrence for those he infected, especially because this particular version had one other notable difference from the main strain.

The accelerated incubation period between initial contact and full-on symptoms.

20

ISABELLA ISLAND, COSTA RICA
5:20 PM CST

"I DID NOT see it until it was almost in the surf," Henri Boucher said over the radio. He was another resort guest, a Frenchman, currently on watch over the north end of the island. Just before calling in, he had spotted a boat approaching one of the beaches. "I am sorry. It is small so not easy to see."

"It's okay," Dominic said. "How many are on it?"

"It looks empty, but I cannot be sure. The area, it is blocked from the sun by part of the island, so have many shadows, you know?"

"Whoever was on board could have already jumped off and swum to shore," Robert said to Dominic. "I'll take some people and do a search before it gets too dark."

Dominic nodded grimly. "Be careful."

As Robert left, Henri's voice came back over the radio. "It is almost to the beach. Hold on." There was a long pause. "*Oui*, it is there now. I do not see anyone moving, though."

"Keep your eyes on it and report if anything changes," Dominic said.

The evening before, they had moved the radio down to the room behind the terrace bar, since the area had become the main gathering point for the Isabella Island survivors, or, as Robert had started calling everyone, the Bellians. The name had yet to stick.

Dominic stepped out of the room, and looked across the bar to see who was nearby. "Mark!"

The lanky, brown-haired engineer from Toronto glanced over.

"Can you find Luis then meet me back here?" Dominic asked.

"Sure."

As Mark left, Dominic caught Renee's attention. "Take over on the radio for a little while," he told her.

"Something up?" she asked.

"Everything's fine," he said for the benefit of anyone who might overhear. There was no sense in getting the others worked up if the boat turned out to be nothing. Once she was in the back room, though, he told her the truth, then said, "Robert's checking if anyone might have already reached shore. I'm going to go take a look at the boat."

"Are you sure that's a good idea?"

"Somebody has to do it."

Back in the bar, he found Luis and Mark waiting for him. "You guys up for a little hike?"

IT WOULD HAVE been faster to take the speedboat around the island to the beach, but due to their limited supply of fuel, they'd decided no boat would be used unless absolutely necessary. For the same reason, all the generators, save the one powering the refrigerators and the radio, were shut down after dark. At nighttime, it was all torchlight or sleep.

So they took the slower route and walked across the island on one of the many resort-maintained paths. Unfortunately, the beach in question was not one of the better ones Isabella offered, so there was no path that went all the way there, and for the final quarter mile, they had to cut their way through the jungle.

"Henri, we're getting close to the beach. If you see movement, that's probably us," Dominic said into his walkie-talkie.

"Okay, I will watch for you."

"Renee?" Dominic asked.

There was a click. "Right here."

"Any news from Robert?"

"Hasn't spotted anyone yet. He's circling around toward you, so you might run into him."

"Good to know. Thanks."

Part of the problem with this particular beach was that, depending on the tide, there was little room between where the waves crashed down and the brush began. Throw in the uneven rocky ground just below the water, and it was enough to keep most people away.

Dominic and his two companions came out of the jungle at the east end, about a hundred and fifty feet from the boat. It was smaller than he expected, probably no larger than a standard rowboat. In fact, it probably *was* a rowboat. It rolled side to side as the wave crashed unevenly into it, pushing it farther up the short beach.

"I don't see anyone," Luis said.

"Yeah, it looks empty," Mark agreed.

Dominic noticed movement in the vegetation at the far end of the beach. He was just starting to think someone *had* made it to shore when Robert and three others stepped out onto the sand.

"Robert, you see us?" Dominic said into his radio while waving his free hand above his head.

"Gotcha," Robert replied. "Any footprints over there of someone who might have run by?"

Dominic and the others looked around. "Nothing."

"Clean over here, too."

"Tell your guys to hang out there while you meet me at the boat," Dominic said.

"Got it," Robert told him.

Dominic told Mark and Luis to wait, and then set out across the beach.

The boat was fifty feet closer to his position than Robert's so he reached it first. It wasn't quite what he'd first thought. Though the size was right, it was a little more robust than any rowboat he'd been in. A personal fishing vessel would be his guess.

He looked at the surrounding beach. No footprints anywhere. Maybe someone just forgot to tie it up and it drifted out on the current.

He walked over to the side and peered in. There was a pile of rope in the front, and an old fishing net. One oar was lying against the hull, but there was no sign of a second. In the back was a jumbled tarp. He reached over and pulled up one end.

With a start, he dropped the canvas and jumped back.

"What is it?" Robert asked. He was about twenty feet away now.

"Stop!" Dominic yelled.

Robert halted. "What?"

"Go back! Don't let anyone near here."

"Dominic, what is it?"

"The boat's not empty."

Dominic had looked long enough to know the body under the tarp belonged to a woman, but how old she had been, he couldn't have said. There was no mistaking what had killed her, though. They had all seen similar bodies on TV over the last few days.

The Sage Flu had come to Isabella Island.

21

COLORADO SPRINGS, COLORADO
7:34 PM MST

THE RECORDS CHLOE and Josie found at Malmstrom Air Force Base said that Brandon had been flown into Peterson Air Force Base, which shared space with Colorado Springs Airport. Unfortunately, there was no mention of where he had been taken after that.

The Resistance's jet landed at the airfield shortly after seven thirty p.m. Chloe went up into the cockpit as they taxied toward the central part of the facility, and scanned the buildings that lined the tarmac to see if there was any indication of which one they should start with.

Five nearly identical buildings straddled either side of the control tower structure. A few additional buildings were located at both the south and north ends. Nothing, though, stood out as *the* place where she and the others could pick up Brandon's trail.

"We might as well start at the control tower," she told Harlan.

The pilot guided the plane across the airfield, and stopped just short of the sign on the ground that said WELCOME TO PETERSON AFB.

"I'm not sure how long we'll be," Chloe said.

"Could you use some extra hands?" Harlan asked as he and Barry powered the plane down. "We'd like to help."

She put a hand on Harlan's shoulder and gave it a

squeeze. "Definitely."

They divided into two groups: the two pilots in one, and Chloe, Josie, and Miller in the other. The idea was that each group would take a building and do a quick check before moving on to the next. If they weren't able to dig anything up that way, they'd go back and do a room-by-room examination.

Chloe and her group started with the control tower complex. Most of the lights inside were off, so they were constantly flicking switches. No one had chosen to die in the building, but that was about the extent of their success, as they could find nothing that pointed to Brandon's whereabouts.

The next building was a combination of hangar and offices. In one of the offices, Chloe found a TV on, the screen displaying only digital noise. She was going to turn it off, but, curious, she flipped through the channels. A majority displayed the same static. Several of the larger cable networks, including all the news stations, displayed a "Technical Difficulties" screen. The only station still broadcasting content was a music video network that must have been fully automated.

She punched the Off button, turned around, and jerked in surprise. Josie was standing in the doorway, her eyes fixed on the TV screen.

"They're all dead, aren't they?" the girl asked.

Chloe wasn't sure how Ash would want her to answer, so she went with the truth. "No. Most are probably still sick."

"But they will die."

Chloe nodded. "Probably."

"What's going to happen then?"

"I…" Chloe paused for several seconds. "I don't know."

By eleven p.m. they still had nothing.

Chloe could see they were all bone tired. "Let's get some rest," she said.

"But…but Brandon," Josie protested. "We can't stop."

"Just a few hours. Right now we're all so exhausted we might miss something."

Josie tried to argue the point, but finally admitted Chloe was right.

Instead of sleeping on the plane, they bunked out in the lobby of the control tower. Josie was the first to fall asleep, and soon after Miller and the two pilots followed suit.

Chloe took longer, Josie's question from earlier repeating in her mind.

What's going to happen then?

What, indeed.

TEMPORARY OFFICE OF THE PRINCIPAL DIRECTOR
LAS CRUCES, NEW MEXICO
11:53 PM MST

"THIS IS INTERESTING," Claudia said, staring at her computer screen.

"What is it?" Perez asked.

"One of our operatives in Denver has been tracking down a rumor concerning kids being taken to a secluded location in the Rockies to keep them safe. It's been a little tough getting anything definitive because of today's escalated death rate, but he was finally able to confirm it."

Perez perked up. Children were something the Project could use. They wouldn't be tainted by adult prejudices, and could be worked more easily into the Project's plans.

"Where, exactly?" he asked.

"Outside Colorado Springs. A place called Camp Kiley." A pause. "It's only six hundred miles from us."

"Do we have a squad available?"

She consulted her computer again. "There's a team that could fly into Colorado Springs first thing in the morning, then drive up. Should be able to wrap it up and be out of there before noon."

Perez thought for a moment. While the Project would soon be activating its plan to identify and deal with survivors, there was no sense in wasting an opportunity.

"Set it up," he said. "If the kids are truly uninfected, have them vaccinated and taken to our nearest facility." He didn't have to add the same wouldn't apply to any adults who might be found.

"Yes, sir."

December 27th

World Population
3,001,589,414

Change Over Previous Day
- 2,842,431,503

22

CAMP KILEY, COLORADO
1:25 AM MST

SOMETHING PUSHED AGAINST Brandon's back. More asleep than awake, he scooted to the edge of his bed to get away from whatever it was.

Another nudge. This time he flopped his arm behind him to push it away. When he realized he was touching someone, he jerked back his hand and twisted around.

"Loni?" he whispered.

She was lying in the bed next to him, her lips trembling.

"What's wrong?" he asked.

"I…I'm scared. I didn't know where else to go."

"We're all scared," he said, trying to calm her down.

"No. I mean someone in my cabin is…is…"

"Is what?"

"Coughing."

He sat up. "Are you sure?"

She nodded.

"Who?"

"I don't know."

Across the room, somebody turned in his bed and sniffled.

Loni's eyes widened. "Oh, no."

Brandon waited to see if a cough would follow, but none did.

"You're sure you weren't dreaming it?" he said.

"I'm sure."

"Which cabin are you in?"

"Six."

He swung out of bed, slipped on his shoes, and grabbed his jacket.

"Where are you going?" she asked.

"To check."

"You don't believe me?"

"I do, but…just come with me."

Quietly, they crossed the room and went outside. Brandon let Loni lead him to her cabin. They cracked open the front door but remained on the stoop. At first all was quiet, and he started to think what she'd heard was probably someone clearing their throat while they slept. His dad did that all the time. But then someone coughed. Deep and wet.

A moment later there was a second cough, only this one came from the other side of the room.

Loni pulled at his arm. "Close it."

She didn't need to tell him twice.

"See, I was right," she said. Her lower lip began to tremble. "That means we're all going to get it, doesn't it?"

One of the videos the Resistance had made explained what to do if someone thought they'd been exposed. Brandon had seen it multiple times. "Go to the showers," he told her. "Scrub yourself as hard as you can."

"The showers?"

"Right now," he said. "If any got on you, you might still be able to wash it off."

It took her a second before she seemed to get it.

As she was turning to run to the showers, he said, "Don't put those clothes back on, and don't touch them after you're done. I'll bring you some clean ones."

She nodded and left.

The first thing he needed to do was wake up Mrs. Trieb and tell her what was going on. Maybe they could separate the sick ones and save everyone else. With the exception of Miss Collins, who was sleeping in the cabin with the younger children, the supervisors were in cabin number eight, two down from Loni's. He ran there and was about to pull open the door when someone inside broke out in a coughing fit.

Backing away, he heard more coughs—not just from numbers six and eight, but from all the cabins except his and the one the little kids were in.

There would be no isolating the ill, but maybe there were a few others he could get out before the infection reached them.

He entered his cabin first and grabbed his pack, but just as he was about to start waking his dorm mates, the person he'd heard sniffle earlier coughed.

It's everywhere!

He headed for the door, but stopped before he reached it. Maybe there were a few here he could still save. He shook the feet of the boys in the four beds closest to the door. Only two opened their eyes.

"What's going on?" a kid named Vincent said.

"We've got to get out," Brandon told him.

"Why?"

There was no need for Brandon to answer. Another cough did the job for him.

Vincent and the other boy, Carter, jumped from their beds.

"Grab your bags but don't open them," Brandon said. He explained about taking showers, and getting rid of the clothes they were wearing. "Wash off your bags first, though. *Then* you can take something out to wear."

Another head popped up, this one a sniffling mess. "Shut up, huh? Trying to sleep."

Vincent and Carter snatched up their bags and headed for the door. Brandon surveyed the room, but knew there was no one else left he could help, so he followed a few seconds after the other two boys.

He headed for the little kids' cabin, and paused outside. No hacks or sniffles coming from inside.

Good.

He reached for the handle, but stopped himself before grabbing it. There had been coughing in his cabin. Was it possible that though he couldn't get the flu himself, he might be contaminated? If so, while he tried to save the kids, he would actually be killing them.

He took a step back. "Don't let them catch it," he whispered. He spun around and ran for the showers.

Entering, he could hear Loni washing off on the other side of the partition.

"I'll bring you something to wear as soon as I'm done washing," he shouted loudly enough for her to hear.

"Okay," she replied.

He scrubbed himself raw, and repeated the process with his bag. When he was done, he pulled out a set of clothes for himself and one for Loni. She was smaller than he, but it was the best he could do for now.

"When you're done," he said to Vincent and Carter as he finished dressing, "meet at the cafeteria. If I'm not there yet, gather up some food. Enough for a few days."

"Where are you going?" Vincent asked.

"To check if there's anyone else we can help."

He tossed the other set of clothes through the opening to the girls' shower, and gave Loni the same instructions he'd given the boys. He then jogged over to the little kids' cabin.

Once again, he paused outside. No sniffles. No coughs. No clearing of throats. Only quiet.

"Thank you," he mouthed.

He opened the door and eased inside. Miss Collins's bed was easy to pick out. Though she wasn't a tall woman, she was twice the size of the kids in the cabin.

Kneeling beside her bed, he shook her shoulder. "Miss Collins? Miss Collins, wake up."

She took in a deep breath and rolled onto her back, but didn't wake.

"Miss Collins, please."

Her eyelids fluttered, then opened. A second passed before she noticed he was there. "Brandon? What are you doing in here?"

"We have to get the kids out."

She blinked, and rose on an elbow. "Why? What

happened?"

"The others are sick."

She stared at him as if she didn't understand. "They…can't…be. We've taken precautions."

"Yeah, I know, but people are coughing in all the other cabins. If we don't get the kids in here out right now, they'll catch it, too."

She swung her legs off the bed and stood up. "What about the staff cabin? Mrs. Trieb? Have you let her know?"

"I couldn't. They're sick, too."

She took a step toward the door before looking back at him. "I…I need to check."

"We don't have time."

"You get the kids up. I'll be right back."

"Don't go inside," he called after her as she ran out the door. "Just listen from outside."

Whether she heard him or not, he didn't know.

Brandon moved quickly through the room, checking each of the kids to make sure they didn't have a fever. When he was confident the flu hadn't infected any of them, he turned on the cabin light and said, "Hey, everyone, time to wake up."

A few groans and some twisting in beds, but no heads popped up. He went around, pulling back their blankets and shaking their feet.

"Come on! Let's go!"

This time several of the children sat up.

"What time is it?" one of the boys asked.

"It's time to get up," Brandon said.

He knew they should all take showers, too, but it would be harder to get them washed up and ready to go. Plus, it would delay their departure, and that was not something Brandon wanted to do.

Hoping none of them had been exposed, he said, "Everyone get dressed. Something warm, okay?"

The girl in the last bed stared at him, a bear hugged to her chest. He walked over to her.

"Ellie, right?" he said.

She nodded.

"You need some help?"

"I don't have any more clothes," she told him.

"That's okay. Let me see what I can find, all right?"

He gathered items from some of the other kids. Like the clothes he'd given Loni, these would be big on the girl, but they'd do.

As he was helping her dress, the cabin door opened and Miss Collins walked back in. It was clear from the stunned expression on her face what she'd discovered.

Brandon helped Ellie pull her jacket on, then, after making sure she had her bear, he picked her up and hurried over to the supervisor.

Stopping a few feet away, he said, "You didn't go in, did you?"

Miss Collins shook her head. "No."

"But you heard the coughs."

A nod.

"Then you know we need to get out of here."

No response this time.

"Miss Collins!" he yelled.

She jerked and focused on him.

"We need you to be okay. You're the only adult."

A stuttering breath and then a nod. "You're right. You're right. I…I'll be okay."

Since she had been near the infected cabins, he told her she should take a shower and change clothes. "I'll take everyone over to the cafeteria, and we'll meet you there as soon as you're done. Don't take long, okay?"

"I…I understand, Brandon. I'll be quick."

He kept everyone away from her as she gathered her bag and left again.

As soon as the door closed behind her, he said, "Okay, we're going over to the cafeteria."

"What about Miss Collins?" one of the kids asked.

"She'll join us in a few minutes. Is everyone ready?"

Tired nods all around.

"Then follow me." With Ellie in his arms, and the others

trailing behind, Brandon went out the door.

TEN MINUTES PASSED before Miss Collins showed up. In the intervening time, Loni, Vincent, and Carter put together several bags of food, while Brandon worked on how they would get out of there.

They could hike, but who knew how far they would have to go before they reached a house or building they could take shelter in. Too far, probably, especially with seven little kids. The only real answer was down at the end of the cafeteria.

Sergeant Lukes's Suburban SUV.

Brandon checked the vehicle, hoping the keys would be inside, but they weren't. He would have to get them from Sergeant Lukes himself in the staff cabin.

Grabbing another change of clothes from his bag, he stopped by the showers first, leaving them on one of benches inside before heading to the staff cabin. The chorus of coughing had increased since his last visit. Even though he knew he was immune, it scared the hell out of him to be so close to the disease, but he also knew it was this immunity that was going to allow him save the others.

He took several deep breaths to work up his courage, and finally pulled the door open. He moved slowly into the room, gently transferring his weight from foot to foot so that the floorboards would creak as little as possible. Sergeant Lukes's bed turned out to be the second one in on the left. Like the others, his breathing was labored.

Brandon found the sergeant's pants folded neatly on top of his shoes beside the bed. He checked the pockets. No keys. The man's jacket was lying on the empty bed beside him. No luck there, either. The only other place to look was in the sergeant's bag, which he found tucked under the bed.

Carefully, he worked it out from beneath. The zipper proved to be a problem, though. There was nothing he could do to muffle the sound it made. He was halfway through when he heard someone stir and sit up. He dropped out of sight between the beds. If it had been Sergeant Lukes, Brandon would have been discovered in seconds, but the sergeant was out cold.

After a few seconds, Brandon chanced peeking over the top of the empty bed next to the sergeant.

Mrs. Trieb was the one awake. She was sitting up, but her head was in her hands. Several more seconds passed before she groaned and lay back down.

Knowing he couldn't chance opening the zipper any more, he slipped his hand in the bag and felt around until his fingers touched the keys.

It took every ounce of will to walk out of the cabin as slowly as he'd walked in, but once he was outside, he raced to the showers.

When he finally returned to the cafeteria, he found the others, including Miss Collins, sitting at tables nearest the door, bags of food piled in front of them.

"Grab as many bags as you can," he said to the three older kids, "and follow me. Miss Collins, you stay with the kids, okay?"

She nodded absently.

He snatched up four of the bags himself, and led the others out to the Suburban. It took them two trips to get everything out and fill up the storage area in back.

When they finished, Brandon went over to Miss Collins and whispered, "Are you okay?"

"Where are we going to go?" she asked, as if whatever they did was going to fail.

"I don't know," he said. "But we'll figure that out later. Right now we just need to get away from here." He paused. "We need you to help us. You can't give up."

"I…I'm not," she said. "I'm just…" She closed her eyes for a second and rubbed her forehead. "Okay, okay. No problem. I'll be fine."

"Can you help with the kids?" Brandon said.

She nodded and stood up. "All right, everyone," she announced. "We're going out to the Suburban. It'll be a bit of a squeeze, but you should all be able to fit."

"Where are we going?" one of the kids asked.

"On a field trip," Miss Collins told her.

"Where?"

"You'll see when we get there."

"This way," Brandon said, opening the door.

With him in the lead and Miss Collins bringing up the rear, they headed out. They were only halfway to the SUV when a voice called out, "What's going on here?"

Brandon stopped in his tracks and twisted around. Mrs. Trieb was standing at the far end of the parking area near the dorms, staring at them. He knew in his gut that if he hadn't disturbed her sleep, she would have never gotten up.

She sniffled and ran a hand under her nose. "I asked you a question. What the hell's going on?"

"Get them in the truck," Miss Collins whispered toward Brandon. She then turned toward her boss. "Alicia, look at yourself."

"Keep going, everyone," Brandon said, getting the kids moving again.

"You're sick," Miss Collins went on. "You've got the flu."

"Sick? What are you talking about? I'm not sick. It's a headache, that's all." As if to emphasize the point, Mrs. Trieb touched her temple and winced. "Get those children back to their beds."

"You *are* sick," Miss Collins told her. "And it's not just you. These kids are the only ones who aren't. I have to get them out of here before they get sick, too. You would do the same. If you don't believe me, go back to the dorms and listen to the coughs."

With another wipe of her nose, Mrs. Trieb started walking toward the group, her balance far from perfect. "Everyone, back to your beds!"

"Alicia, please!" Miss Collins shouted, moving to keep herself between Mrs. Trieb and the others. "If you get too close you'll expose them, too! I know you don't want that."

Brandon ran the last few feet to the Suburban and threw open a side door. "Everybody in. Quick."

The ones closest to him piled in, but those in back looked

unsure of what to do as they glanced between him, Miss Collins, and Mrs. Trieb.

"It's going to be okay," Loni said, urging the younger ones along.

After the last of them was in the car, Vincent and Carter followed.

"You, too," Brandon said to Loni.

"What about you?"

"Just get in and keep them calm. I'll be right there."

Reluctantly, she climbed inside.

"Hey!" Mrs. Trieb yelled as she altered her course toward Brandon. "You get them out of that car right now!"

Miss Collins repositioned herself in front of her boss again. "Alicia! Stop! You don't want to do this!"

"Shut up, bitch!"

Mrs. Trieb was fifty feet away from the Suburban, Miss Collins twenty feet in front of her.

"Get in the car," Miss Collins said to Brandon.

He hesitated a moment before climbing into the front passenger seat. As soon as the door closed, Miss Collins turned and ran for the SUV. When she reached the truck, she circled around the front to the driver's side door.

Unfortunately, Mrs. Trieb had also picked up her pace. Though she wasn't as fast as Miss Collins, she was able to round the hood just as the younger woman pulled on the door handle.

"You're not going to make it!" Brandon yelled.

Miss Collins looked over at her colleague, and realized Brandon was right. She let go of the door and ran around the back end of the truck. Brandon reached over and pressed the door lock button. There was a loud *clunk* as all the locks engaged. Behind him, many of the kids started to cry.

"It's okay," Loni said. "We're going to be fine."

Brandon hopped over the center console into the driver's seat.

"What are you doing?" Vincent asked.

"What's it look like I'm doing?"

Brandon moved the seat as far forward as it would go,

helping his foot reach the pedals.

"You know how to drive?" Carter asked.

"Uh-huh." Brandon started the engine.

"I don't believe you," Vincent said. "Who taught you?"

"My dad," Brandon said. "Now be quiet so I can pay attention." He moved the transmission into Drive and sped forward.

"What about Miss Collins?" Loni asked.

Brandon didn't answer. Before he reached the end of the parking area, he turned the truck back around and stopped there as he scanned the area for Miss Collins.

"Where is she?" he asked. "Do any of you see her?"

"I don't know," Loni said.

Mrs. Trieb had once more changed directions and was now heading for the cafeteria entrance.

Brandon rolled down his window and yelled, "Miss Collins!" When she didn't appear, he honked the horn and called her name again.

Mrs. Trieb turned to look at the truck, twisting her whole body as if the muscles in her neck no longer worked.

"Miss Collins!"

A door slammed somewhere. Not near the cafeteria, but in the direction of the dormitories.

"You kids get out of there," Mrs. Trieb yelled, her voice barely audible above the Suburban's engine. "Go back to your cabins." Miss Collins seemingly forgotten, she lurched toward them again.

Movement to the left caught Brandon's attention. Two of the older boys were coming down the path from the dorms, one holding a hand over his mouth as he coughed.

We have to get out of here, Brandon thought.

"Miss Collins!" he yelled again. "Where are you?"

A head poked out from behind the far end of the cafeteria—Miss Collins, looking nervous and scared.

"Everyone hang on," Brandon said as he rolled up his window.

He switched his foot from the brake to the accelerator, and drove in a wide arc around Mrs. Trieb over to the cafeteria. As he neared the logs that marked the back of the lot, he tried to do one of the tricks his father had shown him, slamming on the brakes as he whipped the wheel around.

The Suburban tipped violently to the left, the wheels on the passenger side all but leaving the ground. Almost everyone in back screamed. The truck rocked back to the right, then left, then right again before settling back down.

"Whoa!" Vincent said. "Your dad taught you *that*?"

Brandon lowered his window again and yelled at Miss Collins, "Hurry!"

She broke from the building and ran around the back of the truck. Just as she got to the passenger door, Brandon pushed the Unlock button. She yanked the door open, and jumped into the seat. The second the door was closed again, Brandon relocked everything.

"You want to drive?" he asked.

She shook her head, her face strained with fear. "You seem to be doing fine."

Brandon did a quick look around. Mrs. Trieb was a good thirty feet away, still heading toward them. The two boys who'd come out of the dorm were standing near the end of the path, and a few others had staggered outside to see what was going on.

"Get us out of here," Vincent said.

Not needing further encouragement, Brandon gunned the engine, slalomed around Mrs. Trieb, and raced out to the road that would take them away from Camp Kiley.

23

FROM THE JOURNAL OF BELINDA RAMSEY
ENTRY DATE—DECEMBER 27, 2:00 AM

THE ONLY THINGS I can get on TV now are infomercials and movies. Most of the stations are no longer broadcasting. Either they have a logo just sitting there or the channel has gone completely dark. In a way, that's even scarier than when they were showing what was going on.

So far, no one has tried to get onto my floor. Thought I heard a noise in the stairwell earlier in the evening, but if it was someone, they didn't come up this high. I think that's probably my best safety feature. Anyone who's sick won't have the energy to climb more than a floor or two, and if what the news had been saying is correct, then pretty much everyone is sick.

The thing that's been worrying me the most has been the elevator. It's the easy way up. I had blocked the entrance, but it wouldn't take much to get through my barricade. I finally decided I needed to take a chance and do something a bit more drastic.

I hunted through some of the other rooms, and found a rain slicker that went down past my knees, some rubber boots, and a pair of skiing gloves. (By the way, if for some reason everything goes back to normal, I'm probably going to be on the hook for the cost of the door to Kendal's room. I just figured it would be cheaper to bust into hers, since she's our resident advisor, and find her master keys than to break through all the doors.) I also took one of the medical masks out of the floor's first-aid kit, and my roommate's swimming goggles.

When I put everything on and pulled the hood over my head, I'd created what would probably be a pretty good Halloween costume. (No, I didn't think that at the time. I'm trying to be clever in hindsight. It's helping me to keep my sanity.)

I dismantled my barrier, and, well…I don't know how long I stood in front of the elevator dressed like that before I finally pushed the button to call up the car. I knew it was risky, but there was no way I was going to be able to sleep very well until I was sure the elevator was out of service.

I moved back as far as I could while still able see inside the elevator when the door opened. My biggest fear was that there would be someone in the car. Dead or not really didn't matter; either would probably mean my death. But if you had asked me at that point which I preferred, I would have said a dead body. The sight of someone stepping out, coughing and sneezing, might have been enough to give me a heart attack.

Thankfully, the car was empty. I had intended to race over right away, then use Kendal's elevator key to put it in fire mode, which, if I remembered correctly, would send the car back to the first floor, where it would stay unless another key was used to reactivate it. But when the door opened, I froze.

"Come on," I told myself after it closed again. "You've got to do this."

I willed myself back to the call button and pushed it again, which wasn't easy. I don't think my hand had ever felt that heavy. As soon as the door reopened, I stepped inside, and pivoted around so I was facing the control panel. The key slipped right into the slot, but I turned it the wrong way first and all the lights inside went off. After cursing at myself, I flipped it in the other direction.

Immediately, the lights turned back on and the door started to close. I nearly panicked, thinking I was going to be trapped inside. Without thinking, I threw my arm in between the doors and broke the electronic beam. I can't even describe the relief I felt when the doors opened again.

I jumped out, but kept a booted foot pressed against the door so it would remain open. With the alarm inside beeping, I stripped off my homemade protection suit and threw it piece by piece into the elevator car, gloves and boots last. The gear would have been nice to hold on to, but I figured I should be able to scrounge up another set if I need it, and I didn't want to take the chance that any of the Sage Flu virus had transferred to the other stuff I was wearing.

As soon as the door was freed, it closed all the way, and the car descended back to the main lobby.

Now I am truly alone but, hopefully, safe. If that means I'm going to be the last person on Earth, I'm not sure how I feel about that. But I have to believe that if I'm able to survive, others will, too.

Of course, survival is contingent on staying away from the virus. What I don't know—and there probably won't be anyone who can tell me—is will I ever be able to leave the building? At some point I'll have to, but will the virus still be active then?

I'm sure starting to wish I'd majored in biology instead of English. I tried looking for more information on the Web, but the Internet connection here at the dorm stopped working around dinnertime. I still have a Wi-Fi signal; it's just that the main modem isn't able to connect to anything. We've had problems with that modem before, so I think it probably just needs to be rebooted. The Internet should still be out there. Whether there's any new information being posted anywhere is a whole other question.

I think the modem is located on the floor below mine. If I can work up the courage, I'll go try to reboot it. I really need to get it working if I'm going to put together an accurate timeline of what's been happening. I've been writing as much about the pandemic as I can up to this point, but most of my information has only come from what I saw on TV. I need more.

Maybe no one will ever read my history of events, but someone has to write it, right? And it's not like I have a lot of other things keeping me busy.

To be totally honest, there's actually a second reason to get the Internet going again. If there are *other survivors, I might be able to find them online. Even if they're halfway around the world, it would be nice to know I'm not completely on my own.*

*Sleep now, though. In the morning, when it's lighter (*if *I can get my courage up), I'll tackle the modem.*

24

OUTSIDE MUMBAI, INDIA
3:24 PM INDIA STANDARD TIME

SANJAY STEPPED WITH care as he approached the back of the building. Dozens of birdcages lined the pathway, two or three chickens in each, some dead, others looking well on the way. It wasn't the flu that was taking their lives, not directly, anyway. It was the fact they had not been fed in at least a couple of days, their owners gone.

Sanjay was tempted to pour some feed into their cages and give them fresh water, but the building needed to be checked before anything else.

"Maybe I should go in first this time," Kusum whispered behind him.

He glared at her to let her know he was more than capable of doing it himself. She merely rolled her eyes and smirked.

He couldn't help but smile a little. He loved her smirk. He loved her eyes, rolling or not. He loved everything about her. Which was a good thing since she was now his wife. The roadside ceremony the day before had been brief. Sanjay had expected Kusum's father to protest, but with death all around them, maybe it wasn't so surprising that his new father-in-law actually blessed their union.

The back door was unlocked. When he pulled it open, he braced himself for the now familiar stench of death, but there was none. Either whoever lived there was still breathing, or they had died somewhere else, a promising possibility.

He stepped across the threshold. "Hello?" he said. "Hello, is anyone here?"

As he moved farther inside, Kusum followed.

"Hello?" he said again. He was just turning back to her to say he didn't think anyone was there, when they heard the sound of movement coming from somewhere deeper in the building.

"I will check," Kusum whispered, pushing past him.

"No." He tried to grab her, but she slipped by. If he could have used both hands, maybe he would have stopped her, but his left arm was still wrapped to his chest, keeping the shoulder he'd dislocated four days earlier as immobile as possible. "Kusum. Come back."

He knew the second he spoke he shouldn't have wasted his breath. Kusum had changed since the outbreak started. Her good qualities were all still there: her playfulness, her smile, her kind words. But she was no longer the somewhat timid person he'd first met. She saw herself now as his equal, and acted as such. That wasn't the way things had been in the world they'd grown up in, where it wouldn't have mattered whether she was actually his equal or not. Stupid times, he knew now. In this new world they had entered, they couldn't afford to continue old, useless customs. She *was* his equal, and he was glad for it.

This, of course, didn't mean she should have gone first.

The building was a maze of rooms and hallways, some piled high with boxes and others with desks and beds. The sign on the road leading to the property had indicated it was a school.

The night after Sanjay had been reunited with Kusum and her family—and, surprisingly, with the group of survivors her family had collected on the way—they had discussed the need to find shelter someplace away from any large population center. There, they could wait out the outbreak and make plans for what they should do next.

Finding the right place, though, was the problem. They drove farther inland, away from Mumbai, in the truck

Kusum's family had arrived in, thinking they might be able to find a farm or small village they could essentially take over. Unfortunately, everywhere they checked was already occupied by those who'd succumbed to the virus.

Though each member of their group had been inoculated with the vaccine Sanjay had stolen, no one was ready to move the dead to free up space. What they needed was someplace empty.

It was Jabala, Kusum's sister, who'd come up with the best idea. "Most schools are on winter break. And if we can find a boarding school, that would be perfect, wouldn't it?"

So for the last two days, they had concentrated on schools. Most of the ones they found were for local children and didn't have any extra housing. While they could've sufficed, Sanjay and the others weren't ready to give up on the idea of finding actual beds.

They had come across the first boarding school the previous afternoon, and a second one that morning. The first had been taken over by another group after the virus had been released, but the flu had not passed them by, and while only a few were already dead, the rest were well on their way.

The school from that morning had been empty, but the condition of the buildings and the furniture inside indicated it hadn't been used in years. They had decided if they could find nothing else in the next day or two, they would come back.

They had found the bordering school where they were now—the fourth one—because of a sign they'd seen along the highway. It was built out in the countryside, with a private, gated road. There were several buildings, probably containing classrooms, a dining hall, and perhaps even a gymnasium. There was a single English-style house near the center that was probably home to the headmaster. The dormitories were located along the back. Since that was most likely where anyone who might still be around would be located, that's where Sanjay and Kusum, as the self-designated search party, headed first.

They heard the sound again. It sounded like a piece of furniture scraping across the floor, in short bursts.

"Careful," Sanjay said as they drew near.

Kusum waved her hand in the air without looking back, telling him she wasn't an idiot.

The sound was coming out a doorway ten feet ahead. The door itself was cut in half, the top portion open, while the bottom was closed.

The scraping stopped, replaced by a short, hoarse *Ap, ap!*

Someone was in there and still alive, Sanjay realized. The place wasn't as deserted as he had hoped. Still, only one person was better than the dozens of dead bodies they'd run into elsewhere.

Kusum hugged the wall as she approached the doorway. When she reached the edge, she leaned forward just enough to spy inside.

Ap! Ap! Ap! Ap!

More scraping.

Kusum laugh as she stepped away from the wall, moving in front of the half door.

Ap! Ap! Ap! Ap!

"What is it?" Sanjay asked, quickly following her.

The space on the other side was a communal toilet area and shower room. Old green tiles covered almost every surface. In the middle of the room, directly beyond the doorway, was a wooden table sitting at an odd angle. The reason for this was obvious. Strapped to one of the legs was a leather leash that, in turn, was connected to a dog about the size of Sanjay's forearm. At the sight of them, it jumped up and down.

Ap! Ap! Ap! Ap!

Its bark was odd, as if its vocal chords had been removed. Perhaps they had been, or, more likely, Sanjay thought, its voice was strained from barking for days on end.

Kusum opened the door.

"Wait," Sanjay said. "It may bite."

"I am sure it will," she said. "Look how hungry it is."

From the bag over her shoulder, she pulled out a stale roll and tossed it onto the ground in front of the dog. The animal instantly pounced on it, and began tearing at the crust.

Sanjay noticed a water bowl against the wall, where the table had probably once been. The bowl was empty, so he took it over to the sink and filled it, then scooted it in front of the dog with his foot.

The dog stopped eating right away and switched to the water.

"We need to finish looking around," Sanjay said.

Kusum nodded, and said to the dog, "We will be right back."

As they walked out of the room, the dog looked up and began barking again.

"I promise we will not be long," Sanjay said.

Ap! Ap! Ap! Ap!

Kusum returned to the dog.

"What are you doing?" Sanjay asked.

"She's afraid of being left alone again."

"She?" Sanjay asked.

Kusum glanced at him, one eyebrow raised. "Please tell me you know how to tell the difference."

Ignoring her comment, he said. "*She* will be fine. We need to finish. The others are waiting."

Instead of getting up, Kusum held her hand out to the dog, who sniffed it, then licked Kusum's fingers.

"See?" Kusum said. "She's friendly."

She removed the leash from the leg of the table. With the dog in tow, she walked back to the doorway. "Let's go, Mr. Impatient."

THEY FOUND THREE bodies at the school—an older couple, who they assumed was husband and wife, in the caretaker's apartment in back of the kitchen; and a middle-aged Caucasian man in the headmaster's house.

Since Sanjay could not help, Kusum and her father—after carefully wrapping themselves in protective clothing—carried the bodies out to a ditch others had dug in the jungle. They burned the bodies, and buried the remains deep enough so that no animal could drag a piece back into the compound.

Once this was done, they divided up the rooms in the main dormitory. That evening, after most of the children were asleep, Sanjay, Kusum, her parents, and the four other adults who had joined Kusum's family on their exodus from Mumbai gathered in the living room of the headmaster's house. The dog, which Kusum had started calling Jeeval, had staked a claim to Kusum's lap.

"There's enough food in the cafeteria to last us a week, maybe two. That is, if you only want to eat rice the second week," Kusum's mother said.

"What about the chickens?" Kusum's father suggested.

"The chickens are weak and skinny. We need to nurse them back. And we will need most of them for eggs."

"Tomorrow we should send out search parties and gather what we can," Sanjay said.

"We should also put together a list of non-food items we need," Kusum suggested. "Medicine and soap and clothes, for instance."

"Excellent idea," Sanjay said.

Kusum found a pad of paper and a pen, and they began brainstorming other things they could use.

After a while, Naresh, one of other adults, said, "A radio would be good."

The woman named Ritu pointed across the room, at a stereo on the shelf next to the television. "There's one right there."

"Not that kind of radio," Naresh said. "One for talking." He looked at Sanjay. "Some people have shortwave radio and can talk to others all over the world. There has to be more survivors. We cannot be the only ones. Maybe they also have radios, and we can connect with them."

"Couldn't we just try using a cell phone?" another woman, Bhakti, asked.

"And call what number?" the man said. "We need to find a shortwave."

Sanjay nodded. This was also an excellent idea. He hadn't even realized that such radios existed, but why wouldn't they? "How do we find one?" he asked.

"They will have a big antennae. Here." Naresh motioned for Kusum to lend him the pad of paper and pen. He quickly sketched something on a clean sheet, then turned it so Sanjay could see. "Like this."

The drawing was no masterpiece, but it got the point across—a crude house, several trees, and a tall pole-like structure towering above them.

"Maybe not so high as this," Naresh said, "but definitely tall, and made of metal. It might also have wires out to the sides to keep it steady."

"I think maybe you should join me tomorrow with the first search crew," Sanjay said.

"Of course."

"With both of us," Kusum said.

Jeeval sat up. *Ap.*

"And Jeeval, too," Kusum added.

25

COLORADO SPRINGS, COLORADO
6:40 AM MST

THE DOOR TO the office Chloe was searching flew open.

"Why didn't you wake me?" Josie said angrily as she entered. "I could have been helping you!"

Chloe looked up from the files she'd been examining. "You needed the rest."

"I can rest later. I need to find Brandon!"

"*We* need to find Brandon. And that's exactly what we're trying to do."

"If you had woken me when you got up, maybe I would have found something by now."

"Or you would have missed it because you'd have been too tired to realize what you were looking at."

"You can't know that."

"And you can't know you wouldn't have, either," Chloe said. "So are we going to argue, or are you ready to help now?"

Josie squeezed her lips together, frustrated. Then, barely parting them again, she said, "Help."

"Good. How are you at computers?"

A shrug. "Good enough."

"You know your way around file systems, that kind of thing?"

"Sure."

Chloe pointed at the computer on the desk next to her.

"See what you can find."

While Josie got busy, Chloe returned her attention to the files.

Somewhere there had to be something that would tell them where Brandon had gone. Keeping detailed records was a military tradition, and if they were moving children around, they would have made doubly sure to account for everything in writing. Even in the face of the end of mankind, those along the chain of custody would be worried about being drawn into a potential PR fiasco if something happened to the kids and the people in charge hadn't accounted for their actions.

So why hadn't Chloe or the others found anything associated with Operation Piper?

She reached the bottom of the stack and tossed it all into the trash.

"Chloe?" Miller's voice came over the walkie-talkie on the desk.

She picked it up. "Yeah?"

"You're going to want to come over here."

"You find something?"

"Yeah, I think so."

Josie bolted out of her chair before Chloe even had a chance to stand.

"Hold on," Chloe told the girl.

Josie stopped a few feet short of the door.

"Where are you?" Chloe said into the radio.

"I know where he is," Josie said.

"Building 123," Miller replied. "The little offshoot with the sloped roof. You'll see it."

"Come on," Josie said, leaning toward the door. "I'll show you."

It took them three minutes to jog to Building 123.

Like most of the other buildings, it had large sliding doors that faced the runway and opened to a hangar. Where this one differed from the others, though, was along the southeast side of the building, where several other structures had been added, including a rectangular extension with a pitched roof.

They found Miller inside, looking at a map tacked to the wall. Both Harlan and Barry were with him.

"Where is he?" Josie asked as soon as she and Chloe entered.

Miller tapped the map. "Right here."

Chloe and Josie hurried over. The point he touched was in the mountains above Colorado Springs.

"I was in Building 121 and found a note taped to a computer monitor." Miller picked up a small piece of paper from the nearby desk and handed it to Chloe.

ALL O.P. INQUIRIES TO
WEINBERG x7223

"At first I thought it meant 'op' like operation, in which case it could mean anything," he said. "But then I realized it's o-period, p-period. The whole thing doesn't mean 'operation,' just the first letter. It still could mean something else, but it's a hell of a lot closer to Operation Piper than anything I've seen so far. I tried to track down this Weinberg guy, but no one with that name was in the directory, so I searched by the extension number. It belongs to a guy named Clarke. This is his office, but when I got here, there were several papers on the desk signed by this Weinberg guy. He must have taken over this room in the last few days."

Chloe nodded at the map. "But how do you know that's where Brandon is?"

He picked up two other pieces of paper and passed them to her. The top one was crinkled, like it had been balled up before being flattened again. On it was a list of names in alphabetical order. The second one down was Brandon Ash.

"Where was this?" Josie, who'd been looking over Chloe's shoulder, asked.

Miller pointed a grocery-sized brown bag with groups of stripes running across it—five white, five red, five white—sitting on the desk. "Burn bag," he said. "It was in a cabinet near the door awaiting pickup. That second sheet was in there, too."

Chloe looked at the second page. It was a printout from Google—turn-by-turn directions to someplace called Camp Kiley.

"I can't tie the two things to each other directly, but both pieces of paper were in the same bag, and, well, it kind of makes sense. If they were trying to protect the kids, they'd want to take them someplace they thought would be safe. Someplace controllable and in the middle of nowhere would be their best bet. This has got to be where they took him." His face tensed. "Should have thought to check for burn bags last night."

"None of us thought of it," Chloe said. "And you found them now." She looked at the directions again. "This says it's forty-six miles away but takes over an hour."

"Mountain roads," Miller said. "Most of it two-lane."

"What are we waiting for?" Josie asked. "Let's go!"

Chloe was silent for a moment, thinking. "All right," she said, glancing momentarily at Josie, then looking at the others. "Harlan, Barry, check in with Matt. If he needs you somewhere else, go. If not, just wait here. Miller, put us together a weapons package." She hoped they wouldn't need them, but it was better to be prepared. She turned back to Josie. "Let's you and I find ourselves a ride."

IT WASN'T SURPRISING that the only cars parked near the airfield were military vehicles, any civilian ones undoubtedly used by their owners to get home before or after they'd become ill. While the sedan they chose was adequate, it was far from comfortable, so when they drove through Colorado Springs, they exchanged it for a brand new Audi A3 right off the lot, and headed into the mountains.

No one spoke for the longest time. Finally Josie said, "He'll be okay, right?"

"Of course," Chloe said. "They were trying to help him, not hurt him."

She glanced at Josie via the rearview mirror. The girl was chewing on her lower lip, her gaze unfocused.

"Hey," Chloe said.

Josie looked up.

"He'll be fine."

Twenty minutes outside Colorado Springs, Josie's satellite phone rang. The display indicated it was coming from the Ranch.

"Yes?" she said, answering it.

"It's Matt. You have a problem."

HARLAN HAD JUST finished checking in with Matt when Barry said, "Do you hear that?"

Harlan cocked his head and listened. An engine. A *jet* engine.

They looked out the cockpit window but saw nothing, so they moved back to the plane's exit. Before Barry could climb outside, Harlan said, "Be careful. If it's the air force, it might be better if they don't see us."

"They're going to see the plane."

"Yeah, but they might ignore it. People, not so much."

Barry nodded.

Outside, they stayed tight to the fuselage of their jet and scanned the sky.

"There," Harlan said, pointing.

A plane was approaching the runway, a small jet like theirs. Right before it touched down, the two men scrambled back inside, shut the door, and monitored the other plane's progress from the passenger cabin. Once the other aircraft started taxiing, it turned toward the air force side of the airport.

"Military?" Barry asked.

Harlan studied the new arrival. There was nothing on it to indicate any kind of association, military or otherwise. Just a plain white fuselage with its identification number painted on the side and tail. "I don't know," he said.

They both knew if it was carrying US military personnel, the two of them could be in a whole lot of trouble if found. Hopefully, whoever was on board would assume the Ranch's jet had been at the airport for a while and ignore it.

The plane slowed as it neared the control tower, and Harlan was sure it would pull in right beside them. But after a few minutes, the noise of its engines increased again, and it began rolling faster toward the next building over. A hundred feet from the structure, it came to a complete stop, its engines shutting down.

The door opened and half a dozen men in fatigues piled out.

"Oh, shit," Barry said.

"Grab the binoculars," Harlan said. There was something about the soldiers that troubled him.

Barry went into the cockpit, and returned thirty seconds later with the glasses. "I don't know if you should use these," he said as he handed them to Harlan. "What if the lens catches the light? They might see us."

"Relax. That's not going to happen."

To be safe, though, Harlan didn't press the binoculars directly against the window, but instead looked through them from a few feet away in the dimness of the cabin.

The six soldiers had been joined by a seventh, who, given the fact he was doing all the talking, seemed to be the one in charge. After a moment, two of the men broke from the group and jogged around the side of the building, out of sight. Harlan returned his attention to the men still near the plane. Each had a rifle slung over his shoulder, and two were carrying duffel bags that Harlan figured held ammunition and more weapons.

He concentrated on their uniforms. There were no patches or anything else that identified which branch of the military they belonged to. Suddenly, the one in charge raised a walkie-talkie to his mouth.

"Here," Harlan said, handing the binoculars to Barry. "Keep an eye on them. I'll be right back."

Staying low to prevent the soldiers from noticing any movement, he returned to the cockpit, where he donned the headphone for the plane's enhanced radio. He searched around until he located the channel the men outside were using to talk on their walkie-talkies.

"...for now," a voice said.

"Yes, sir," another replied.

There was dead air for several seconds.

"Keys located," the second voice said. "We'll be right there."

"Copy that." A pause, then the first said, "Stevens?"

"Yes, sir."

"We should be back by noon, latest. Check in with NB219. Let them know we're on schedule and should be at Camp Kiley within an hour."

"Copy that."

Harlan's blood would have gone cold at the mention of Camp Kiley if it hadn't already turned to ice when the man said NB219. NB was the designation Project Eden used to identify its facilities. There was no way Harlan would believe the use of the letter-number combo was a coincidence.

He heard the rumbling noise of a diesel engine. He slinked back into the passenger cabin and looked outside. A sedan and a troop-transport truck came out from between the buildings and stopped near where the remaining soldiers were gathered. The men divided themselves up and climbed aboard the two vehicles. Then, with the sedan in the lead, they drove off.

"What the hell do you think that was about?" Barry asked.

Instead of answering him, Harlan retrieved the satellite phone and called the Ranch.

THE TURNOFF WAS crowned by an old wooden sign arching over the entrance, with the name of the camp painted on it.

"See anyone?" Chloe asked.

Miller scanned the woods to either side. "No."

It was a logical place for a guard to be positioned, but apparently those at the camp either didn't have the manpower or thought it unnecessary.

Chloe turned down the road. The pavement ended after only half a mile. Past that point, the ground was a mixture of frozen mud and gravel that thrust up and down at random and forced her to reduce their speed. That was something she was loath to do, given the news Matt had told her about the Project Eden squad heading their way.

About a quarter mile shy of the camp, they came across an EMT truck parked at an angle along the side of the road. Painted on the door were the words BOULDER FIRE-RESCUE.

Chloe eased past it and stopped.

"Stay here," she said to Josie.

She and Miller hopped out and cautiously approached the truck.

"Looks empty," Miller said. "Maybe it's just here in case they felt the need to block the road."

A possibility, Chloe thought. But it seemed odd.

They looked through the windows without touching the vehicle. Definitely unoccupied. Chloe motioned for Miller to circle around one way while she went the other.

"Anything?" she asked when they met back up.

He shook his head. "Whoever left it here isn't around anymore."

Chloe glanced down the road. "Camp's just around that bend. We should hike in from here. Get an idea of what's going on."

Miller shot a quick look back the way they'd come. "What about the others?"

She checked her watch. "We should be able to do a quick recon, then get in and out of there with Brandon before the Project Eden assholes show up."

"*Should* be able to."

"That chance goes down the more time we waste here. Come on."

As much as she would have like to leave Josie in the car, there was no telling who might show up while she and Miller were off in the woods, so, after Miller retrieved their bag of weapons, the three of them headed out together.

"Look at this," he said a minute later.

On a small patch of snow in front of him was a set of footprints.

"The person from the truck?" Chloe suggested.

"Got to be, right?"

Camp Kiley came into view a few minutes later. Closest to them were several long, rectangular structures in two rows. Staying under the cover of the forest, Chloe led them to the right so they could get a better look at the rest of the camp. From their new position, they could see a dirt parking lot and a couple larger buildings.

"Chloe!" Josie whispered harshly. "Is that…is it…"

Instead of finishing, she pointed at a dark shape lying in the lot.

A body. No question.

"Both of you wait here," Chloe said.

"No. I'm coming," Josie told her.

"You're staying." Chloe shot a look at Miller.

He put a hand on Josie's shoulder. "We'll be right here," he said.

"What if that's Brandon?" Josie argued.

"It's not," Chloe said, as she pulled one of the pistols out of Miller's bag before leaving.

When she reached the tree line, she stopped and scanned the camp. She spotted three more bodies along the path leading down from the rectangular buildings. The rest of the camp was quiet. Much too quiet. Her pistol at the ready, she stepped out of the woods and crossed the dirt lot.

A dozen feet from the first body, she stopped. It was a woman, middle-aged. The clear signs of the flu were etched on her face.

Her chest tightening, Chloe turned and looked toward the other bodies. Though they were farther away, there was no question they had also been downed by the flu.

It seemed as though the planned safe haven hadn't worked out the way the government had intended.

She cupped her hands around her mouth and yelled, "Brandon!"

His name echoed off the buildings and across a small

lake.

She turned to the larger buildings. "Brandon!"

There was a noise behind her. She whipped around and saw two teenage girls emerge with some difficulty from one of the rectangular buildings.

After a false start, one of them managed to call out, "Are you here to help us?"

Chloe took several steps toward them. "I'm looking for a friend of mine. A boy."

"Everyone's sick here," the other one said. "You should go. It's not…safe."

"My friend's name is Brandon."

"Brandon?"

"Yes."

"He's not here," the girl said, wincing in pain.

Chloe's brow furrowed. "I'm sure he was brought here."

"I mean…he's gone. Him and some others. They got away last night."

Got away? "How? Where did they go?"

A man wearing an army uniform staggered out from between two of the other buildings. "You can't be here," he said.

"I'm not staying," Chloe told him. "I just need to—"

"This is a private…facility," he went on as if he didn't hear her. "You can't…be…here."

"I said I'm leaving." She looked back at the teenagers. "Do you know where the others went?"

"No," the first girl said. "But they're in the…in the…truck."

"What kind of truck?"

"Like an SUV but…big."

"A Humvee?"

"No. Like a…um…"

"A Suburban," the other girl said. "It was a Suburban."

Out of the corner of her eye, Chloe saw the uniformed man raise a gun into the air.

"I said you need to leave!"

She started to back away. "I'm going, all right? See?"

Whether he believed her or his weapon was too heavy for his condition, it dropped back to his side.

When she reached the edge of the parking lot, she turned and sprinted into the woods.

"Come on!" she yelled at Miller and Josie as she neared them. "Back to the car!"

"What about Brandon?" Josie asked.

"He's not here."

"Where is he?"

"Come on!"

Chloe raced past them and back to the road, confident they would follow. As soon as she reached the car, she got behind the wheel and started the engine. Several seconds later, Josie and Miller climbed in, too.

"If Brandon's not there, where is he?" Josie asked, breathing hard.

Chloe swung the Audi into a Y-turn and headed back to the main road. "I don't know," she said.

"We could hear you talking to someone. Didn't they know where he was?"

"Josie, please. Just wait until we get out to the highway, okay?"

Chloe checked her watch. Scouting the camp had taken longer than she'd planned. The last place she wanted to be was on this dirt road when the Project Eden team arrived. She pushed the Audi as fast as she dared, the bumps and jerks doing more to keep Josie from asking more questions than Chloe's request had.

When they finally reached the highway, she slowed momentarily, and peered down the road in the direction of Colorado Springs. Less than half a mile away it turned out of sight. What she could see of it was clear, but she knew going that way would be too risky.

It turned out not to matter one way or the other. As she turned left to take them farther up the mountain, Miller said, "There they are!"

She looked over her shoulder. Sure enough, a dark-colored sedan, nearly identical to the one they'd originally taken from the base, had come around the far corner. Chloe gunned the engine and the Audi accelerated up the slope.

"What are they doing?" she asked.

Miller, looking back, said, "They've seen us. They're speeding up."

Chloe banked around a curve, putting part of the mountain between them and the other car. When the sedan appeared behind them again, it was closer than she expected.

"What the hell?" Miller said.

Chloe increased their speed as the road continued to wind back and forth like a snake.

"Careful!" Josie screamed as they went wide around a curve.

"Not helping," Chloe said.

"Sorry."

The highway straightened out for a bit. Chloe glanced at the rearview mirror. The sedan was about the same distance behind them as it had been at the last check.

Great, she thought. Leave it to the air force to be sure their cars performed above expectations.

Once more the sedan disappeared as Chloe rounded another bend. They passed a sign indicating an intersection ahead. If she could get there before the other car appeared again, she could take the new road and maybe lose them.

She pressed the pedal to the floor, hoping they wouldn't hit any hidden ice.

The turn was nearing.

Going right would be the logical way. The easy way. The way most people would turn.

She went left.

The new road dipped into a shallow valley full of trees. Without reducing their speed, she raced through it and up the other side. Just beyond the ridge, she spotted a dirt road leading into the forest. She took the turn, and didn't stop until they were a good two hundred feet within the trees. There, she found a wide spot, turned the car around, and killed the engine.

"Everyone out," she said.

"Why?" Josie asked. "Aren't we safer in here?"

"I need your ears."

They exited the Audi.

"Listen for them," Chloe instructed.

"What are you going to do?" Josie asked.

"I need to make a call."

Chloe walked farther down the road so that the sound of the other car wouldn't be masked by her voice. When far enough away, she called the Ranch.

"Yes?"

Chloe recognized the voice. "Devin, I need to speak to Christina."

"Who is this?"

"Chloe."

"Did you find him?"

"Working on it. I need Christina."

"Hold on."

The line was silent for a few seconds before Christina picked up.

"Chloe? What's going on?"

"Do you still have satellite access?" Chloe asked.

"For the most part. There've been some access issues cropping up on a few systems. Why? What do you need?"

Chloe gave her the location of Camp Kiley. "Sometime in the last twelve to eighteen hours, a Suburban left there and didn't come back. I need to know where it went."

"Could be difficult. How are the skies?"

Chloe looked up. "Clear. Have been since we arrived last evening."

"That'll help. Let me see what I can do."

"Thanks, Chris."

Chloe hung up and returned to the others. "Anything?"

Miller shook his head. "Quiet."

"What happened back there?" Josie asked.

Chloe hesitated, then said, "Everyone at the camp was sick. Brandon and some others must have realized this, and got out of the camp last night. I know what kind of car they were in, so I've asked Christina to figure out where they went."

"Can she do it?"

"She's trying."

Josie was silent for a moment, then nodded. "She'll find them."

"Shhh," Miller said, tapping his ear.

Chloe cocked her head, and after a second, heard it, too—a car on the main road, heading their way.

"Everyone in," she ordered.

While the other two climbed back into the Audi, she paused by her door and tracked the other vehicle's progress. The sound of the engine dipped for a moment as the other vehicle passed through the nearby valley, then it grew louder and louder as it neared the top of the ridge.

She held her breath as it crested the top, knowing the entrance to the road she and her friends were on was now visible to those in the sedan.

"Don't you dare stop," she said under her breath.

Closer and closer it came. If it was going to take the turn, it needed to start slowing immediately, but the hum of the engine remained unchanged as the car raced past them and continued down the highway. Once the noise dwindled to almost nothing, she climbed back into the car.

"Aren't we going?" Josie asked.

"Not yet," Chloe said.

"Why not?"

"Where exactly are we supposed to go?"

Josie was silent for a moment. "So…we wait?"

"We wait."

26

ISABELLA ISLAND, COSTA RICA
8:18 AM CST

BY THE TIME Robert had returned to the resort the night before, all the residents knew about the boat that had washed up on shore with the body on board. They also knew that Dominic was the first on the scene, and was now trapped out there in case he had been exposed to the virus.

No one knew who had started calling it Dominic's Beach, but the nickname quickly took hold as a spirited discussion ensued over what, if anything, should be done. The most militant in the crowd insisted that Dominic needed to get into the boat and row it back to the mainland, while the more fatalistic had said, why bother? They were all going to die now anyway.

Robert let them go on for a while before informing everyone they would be sticking with Dominic's self-imposed quarantine zone, and wait to see what happened.

Robert and Luis then hauled a cot, some food, water, and other supplies across the island and put them at the edge of the beach. After they had retreated into the jungle, Dominic retrieved everything.

"Thanks!" he yelled.

"You're welcome," Robert called back. "Still think you planned this so that you could have a little vacation."

"If I'd planned it, I would have chosen a bigger beach."

"Yeah, I'd definitely suggest that next time."

"I'll try to remember…" Dominic paused. "Hey, what are these for? A campfire?"

Dominic was holding up two one-gallon containers of gasoline.

"Thought it might be best if you burn the boat," Robert said.

That was not something Robert had mentioned to everyone. While he was sure many of the others would see the benefit of burning the boat, some would be sticking with the idea that Dominic needed to float away in it. That was not something Robert could stomach, so the boat had to go.

"That's probably a good idea," Dominic said, not sounding very enthusiastic.

"Just splash some gas on the sides and throw the cans in. You won't have to get that close."

Dominic repositioned his supplies farther up the beach, away from the water. Once that was done, he carried the gas cans over to the boat. It was low tide so it was fully stranded on the beach. Carefully, he tossed gas over the wooden hull, quickly emptying the first can. He added more from the second, then tossed both cans on board.

With the soft onshore breeze, it took him a few tries before he could get one of the matches that had been in the supplies to stay lit long enough to ignite the boat. But when the fire took hold, it spread quickly, its flames rising high.

Dominic, caught off guard, stumbled backward and fell onto the sand.

"You all right?" Robert shouted.

"I think I singed my eyebrows."

"That's a good thing. They were too bushy before."

"Gee, thanks," Dominic said. He stood back up and took several steps farther away from the fire.

Robert, Dominic, and Luis watched the blaze consume the boat until only the gutted keel remained intact. Robert had then bid his friend goodnight and gone back to the resort.

Upon waking that morning, he'd asked Juan, one of the resort's cooks, to whip up Dominic's favorite omelet. As soon as it was ready, he went down to Dominic's Beach to deliver the meal.

"Hey! You hungry?" he yelled when he reached the edge of the jungle. "Brought you something you're going to like."

He looked at the beach. Much of the burned-out boat had been washed away in the high tide early that morning, and only the keel remained. Dominic had set up his cot near the trees at the center part of the beach, but it was empty.

"Dominic?" Robert yelled. In a panic, he took a step onto the beach. "Dominic, where are you?"

*Surely he hasn't gone into the jungl*e. Dominic was the one who had first insisted on being isolated, setting up the boundaries himself.

Robert looked out at the ocean. Had he gone for a swim?

"Dominic!"

"I'm here. Relax."

Dominic stepped out from behind some rocks just beyond where his cot was set up.

"What the hell, man?" Robert said. "Don't tell me you couldn't hear me."

"Sorry, had to take care of a little business, you know? Kind of hard to answer when you're in the middle of things."

Robert chuckled, both relieved and a little embarrassed. "Brought you an omelet." He set it on the ground. "You'll want to eat it before it gets cold."

"Thanks."

Robert stepped back into the jungle. "How you feeling this morning?"

"Could use a shower, but I'm okay."

"That's great."

"How are things at the hotel? Anything new on the news?"

Robert shook his head. "Most of the channels went off air last night."

"You're kidding."

"Nope."

"That can't be good," Dominic said. He paused for a moment, looking tired. "Listen, you need to start planning long-term. I have a feeling it's going to be awhile before anyone here can leave the island."

"As soon as you can come back, you and I will do that."

"Sounds good," Dominic said. "Now get out of here so I can come over and get that omelet before some bird flies off with it."

"All right. I'll come back in a few hours to see how you're doing."

"If I'm asleep, don't wake me up!" Dominic admonished him.

"I'll keep that in mind."

With a wave, Robert headed back to the resort. For the first time since discovering the boat, he felt okay. He was sure now that Dominic would be fine.

Thank God.

DOMINIC WATCHED HIS friend disappear into the jungle, then waited another minute to be sure he was gone. Satisfied he was alone, he glanced behind the rock where he'd been when Robert had shown up.

Contrary to the impression he'd given his friend, he hadn't been relieving himself or taking a crap. He'd been throwing up, and not for the first time.

The pains had come on right before dawn. Not only in his stomach, but in his chest and neck, too. Surprisingly, he wasn't experiencing the congestion they'd talked about on TV, but there was no question in his mind that this was the flu. Maybe it changed from person to person. He knew other diseases could hit one person one way and someone else another.

It didn't really matter. What did, though, was the fact that he knew now he was going to die. What he needed to figure out was how to do it without harming anyone else.

Dying on the beach was a problem. The same birds he'd pretended to be worried about stealing the omelet could pluck away at him, and carry some of his diseased flesh back to the resort.

And swimming out to sea? He didn't know if he was

strong enough to get to a point where the currents wouldn't pull him back to the island.

Someone else might not have cared, but he was the manager. The safety of the guests was his responsibility, even if it meant protecting them from him.

So how the hell was he going to do that?

As he tried to come up with a solution, his stomach clenched again.

27

RIDGECREST, CALIFORNIA
8:10 AM PST

THE KNOCK ON the door was loud and unwanted.

Martina pulled the spare pillow over her head, and turned so that her back was to the noise.

Another knock. "Hey, Martina. Wake up."

"Who's that?" Riley asked sleepily from the other bed.

Martina glanced at the clock and groaned. A few minutes after eight. Only five hours since she'd fallen asleep. She flopped onto her back and yelled, "Just a minute!"

The evening before, she and her former teammates had decided that staying together made a lot more sense than going their separate ways every night. So, after Martina picked up Riley, they had all gone over to the Carriage Inn and taken rooms.

They'd ended up talking into the wee hours of the night, which was why she hadn't planned on getting out of bed until noon.

She sighed as she stood, and shuffled over to the door. Sunlight poured in the moment she cracked it open. She blinked several times and finally settled on a squint so she could see who thought waking her was a good idea.

It was Noreen. She was dressed and looked anxious.

"What's going on?" Martina asked.

"I heard a car."

"What?" Martina said, not quite understanding the

significance.

"I heard a *car*. Sounded like it was racing. You know, really loud. It was—" She pointed to the south. "That way."

"So what?"

"Martina! A car! Not one of ours. I'm the only one up."

Martina looked out at the parking lot. All her friends' cars were still there. "You're sure?"

"Yes."

"When did you hear it?"

"Five minutes ago. Tires squealing and everything."

"Hold on."

Alert now, Martina closed the door.

"What's going on?" Riley asked.

Martina went over to her clothes and pulled on her jeans. "Noreen thinks she heard a car."

"Seriously?"

"We're going to check it out."

"Can I come?"

"How you feeling?"

Riley considered the question. "Still a little stuffy, but my throat's better, and I don't feel as tired."

"All right. Hurry up."

By the time Martina finished dressing and using the bathroom, Riley was ready to go.

They decided to take Noreen's car. Though the morning was cool, they kept their windows down so they could listen for the other vehicle.

"It had to have been somewhere in this area," Noreen said as they passed the police station. "I'm sure of it."

"I don't hear anything," Riley said from the backseat.

"Me, either," Martina chimed in.

Noreen looked both frustrated and disappointed. "I know it was a car."

"I believe you," Martina said. "It's just not here now."

As they continued down China Lake Boulevard, they scanned the parking lots and side streets, looking for any signs of movement, but there was none.

They passed Ridgecrest Boulevard, Carl's Jr., and finally

Walmart, where the road took a gentle curve to the west along the southern edge of town.

Noreen pulled her car to the side of the road. "It must be gone," she said, defeated.

"It's okay. I'm sure we'll hear it again," Martina said, though she was beginning to wonder if her friend had dreamt the noise.

Noreen pulled a U-turn and headed back into town.

As they were nearing Ridgecrest Boulevard again, Martina said, "Let's make a stop at CVS. Pick up some drinks and snacks. I'm buying."

Though no one laughed, Noreen did crack a smile.

"Maybe they'll have a container of Pringles. Barbecue favor," Riley said. "I love—watch out!"

Riley screamed the last part as a shiny, black Ford Mustang roared into the intersection directly in front of them. Noreen slammed on the brakes while Martina instinctively braced herself against the dash.

They all watched as the other car raced across their path, barely getting out of the way before they skidded behind it. The driver of the other vehicle, his face turned toward them, looked as surprised to see them as they were to see him.

The moment they were out of each other's way, the Mustang began to swerve. The driver tried to compensate by cutting sharply to the left. He overcompensated and his tires lost their hold on the road. The car flipped up then over and over and over, coming to rest back on its wheels partially in the entrance to the Denny's parking lot.

"Oh, my God!" Riley said.

Martina threw her door open and raced down the asphalt toward the other car.

The roof was crushed halfway down, the safety glass of the windshield an ocean of cracks. The rest of the car was dented and twisted.

She reached the driver's door and looked in. The airbags had deployed and now lay deflated over the steering wheel and across the door. The driver was slumped to the right.

She jerked on the handle, but the door wouldn't open.

"Hey! Hey, are you all right?" she yelled.

The guy didn't move.

As she circled around to the other side, she saw Riley and Noreen running over. The passenger door was also jammed.

"The windshield," Riley said, pointing.

Martina looked at the front window. The upper corner nearest her was out of the frame. She climbed up onto the hood and kicked down on the glass. It moved. After several more stomps, there was enough of a gap to allow her to pass inside.

The driver still hadn't moved.

"Hey," she said, putting a hand on his shoulder. "Can you hear me?"

No response.

She hesitated, unsure what to do. If he'd broken his back, she knew she shouldn't move him. Then again, if he *had* broken his back, would he have to stay in the car forever?

She said a silent prayer, hoping she wouldn't hurt him, and then pushed him into sitting position. When the Mustang had driven by them, Martina had only had time to register the driver's surprise, but not get a good look at him. She'd assumed he was an adult, but the guy she was looking at couldn't have been more than sixteen or seventeen.

She tried to check his pulse, but he tensed and jerked his hand away as he groaned.

At least he was alive, but there was something definitely wrong with his wrist.

She grabbed his chin and wiggled it back and forth. "Wake up. We've got to get you out of here."

Another groan, then a wince as his eyes parted.

"Good," she said. "You're with me, right?"

She wasn't sure if he was moaning or saying yes, so she decided to assume it was the latter.

"What's your name?"

"Cra…"

She waited.

"Craig," he whispered.

"Okay, Craig. Can you move your legs?"

Another wince. "I don't know."

"Give it a try."

She watched as each of his thighs moved up and down.

"Excellent. I'm going to undo your seatbelt. Then you and I are going to crawl through the window."

He looked dubious.

"It's the only way out," she told him. "Are you ready?"

A nod.

She held on to him with one hand in case he lost his balance, and unbuckled his belt with the other.

"Noreen!" she shouted. "Get up on the hood, and help him out the window. But watch out for his right wrist." She focused back on Craig. "We need to switch seats." She glanced into the back of the car, thinking she might be able to move there and get out of his way, but the roof was crushed too far down. "I'm going to have to crawl over the top of you while you shift over here. You can do that, right?"

"I think so."

The transfer was awkward, and not without pain on Craig's part, but successful.

"Now through the window," she said.

"I'm not sure I can."

"It's either that or stay in here the rest of your life, because I'm pretty sure the fire department's not coming."

He seemed to actually be considering the choice.

"Come on. Let's go," she said as she gently pushed his shoulder.

With reluctance, he leaned over the dash and stuck his head through the window.

"Let me help you," Noreen said, outside.

Working from either end, the two girls maneuvered Craig out of the car. As soon as he was clear, Martina followed.

"Let me take a look at that wrist," Martina said.

He gingerly held out his right arm.

After she pushed back the sleeve of his sweater, she nodded. "Oh, yeah. That's broken." Though no bones were sticking out of the skin, the arm was already bruised.

"Hurt anywhere else?"

"Everywhere else," he said.

"Achy painy or really hurt?"

He shrugged. "Achy painy, I guess."

"All right. We should wrap up that wrist. Come on."

As they walked back to Noreen's car, Martina asked, "Tell me, hotshot. How long have you had your license?"

"What does it matter?"

"Well, you did nearly kill us, so that gives me the right to know."

"I've had it long enough."

She smirked. "Wasn't your car, was it?"

"Yeah, it was."

"It looked pretty new to me."

Looking guilty, he said, "No one else was going to use it."

She rolled her eyes, and opened the passenger door of the car. "Get in."

Before Riley could get in on her side, Martina said, "Do you know him?"

A shrug. "I've seen him around, I think."

"And?"

"And what?"

"And why are you acting like you don't like him?" she asked, because that was exactly what Riley had been doing since they'd pulled Craig out.

Her friend shrugged. "No reason."

"Uh-huh," Martina said, unconvinced.

"You guys getting in or not?" Noreen called from the driver's seat.

Riley opened the back door and got in, but kept as much distance between herself and Craig as she could. He didn't even seem to notice her. That's when the truth dawned on Martina. It wasn't that Riley *didn't* like Craig. It was the opposite.

The realization made her think of her own boyfriend. If she had survived the flu, Ben must have, too. He'd also lived through the original Sage Flu outbreak, after all. That was how they'd met.

She wondered where he was.

She wondered how he was doing.

But most of all, she wondered if she would ever see him again.

"Martina, let's go!"

CRAIG'S APPEARANCE MADE the girls curious how many others were still alive. They decided to split up and drive through town, honking their horns and making as much noise as possible to see if anyone else came out.

Martina also drove by Coach Driscoll's house because she should have been immune, too, but no one was home. That made sense, though. Coach usually went back east for the holidays.

Sadly, when they regrouped two hours later, the only people anyone had seen were a handful of the sick still strong enough to look out a window.

"How long until you think they're all dead?" Ruby Gryting asked.

"A few days, maybe a week," Martina said.

"And then what?" Jilly asked.

When no one seemed to have an answer for that, Craig raised his unbroken arm.

"You don't have to do that," Martina told him. "Just say what's on your mind."

He lowered his arm. "Sorry."

"What did you want to say?"

"Um, well, I think that what we do next, well, we should look for others who are still alive."

"We just *did* that," Valerie said. "No one's left but us."

"I don't mean here. There's got to be others in other places right? Look at us."

"We're alive because we all had the flu before," Amanda said.

"I didn't," he said. He looked at Riley. "Did you have it

before?"

A slight blush came to her cheeks as she shook her head. "No."

"We can't be the only two. But even if we are, what about all those other people who survived the outbreak last spring? There has to be at least a few hundred."

That made everyone think for a moment.

Martina nodded. "You're right. We do need to find whoever's left. Life is never going to go back to normal. The more of us together, the better."

"But how are we supposed to do that?" Valerie asked. "Drive from place to place and honk our horns again?"

More silence.

"I know how," Martina said, recalling her experience the previous spring. "Radios. CBs."

"Don't those have limited broadcast?" Amanda asked.

"Yeah, and aren't they just for truckers?" Valerie said. "What if no one's in a truck?"

"Don't you think other people will think about this and try it, too?" Martina argued.

Valerie thought for a moment, then said, "I guess it couldn't hurt, huh?"

Martina stood up. "We can pull one out of a truck, or maybe one of the stores in town has one, and set it up here."

There were voices of support and nods from the other girls.

"Um, there are other things we could try," Craig said.

"Okay," Martina said. "Like what?"

"Ham radios. Those go farther," he said. "A friend of my dad's has one set up at his house."

"Great idea."

"And…"

When he didn't continue, Martina said, "And what?"

"Well, I was thinking, what about K-Ridge?" he said.

Martina looked at him, confused. "K-Ridge, the radio station?"

"Yeah."

"They only broadcast, don't they? We couldn't talk back

and forth."

"Yeah, but couldn't we broadcast how to get ahold of us on a ham radio?"

Martina stared at him. "That's...not a bad idea, either." She looked around the room. "Does anyone know how to operate a radio station?"

As expected, no one answered.

"All right. Who wants to learn?"

28

ROCKIE MOUNTAINS, COLORADO
9:57 AM MST

WHERE THE HELL did the Audi go?

Isaac Judson searched the road ahead, knowing he wasn't going to spot it. Playing a hunch when they'd reached the intersection, he had instructed the man driving his car to go left. But here they were, several miles in, and no sign of the other vehicle.

He should have probably let the car go, but it had come from the direction of the camp, and raced away from him the minute they saw each other. That's what had piqued his curiosity. Why would they run? In a world where almost everyone was dying, wouldn't they wait when they saw someone else on the road?

His sat phone rang.

"Yes?"

"Sir, it's Peyton. We've reached the camp."

Judson told his driver to pull over, then said into the phone, "And?"

"Whole place is infected. At least thirty people, mostly kids. We've got a few more buildings to check, so I expect that number to go up."

"Dead?"

"No one yet, but give it a few hours and that'll change."

So their trip to Colorado was a waste of time. The people in the car had probably been sick, too, he thought.

"Turn around," he told his driver. To Peyton, he said, "No need to continue the search. Let's get back to the airport and out of here."

"There's something you might be interested in."

"What?"

"We talked to one of the girls here. She wondered if we were with the people who had just left."

"The ones in the car we've been after?"

"I assume so. Apparently they weren't from the camp. They'd stopped here looking for a kid who was."

"I don't see how this is important. Probably parents wanting to get their kid before they thought it was too late."

"I don't think so. The woman was black, and the kid she was looking for was white."

"A friend, then."

"Possibly," Peyton said. "The thing is, this kid escaped last night in a Suburban with several others. The girl I talked to said they didn't look sick."

Now this was interesting. "Where did they go?"

"She didn't know."

A call to base might solve that riddle. They could check and see if there was any satellite imagery of the area that caught the fleeing car.

"One other thing, sir. Actually, this is the item I thought you'd find most interesting."

Judson sat up straight. "Okay. What?"

"This kid the others were looking for, the girl said his name is Brandon. We found a list of the children that had been moved up here. There's only one Brandon on it. Brandon Ash."

Judson said nothing for a moment, caught off guard. "You're kidding me."

"No, sir."

It could be a coincidence. Ash wasn't exactly a common name, but it wasn't uncommon, either. And Brandon? You could throw a stone though a crowd and hit at least a couple of them. That was, if you could gather up a crowd anymore.

Still, Brandon Ash. The same name as the son of Captain

Daniel Ash, well known in the Project because of the part his blood played in creating a vaccine for KV-27a that allowed them to move forward with Implementation Day.

If the boy was that Brandon Ash, he would be worth spending a little more time searching for.

Yes, a call to base would definitely be in order.

THE BUNKER, MONTANA
10:07 AM MST

CHRISTINA TAPPED REPEATEDLY on the right arrow key, so that the time-lapse image on screen moved forward at a pace slow enough for her to get a sense of each frame. What she was looking at was a series of satellite photos taken the previous night over the Rocky Mountains surrounding Camp Kiley, the shots coming at one-minute intervals.

The camp remained quiet until 1:42 a.m. That's when a pair of headlights switched on, and a vehicle, after remaining in the camp parking area for a few minutes, headed down the road to the highway. She flipped to the infrared image and was ninety-nine percent sure the vehicle was a Suburban. It had to be them.

When it reached the highway, it stopped for at least three minutes. The next shot revealed that it turned left, going up the mountain. She traced its route, tapping and tapping and tapping, until the SUV finally turned again, stopped, and killed its lights. Flipping between IR and visual spectrum, she realized it had parked in front of a house. Several frames on, the house started to heat up.

She noted the GPS location, and was about to call Chloe with the information when a warning window opened on her screen.

DUAL ACCESS
MESSAGE 634X179

Dual access? She opened the log and rooted around for a moment.

"Oh, great," she said to herself.

She grabbed the phone.

"It's me," she said, after Chloe answered her call. "I've traced the car to a house about seventeen miles from your current position."

"In the mountains or below?"

"Mountains. Hold on." Christina accessed the texting function, typed in the GPS code, and hit SEND. "You should have the coordinates now."

There was a pause. "This is where he is?"

"It's where he went last night. I haven't followed the images forward enough yet, but thought you should get going."

"Might be better if we wait until—"

"Chloe, someone else just accessed the same satellite data. Project Eden's hunting for him, too."

ROCKY MOUNTAINS, COLORADO

"CALL ME AS soon as you can confirm." Chloe hung up the phone without waiting for Christina to reply.

"Did she find him?" Josie asked.

Chloe tossed the phone to her. "I just got a text. Copy the number and enter it into the cell's map function. It's GPS coordinates."

"For where Brandon is?"

"Was, at least." Chloe shifted the car into Drive and returned to the highway. "So, which way?"

"Left," Josie said.

They sped through the valley and up the other side.

When they reached the intersection that had earlier aided in their escape, Josie said, "Left."

Not long after they made the turn, Chloe's phone rang again.

"It's the Ranch. You want me to answer it?" Josie asked.

"Put it on speaker."

It was Christina.

"I was able to trace the rest of the satellite history," she said. "As of two minutes ago, the Suburban is still parked in front of the house."

"Finally some good news," Chloe said. "We should be there in fifteen minutes, tops."

"You won't be the first."

"Wait a minute. What?" Josie said. "What do you mean?"

"Where are they?" Chloe asked.

"On the road about three miles in front of you."

"The truck or the sedan?"

"Both."

"The Project Eden people?" Josie said. "They know where Brandon is, too?"

"Is there a back way?" Chloe asked Christina. "A back road that'll give us the chance to get ahead of them?"

"There's only the one route," Christina said.

Chloe tensed. One way or the other, they would have to deal with these assholes head on.

"We'll try to take them out on the road before they can get to the house," she said.

"Wait, wait, wait," Christina said. "I might have a better idea."

"Let's hear it."

"I need to check something first. For now, try to get as close to them as you can without letting them know you're there. I'll call you back in a minute."

"Hold on," Chloe said. "What's the idea?"

The line was already dead.

FOR THE FIRST few hours after they had broken into the house, Brandon had been unable to sleep. When he finally did, he was greeted with nightmares of chases and monsters and death.

It was a shake of his arm that woke him.

He opened his eyes to find daylight streaming into the house. By the angle, he guessed it was at least midmorning.

Ellie was sitting on the floor next to him, clutching her bear to her chest.

"Something wrong?" he asked.

"Everyone's asleep," she told him.

"Well, you should be, too."

"I can't. I'm…I'm scared."

He sat up. "You don't have to be scared now. No one here's going to hurt you." When her expression didn't change, he said, "Come here."

He opened his arms and she crawled onto his lap. Remembering how he'd loved to be rocked by his mom whenever he felt scared, he gently moved side to side, hoping it would help the girl. After a minute or so, he could feel her relax.

"How about something to drink?" he asked.

It took a few seconds, but finally she bobbed her head up and down.

"All right. Hop up."

He tickled her ribs. She didn't laugh, but she did squirm in protest as she rose to her feet.

Spread around them were Miss Collins and the other children. No one had wanted to be separated, so despite the fact that there were three bedrooms, they had all slept in the living room.

Brandon led Ellie around the others and into the kitchen. He located a glass and filled it with water.

After she took a drink, she said, "Breakfast?"

"Breakfast? Don't tell me you're hungry," he teased.

She looked at him with sad eyes and nodded.

"I'm just kidding," he said, tousling her hair. "Let me see what I can find."

He opened the refrigerator, totally forgetting that he had checked it the night before, and quickly shut it again. Still empty. The pantry, though, was half filled with canned goods and boxes of crackers and cereal and the like. He found some

Ritz crackers and an unopened jar of peanut butter, from which he made half a dozen tiny sandwiches and put them on a plate for them to share.

"This isn't breakfast," Ellie said.

"Oh, well, then I'll eat it all myself."

He pretended to pull the plate away.

"No, no," she said, grabbing his arm.

"So you do think this is okay for breakfast?"

She thought for a moment, then nodded.

The dozen miniature sandwiches disappeared in a hurry, so he made another set.

He had just popped one into his mouth when something rang, loud and close. Startled, he jumped and nearly choked on the cracker.

When it rang again, he realized it was coming from the cordless phone, sitting on the counter next to the refrigerator. From the living room, he could hear people stirring.

"What is that?" Miss Collins asked.

Brandon was about to answer her, when behind him Ellie said, "Hello?"

He whipped back around. The little girl had the phone to her ear.

"I'm Ellie," she said, and listened for a moment. "Uh-huh. Yeah. You want to talk to him? Okay." She held out the phone. "For you, Brandon."

"Me?" he said.

She nodded.

He assumed the person on the other end was asking for someone older than Ellie. He took the phone and raised it to his ear. "Hello?"

"Brandon? Is that you?"

"Who is this?"

"Christina. From the Ranch. God, I wasn't even sure the phone would work there."

"Chr-Chr-Christina?" He could hardly allow himself to believe it.

"Yes. You need to listen to me. There's—"

"Where are you?" he asked.

"At the Ranch."

"You're alive?"

"Yes." She sounded confused at first, then she said, "Oh, God. You don't know. We're fine. We survived."

"My sister?"

A slight hesitation. "Your family's fine."

"You mean Dad, too? You've heard from him?"

"He's here."

"Please, let me talk to him!"

Miss Collins stepped into the kitchen, her brow furrowed. "Brandon, who is it?"

He looked at her. "A friend of mine." To Christina, he said, "I just want to talk to him."

"He's…not in the room with me, but he's anxious to see you."

"Well, have someone go get him."

"There's no time. Brandon, some bad people are on the way to the house you're in. How many others are there with you?"

"Um, eleven."

"Eleven?" she sounded surprised. "Okay. Well, you need to get them out of there right now."

"Where are we supposed to go?"

"Take them into the woods. Find someplace to hide."

"Wait. On foot? We have a car."

"I know. A Suburban, but the people coming for you can track it. If you can go out the back of the house, that would be best. The woods come right up to it, and if you stay under the trees at all times, you'll be safe."

"They're Project Eden, aren't they?"

A pause. "Yes."

Brandon could feel his skin grow cold in fear. "If we go into the woods, they'll just come after us, won't they? We should at least try the car."

"No. Chloe is only a few minutes behind them."

Chloe? "By herself?"

"No."

His heart rate started to decrease. He trusted Chloe. If

she was coming, they had a chance. "Okay. We'll go into the woods."

"Get them moving right away. The sooner you're out of there, the better chance you'll have."

"I understand."

He hung up the phone.

"What was that all about?" Miss Collins said.

He knew she was going to be the hardest to convince. He was only a kid, after all. Then again, he had proven himself already, so…

"You trust me, right, Miss Collins?"

"Trust you? Um, sure. But what's that have to do with–"

"There are some bad people on their way here."

"What bad people?"

"People who want to hurt us!"

She looked skeptical. "Brandon, relax. Now, who was that on the phone?"

He huffed. "We don't have time for that. We need to get everyone out of the house *now*. Please trust me on this."

"It's cold outside. Everyone's tired. We're safe here."

"We are not safe! These people have already killed friends of mine! They…they killed my mom!"

"Your mom?"

Project Eden had actually killed friends and family of everyone, but he knew saying that would complicate matters. "Miss Collins, I was right about last night, and I'm right about this. If you want to stay, you can, but I hope you don't." He raced into the living room, intending to wake everyone up, but they were all sitting up and staring at him, scared.

"Is that true?" Loni asked.

"Yes," he said. "Everyone up! Put on your jackets and shoes. Right now. Hurry!"

Loni immediately jumped up. The others hesitated a second before joining her.

"Hold on," Miss Collins said. "I think we first need to take a minute and figure out what's going on here."

A couple of the kids stopped what they were doing, while the rest continued getting ready.

"We don't have a minute," Brandon said. "Even if I'm wrong or…or lying, it's not going to hurt us to go out for a little bit, right?" He could see she still wasn't buying it. He thought for a moment. "I saved you last night. You owe me for that."

"Brandon—"

"Just do this for me and we're even." He stared at her, and added, "Please!"

Not looking happy, she said, "Fine, we'll leave, but when someone starts feeling cold, we're coming back in."

"Okay, okay. No problem."

When everyone was ready and gathered at the back door, Brandon said, "Miss Collins, I'll be in front. Can you be in back?"

Still looking uncertain, she said, "Sure."

"Loni, Vincent, and Carter, you three spread out between us and make sure the little kids don't wander off."

"Okay," Loni said. The other two nodded.

"All right. This is really important. Everyone keep quiet, okay?"

"I need to potty," one of the younger kids said.

"Can you hold it?"

"For a little."

Brandon gave him a smile. "Good. The faster we get out of here, the sooner you can go. I promise."

"Okay."

"All right, everybody. Follow me."

He led them single file out the door and into the forest.

Less than two minutes later, as they were climbing a small rise behind the cabin, Brandon heard the unmistakable sound of a car engine in the distance. He caught Miss Collins's gaze, and saw from the surprise on her face that she'd heard it, too.

29

ISABELLA ISLAND
11:07 AM CST

THE ANSWER TO Dominic's problem was right in front of him. Perhaps if he'd been feeling better, he would have seen it sooner. As it was, it took him nearly thirty minutes to realize what he'd been staring at was a way to prevent him from exposing the others to his disease-ridden body.

He'd been sitting on the beach, looking out at the ocean. With each passing minute, the water pulled farther and farther back from the island.

The tide was moving out.

He'd been on the island long enough to know low tide was still a few hours off. Though he had dismissed swimming out as an option before, he hadn't taken into consideration an assist from the receding ocean. The tide could do a lot of the work for him, and he could then use what energy he saved to swim out into the current that swept past the island toward the mainland.

As he stared at the water, wondering if he could really do it, he coughed, deep and violent. Phlegm flew out of his mouth and landed on the beach. It was a blood-speckled, sickly yellow blob. He covered it with dirt and rose to his feet. The longer he waited, the less chance he had at succeeding.

The water was warm on his bare feet. He was tempted to

leave behind the shirt and shorts he was wearing, but he knew the virus could very well be clinging to their fibers.

He looked back. His shoes were sitting near the supplies he'd been given. He should take those.

The supplies, too, he thought. Everything could be tainted.

But there was no way he could haul it all out with him. Perhaps he should write a message in the sand, warning people to stay away.

Robert will figure it out, he told himself, as he stepped farther into the surf.

AFTER DELIVERING DOMINIC'S breakfast, Robert returned to the hotel to find a small group gathered in the bar, discussing the possibility of returning to the mainland.

When he realized what was going on, he said, "Do you not get it? Did you not see what's been going on everywhere else?"

He looked at the TV. Though the news channels had gone off the air, one of the movie channels was still broadcasting as if nothing was wrong. Its current selection: an old black and white gangster film.

"It *can't* be everywhere," one of the men at the table said.

"Maybe not, but it's in Costa Rica. Where else are you going to go?" Robert asked.

The man shared a look with the others. "We thought we'd head north. For Texas."

Robert stared at him. "And how exactly are you going to get there?"

"One of the boats."

"First off, due north is Cuba, not Texas. And even if you did take a boat, which is *not* going to happen, there's not enough gas on the island to even get you as far north as the Nicaraguan border, let alone all the way to the US."

This last fact seemed to throw a wrench into the group's plans. They grumbled for a few more minutes, then scattered, no doubt hoping to come up with an alternative idea.

Robert found Renee in the office, and they went over the inventory list.

"So this gives us, what? A month before we run out of food?"

"Maybe six weeks if we don't do anything else," she said. "But once we start fishing, we should be fine."

He nodded. The sea would become their main food supplier if they were going to be on the island for an extended period of time. He and Dominic had discussed using the scuba boats to fish beyond the island, but had agreed it would be a good idea to wait until everyone settled in and got used to the idea they weren't on vacation anymore.

"We'll start up in a few days," he told her. "Do we know if there's anyone who can—"

"Come in, base," a scratchy voice over the radio speaker said.

Robert snatched up the mic. "This is base. Who's this?"

"Chuck Tyler."

"Go ahead, Chuck."

"Um, I think there's someone in the water."

Robert and Renee shared a puzzled look. "A body?"

"No, swimming. Away from the island." A pause. "I think it might be Dominic," Tyler said.

"Dominic?"

"Looks like whoever it is came straight out from his beach."

Robert was sure Tyler had his geography wrong, and was about to say so when he remembered something from his visit with Dominic that morning.

His friend nowhere to be seen. Robert calling him, his panic growing. Then Dominic stepping out from behind a rock and telling him to relax, that he was just relieving himself.

Was that really what he'd been doing? He could have answered Robert even if he was in the middle of taking a piss. And why had Dominic stayed by the rocks while they'd talked? On other occasions, he'd always come a lot closer so conversation could be easier. And he had looked tired that morning. Robert had assumed that was from worry over his ordeal, but could it have been something else?

"Oh, my God," he said.

He grabbed a spare walkie-talkie and raced out of the office.

"Where are you going?" Renee called after him.

Not answering, he ran through the bar and down the path to the bay. The two speedboats rocked calmly in the water next to the dock. He untied the lines mooring the nearest one and jumped on board. The engine rumbled to life on the first try, and instead of easing the boat away from the pier like everyone was supposed to do, he gave it all he could, and the boat shot away from shore like a rocket.

Dominic's Beach was on the opposite side of the island from the bay. So even going all out, it took Robert fifteen minutes to get there. As the beach came into view, he raised the walkie-talkie to his mouth.

"Come in, Chuck."

"This is Chuck."

"Give me an update."

"That you in the boat?"

"Yeah."

"He's a lot farther out now. Ahead and to your left. Uh, what is that? Port?"

"How far?"

"A couple football fields, I think. Hard to tell."

Robert veered a few degrees to port. "Am I on line with him now?"

"A little bit more."

Robert turned the wheel again.

"That's it," Chuck said.

"Give me a heads-up when I'm getting close."

"You got it."

Keeping his speed down so that he didn't accidentally run over his friend in the water, Robert guided the boat carefully across the swells.

It wasn't long before Chuck's voice came over the radio

again. "Slow down. You're almost there. Right in front of you, maybe a hundred feet."

Robert craned his neck, searching the water ahead. At first, he didn't see anything, then a swell passed by and suddenly there was Dominic. Robert brought the boat up alongside his friend and cut the engine.

Dominic's arms moved back and forth in a less-than-successful attempt to keep his head above water. He looked exhausted, his eyelids half closed.

Robert leaned over the side and reached out. "Give me your hand."

Dominic bobbed up so that his mouth was above the waterline. "No. I'm…" The lower half of his face slipped into the water again, and it took a moment before he could get his mouth clear. "I'm sick. You'll catch it."

His hand still out, Robert said, "You're fine. You just need some rest."

"Robert, I'm sick. I've been throwing up and…" Under the water, then up again. "And coughing. I wanted…wanted to get…" He nearly choked as a wave slapped into his face. "I'm trying to get away so no one else…gets it. Trying to get to the current."

Robert looked out at the open sea, toward the current that ran toward the Costa Rican coast. It was still a good half-mile away. What Dominic was trying to do was admirable but crazy.

"You're never going to make it," he said. "You'll have to let me take you back."

Dominic closed his eyes as if defeated. When he opened them again, he stared straight at Robert. "You have to help me."

"Dominic, come on. Let's get you home."

"You have to help me. Throw me…a rope, and pull me out there."

"Absolutely not. No way."

"You don't have…a…choice." Dominic's head went all the way under. When he popped back up, he gasped for air. "If you take me back…everyone dies."

Robert pressed his lips together, his jaw clenched. "I'll take you back to the beach," he said after a moment. "You'll be okay there."

Dominic silently treaded water, then said, "It's okay. Never mind. I shouldn't have asked you."

He started moving his arms again, breaststroke-style, swimming at a snail's pace.

Robert stood rooted to the deck, confused and stunned. He had three choices, none of them good.

First choice: Forcibly bring his friend back to the island, which would entail exposing himself. It wasn't that he didn't want to die—of course he didn't—but if he got sick, it would be as Dominic had feared, and others would likely fall victim, too.

Second choice: Return to the dock and let his friend go on. But there was no way Dominic would reach the current, so when the tide started coming in again, he would, too. No matter which beach he washed up on, he'd be bringing the flu back with him.

Third choice: Do as Dominic had asked. It was the only choice that would ensure no one else on the island became infected. But it would also mean playing an active role in his friend's death.

Dominic had moved about fifteen feet closer to the current, every stroke he took a struggle.

Robert squeezed his eyes shut, the pain of the only real choice he had unbearable. When he opened them again, a tear escaped from the corner of his eye.

With sudden determination, he wiped it away, and removed a coil of rope from one of the seat lockers. He tied one end to a life preserver, which he tossed into the water next to his friend.

Hearing the splash, Dominic looked back.

"Grab on," Robert said.

"I'm…not going back to shore."

"I'll take you where you want to go."

Dominic studied him for a moment before he reached out and grabbed the life preserver. Robert tied the other end of the rope to a cleat, checked to make sure his friend was secure, and started the engine again.

Keeping his speed slow so Dominic wouldn't be pulled off, he aimed the boat toward the current.

"What are you doing?" Chuck asked over the radio.

Robert left the walkie where it was.

"What's going on?" Renee's voice this time.

"He's pulling Dominic farther out," Chuck said, then started to tell her what he was seeing.

Robert reached over and turned the radio off.

Going as slowly as they were, he was able to feel the shift when they entered the current. He went a hundred yards in, and stopped so that the boat was alongside Dominic again. His friend looked even more tired than before, as both he and the boat began moving silently toward Costa Rica.

"I can take you all the way to the mainland," Robert offered.

"A waste of…fuel. And you wouldn't have enough to go back," he said. "Besides…I'd never make it all the way."

He struggled out of the life preserver.

"I don't care about the fuel. And you might make it. It would give you a chance."

Dominic tried to smile. "Thank you, Robert. You're a good man and a good friend. That's why they need you here. It's up to you to make sure everyone survives."

Before Robert could reply, Dominic let go of the preserver and slipped under the water. Robert nearly jumped in after him to pull him up, but caught himself.

A few seconds later Dominic appeared again, already thirty feet away from the boat.

Robert watched his friend go under again. This time Dominic didn't come back up.

He remembered little of the ride back to the island. When he reached the dock, Renee and several others were waiting.

"What happened?" she asked.

"Dominic's gone."

"You left him out there," someone else said accusingly.

Robert narrowed his eyes. "I took him where he wanted

to go."

"But why?" Renee asked.

"Because it was the only way he could save us."

He pushed through the crowd and headed for the bar, intending to start with the first bottle he saw, and work his way through the last.

30

ROCKY MOUNTAINS, COLORADO
11:43 AM MST

JUDSON SMILED AS they neared the house. The car that had been traced via satellite was still parked in front. It was indeed a Suburban.

He ordered the truck to stop in the driveway and block the exit in case the Ash kid and his friends were able to somehow get to their car. While the driver stayed with the truck, Judson and the rest of the team approached the house, weapons ready.

"Everyone, comm gear on," he whispered.

The men did as instructed.

"You three," Judson said, pointing, "around back. Let me know when you're in position."

"Yes, sir," the men said, then moved off.

Judson and the two remaining men walked quietly up to the front door. It was locked, but that wasn't a problem. There was a thin, decorative window next to the door that had been broken at the same height as the doorknob. Someone had taped cardboard over the hole, but it was easy enough to remove with very little noise. This was obviously the way the group from the camp had gotten inside.

Judson slipped his hand through the hole, unlocked the door, and opened it a few inches. He was surprised by how quiet it was inside. It was late morning, and he thought some of the kids would be making noise.

"In position," one of the three at the back of the house reported.

"Hold there," Judson said. "We'll go in first. You follow in thirty seconds." He looked back at his two companions. "Ready?"

Both men nodded.

"Let's go."

He pushed the door open and they crept inside.

WHEN THEY HEARD the cars approach the house, Brandon looked back at Miss Collins again. It appeared as if she was going to say something, so he quickly shook his head and raised his finger to his lips.

They moved down into a swallow ravine, but instead of climbing up the other side, Brandon decided to go to the right and follow the less strenuous path, so they could quickly put as much distance between them and the house as possible. As they walked, Brandon continually scanned their surroundings for anywhere that might be a good place to hide, but so far he'd seen nothing useful.

"Brandon, I really gotta pee."

The little boy from before had stopped and was rocking back and forth, his face all scrunched up.

"Okay. We'll take a break here," Brandon said. "Anyone else need to go?"

Several hands shot up, including Ellie's. He set the girl down.

"Everyone, just find a tree, I guess."

More than one kid said, "What?" while the others looked at Brandon, confused.

"How about this?" Miss Collins said. "Boys, you go over there behind those trees." She pointed at a small cluster of pines to the right. "And girls, we'll go over here." She motioned toward a similar group on the left.

"We just go outside?" one of the kids asked.

"Uh-huh," Miss Collins said. "Right on the ground."

While the boys looked excited about this prospect, the

girls didn't appear to be happy at all.

"We've got to make it fast," Brandon said. "So everyone get going."

When the groups separated and did their business, Brandon and Loni ended up being the only two who didn't need to take a break.

"Who are these people we're hiding from?" Loni asked.

"You wouldn't believe me."

She looked almost hurt. "Yeah, I would."

He realized she was probably right. "They're the ones who've made everyone sick."

"Are you serious?"

He nodded.

"And they want to make us sick, too?"

"Probably."

The others started returning.

"I'll tell you more later," he whispered.

"Promise?"

"I promise."

Ellie ran back to him and held her arms out, but instead he grabbed her hand. "Need you to walk for a little bit, okay?"

She looked disappointed, but nodded.

He was about to tell everyone, "Time to move," when they all heard a voice yell back toward the house, just loudly enough for them to make out the words.

"Come on back! No sense in hiding! We're here to help you, not hurt you!"

Several of the kids looked at Brandon, wondering if he'd made a mistake.

"Get back here! Now!" The last was shouted in a harsh burst, like there'd be trouble if the order wasn't followed.

"We need to keep moving," Brandon said. "Let's go."

THEY HAD BEEN here. They just weren't here anymore.

The living room was covered with blankets and pillows and makeshift beds. There were several personal bags, too, and an open jar of peanut butter and a box of crackers in the kitchen, all of which led Judson to believe they'd left in a hurry not that long ago.

The fact that the Suburban was still there meant that either someone had picked them up—which seemed highly unlikely—or they had left on foot. A quick search around the perimeter revealed a few footprints out back leading into the woods. Unfortunately, because the cold had made the ground hard, the tracks soon disappeared.

"Goddammit," Judson said. They were just kids. Why did they have to complicate things?

He looked all around, trying to get a sense of where they might have gone, but each direction was as good and as bad as another.

What he needed to do was flush them out. He cupped his hands around his mouth and yelled, "Come on back! No sense in hiding! We're here to help you, not hurt you!"

In the silence that followed, he listened for any sound of movement, but there was nothing.

Dammit, dammit, dammit.

"Get back here! Now!" he shouted, anger sneaking into this voice.

Control yourself, idiot.

A crack off to the right—slight, distant. A branch breaking. It could have been anything, or it could have been them.

He looked back at his team, and pointed in the direction of the sound. "Spread out."

BRANDON SPUN AROUND the moment he heard the crack.

A dozen feet behind him, Billy looked horrified, his foot still on the branch he'd snapped in two. "Sorry."

Brandon looked past him in the direction of the house. They were probably far enough away that it wouldn't matter, but still…

"We need to move faster," he said. "Watch your step, but

try to keep up."

He started out again, his pace doubled.

He hoped it would be enough.

CHLOE PULLED THE Audi to the side of the road. A hundred feet ahead was the driveway to the house where Brandon had apparently spent the night. As she started to open her door, she could hear Josie doing the same in the backseat.

"Uh-uh. You're staying here," she said.

"No way," Josie said.

"There are armed men up there."

"Yeah, I know. And what if one of them finds me here while you're gone?"

Chloe frowned. She didn't think that was likely, but it didn't mean it couldn't happen. "Okay, but stay behind us, and when I say down, you get down."

"I will."

Once out of the car, Chloe and Miller supplemented the guns they were already carrying with additional ammunition and, in Chloe's case, a seven-inch KA-BAR hunting knife from Miller's duffel bag.

"What about me?" Josie asked. "I know how to shoot. Dad taught me."

"At targets, yes," Chloe said. "Not at a person."

"I could if I had to."

Chloe looked at her. "Maybe, but not today."

They ran along the edge of the road, then turned into the woods and worked their way toward the house, parallel to the driveway. It wasn't long before they spotted the large troop truck. It was stopped in the middle of the driveway, blocking access.

Chloe motioned for the other two to wait. She continued forward through the trees until she was even with the vehicle's cab. Not seeing anyone inside, she switched her attention to the area beyond the vehicle. She could see the house now. It was a large, modern vacation home that, at the moment, had its front door halfway open. Parked in front of the house were the Suburban and the military sedan that had been following the Audi.

Standing between the two cars was a member of the Project Eden team, holding a rifle. Chloe double-checked to make sure he was alone, then made her way back to Miller and Josie and described what she'd found.

When finished, she locked eyes with Josie. "This time, you stay right here until I motion for you to join us, understand?"

Josie nodded.

Chloe and Miller went around the back of the truck and into the woods on the other side. From there, they worked their way toward the house, stopping just shy of the parking area.

From this angle the soldier's back was to them. Chloe pantomimed what she wanted to do, and Miller nodded.

Chloe moved in silently behind the soldier, while Miller held back several feet, covering her with his gun. Five feet away, she launched herself, arm flying around the guard's neck. He tried to bash her with his gun as he struggled to throw her off, but Miller moved in and ripped the rifle from his hands.

The man attempted to yell through his constricted windpipe, but managed nothing more than a feeble gasp. His face started to turn red as she clamped down harder. His desperation grew, even as his attempts to free himself weakened.

Finally, his body went limp, but Chloe didn't release her grip. She had zero compassion for anyone associated with Project Eden. They had taken her past from her and killed her friends, not to mention the little matter of the genocide they were in the middle of committing.

No, she had no compassion at all.

When she was sure he was dead, she laid him on the ground and looked at Miller. He'd been keeping watch while she finished off the guard. He shook his head, letting her know the noise had gone undetected.

Harlan had reported seven men in the Project Eden team that had gone into the mountains. Six more to go.

They moved to the open door of the house, expecting to hear noises inside, but the house was eerily silent.

Keeping low, Chloe crept into the foyer, and peeked around the corner into the rest of the house. Blankets and pillows were scattered all around the living room, but the room itself was unoccupied.

Good, Chloe thought. Christina's warning had worked, and Brandon had gotten them out.

The question was, had the Project Eden team found them yet?

Chloe and Miller located the back door and headed outside, hoping they weren't too late.

"WHAT'S THAT?" LONI asked.

Brandon looked in the direction she was pointing. There was something to the left, through the trees. Something manmade. It was white, or at least had been once. A cabin, or perhaps a shed.

"Everyone wait here for a moment," he said.

"Something wrong?" Miss Collins asked.

"I want to check something." He looked down at Ellie. "I'll be right back, okay?"

She didn't look happy but she nodded and let go of his hand.

As he ran toward the structure, he heard someone following him. He glanced over his shoulder to find Loni keeping pace with him a couple yards back.

"I want to see what it is, too," she said.

He contemplated telling her to go back, but decided there was no reason to, so he ran on.

The structure turned out to be neither a cabin nor a shed, at least not in the traditional sense. It had once been a mobile home, but now was a wreck. Three quarters of the roof had collapsed, and an entire sidewall was lying on the ground in pieces. Holes from shotgun blasts covered much of the walls that were still standing.

It had been a long time since anyone had ever called this place home, Brandon thought. He scanned the small clearing surrounding the trailer. How had it arrived here? For that matter, how had the people who lived here gone to and from civilization? There had to be a road, one wide enough for the trailer.

He finally spotted an opening in the trees on the other side of the clearing, and jogged over. Though the forest had started to reclaim it, signs of the old road were still there.

He looked back at the trailer. It could be a passable shelter, but if the Project Eden people spotted it, they would check it for sure.

The road, though, would provide an easier route through the forest, and allow them to get farther faster.

"Come on," he said to Loni as he started running back to the others.

A CLICK OF a tongue.

Judson looked toward the noise. One of the men ahead of him had paused and was waving for him to come over.

"What is it?" he whispered when he got there.

The man pointed at a broken branch on the ground. Judson bent down for a better look. It had been snapped cleanly in two, as if someone had stepped on it.

Excellent, he thought as he rose back up. He knew it wouldn't be long now. The Ash kid and his buddies couldn't be more than seven or eight minutes ahead of them.

He pointed ahead, and the team started out again.

WHERE ARE THEY? Josie wondered.

Chloe and Miller should have been back by now. Josie had heard something a few minutes earlier, grunting and what sounded like feet scuffing the ground, but after that, nothing. The problem was that she couldn't see a thing. The truck was not only blocking the road, but also her view of everything on the other side.

She stood there, frustrated, torn between her promise to Chloe to remain where she was and her desire to know what was going on.

Maybe she could move down until the truck was out of the way. She'd still be in the forest, so that wouldn't be breaking her promise, right?

Staying within the woods, she crept forward until the truck was no longer obstructing her view. She could see the house now and the two vehicles parked in front. The front door of the home was open.

As she looked around for Chloe and Miller, she spotted the lower half of two legs lying on the ground, sticking out from between the cars.

Miller? she wondered.

Fear squeezed her heart.

Where's Chloe?

She whipped her head around again, but Chloe was nowhere to be seen, so she looked back at the feet. If the cars mostly hid one body, they could easily be hiding two. And if Miller and Chloe were dead, it would be up to Josie to save her brother.

Deciding her promise was no longer valid, she shot out from the cover of the trees and crossed over to the body, not daring to breathe again until she was safely between the two cars.

The dead man was not Miller. Nor was there a second body.

Her relief was tempered by her concern about where Chloe and Miller were. In the house? It seemed awfully quiet there. If they were confronting the rest of the Project Eden squad, wouldn't she hear something?

What if they were in trouble?

What if they needed help?

Her father had been training her and Brandon to handle these kinds of situations. She *did* know how to shoot a gun. True, she had never shot at a person before, but if someone she cared about was in trouble, she knew she could pull the trigger.

She glanced down at the dead soldier, at the rifle lying beside him.

ANOTHER TONGUE CLICK, this time from the man farthest to the left. He was pointing at something hidden in the trees, not too far off.

A building, Judson thought, smiling. The kind of place a group of kids might think was a good place to hide.

Using hand signals, he redirected his team toward it.

CHLOE HELD UP her hand, stopping Miller. She'd heard something, a noise. Kind of like the sound a woodpecker would make if it hit a tree only once. She had no idea if woodpeckers ever came to this part of the country, but she was pretty damn sure one wouldn't be knocking away at a trunk during the winter.

She waited, hoping to hear it again, but there was no reprise.

She nodded in her best guess of the direction it had come from. "That way."

JUDSON CURSED TO himself.

The structure, which turned out to be an abandoned mobile home, was empty. He'd been so sure he was going to find them there.

"Sir," Williams, one of his men, whispered over the comm.

Judson turned away from the trailer.

"Footprints," Williams said.

He was at the edge of the clearing near a gap in the trees. Judson walked over.

Williams pointed at the ground. "There, sir."

In a patch of loose dirt were several footprints, all of them too small to belong to an adult. They were aimed toward the gap in the trees.

Not only a gap, Judson realized. A road.

"This way," he said, going through the opening. "Double time."

"I'M TIRED," ONE of the kids shouted.

Before Brandon could react, Loni said, "Quiet."

"Can't we stop?" another asked.

"We have to keep going," Brandon said.

"Why?"

"We don't want the bad men to find us."

"Brandon," Miss Collins said. "They need to rest. Just for a little bit."

He could see all the kids looked beat. Even Billy and Carter seemed to be dragging. He stopped. "Five minutes. Then we gotta go again."

Most of the kids plopped down right where they'd been standing.

Miss Collins walked over to Brandon. "They can't keep going like this. They're too young. They don't have the strength you do."

"Just a little longer," he said. "I'm sure we'll find someplace we can hide."

She looked around, her expression a mix of compassion and resignation. "Where?"

Before he could answer, Ellie, who was still beside him, said, "I need to go potty."

"I'll take you, sweetie," Miss Collins said.

Ellie shook her head. "Brandon."

"Actually, I think it's better if Miss Collins takes you," Brandon said.

Ellie looked doubtful.

"It's okay. I'll be right here," he told her.

Reluctantly, she let go of his hand and went with Miss Collins.

After they left, Brandon decided he needed to relieve himself, too. He chose a tree not too far away, circled behind it, and unzipped.

"Brandon!" It was Miss Collins. She sounded odd.

"Just a sec," he said.

He finished and zipped up. He circled back around the tree, but immediately stopped.

Miss Collins was standing not too far beyond the spot where they'd parted a few minutes earlier. Behind her was a man holding a gun to her head. Two other men were behind him.

The man with the gun grinned. "So, you're Brandon?"

Brandon's mouth went dry. "Um, yes," he said, barely loudly enough to be heard.

"Brandon *Ash*?" the man said.

It wasn't a chill that shot up Brandon's spine. It was an arctic blast.

ONCE THEY DISCOVERED that the kids had gone down the road, it didn't take long before Judson and his men heard them ahead.

Judson ordered three of his men to quietly follow the kids, while he and the other two moved into the forest, intending to arc around to get in front of their prey and overwhelm them from both sides. But the kids stopped in the middle of the road before Judson's small squad was in place.

"Hold," Judson whispered, crouching down behind some brush.

Through the branches, he examined the group of children. Ten kids. No, eleven. But only one adult. A woman. Judson had figured there would be at least two, if not three. This would make things even easier.

"Williams?" he said softly into his mic.

"Go for Williams." He was one of the three left behind the kids.

"Get ready to move in."

"Copy."

"Let us—" Judson cut himself off.

The woman and a small girl were heading into the woods

in their direction. As they drew nearer, he could hear them talking.

"…than that," the woman said. "It won't be much longer now."

"My feet hurt."

"I'm sure they do." The woman paused. "Let's go right behind that bush."

"Okay."

'That bush' was only fifteen feet ahead and to the left of Judson's position.

"Everyone hold," he whispered.

The woman and the girl circled around the bush and stopped.

"Here?" the girl asked.

"Here's fine."

The woman turned her back to Judson to help the girl. As soon as the girl finished going to the bathroom, the woman leaned down to assist her again.

Judson took that as his cue and moved out from his hiding place, motioning for the two men with him to follow. He was able to get in right behind the woman a moment before she stood up.

The little girl sucked in a breath when she saw him. The woman started to turn, but Judson grabbed her and placed his gun against her back.

"Quiet now," he said. "If you cooperate, no one will get hurt. All right?"

She nodded.

"Let's go back to your other friends."

"Come on, Ellie," the woman said, holding her hand out to the girl.

"These are the bad men," Ellie said.

"It's okay," the woman told her. "Come on."

Ellie hesitated a second, then took the woman's hand.

Keeping the gun at her back, Judson guided them over to the other kids.

"Which one's Brandon?" Judson asked.

The woman looked around. "He's not here."

He moved the gun to her head. “Don’t lie to me. Which one?”

“I’m not lying. He *was* here, but he’s not now.”

“Call him.”

The woman said nothing.

“Call. Him.” He twisted the gun’s muzzle against her temple.

“Brandon!” she yelled.

“BRANDON!”

Chloe and Miller froze.

The voice belonged to a woman, and had come from fifty yards away at most.

Chloe and Miller moved into woods to cut down the chance of being seen, and continued on. As they got closer, they could hear another voice, a man’s. Though he was too far away for them to understand him, his tone suggested he was giving orders.

Another twenty feet on, Miller grabbed Chloe’s shoulder and pulled her to a stop. He pointed back at the road. Three soldiers had stepped out of the trees on the other side. They paused in the middle, talked for a moment, then two headed toward the voices, while the third stayed where he was.

There was no question in Chloe’s mind about what was going on. The Project Eden team had found Brandon and the others. The man waiting on the road was the safety net in case someone tried to escape.

That was something they could use to their advantage.

Chloe whispered her plan into Miller’s ear. He nodded, and made his way silently to a point about forty feet deeper into the woods, nearly level with the man’s position. Chloe went in the other direction, stopping just inside the forest.

Right on schedule, Miller scraped a foot across the ground, and walked in place loudly enough for a few footfalls to be heard.

The guard whipped his head to the right, peering into the darkness.

Miller waited a second before he scraped the ground again.

The guard glanced down the road where his friends had gone, then looked back into the woods.

"Someone's out here," he said.

Radios, Chloe thought. *Crap.*

She would have to be extra careful.

The man was quiet for a few seconds, then nodded. "Copy."

Holding his rifle tightly, he headed into the woods. The moment he passed Chloe's position, she moved in behind him.

His first indication that something was wrong was her hand on his mouth. His second was the knife plunging into his chest.

Chloe dropped him to the ground. *Two down.*

"YOU'RE CAPTAIN ASH'S son, right?" the man with the gun asked Brandon.

Brandon remained silent.

"That's a yes, I take it. My bosses will be very interested to talk to you."

"You don't have to hold your gun against her like that," Brandon said. "I'm not going to run."

The man smiled, and pulled the gun away from Miss Collins's head. "All right. But if you *do* try, I'll kill her."

One of the kids started to cry, while a few others looked on the verge of doing the same.

"I said I won't."

The man smiled at Brandon, and looked at the others. "Listen up. This is what's going to happen. I'll give you another…" He paused. "Two minutes to rest, then we're going to walk back to the house."

"What happens then?" Carter asked.

"That depends on how well you behave." The man surveyed the kids. "Any other questions?"

No one said anything.

"Good," he said. He let go of Miss Collins. "You should rest, too."

He took a step back, and motioned for his two men to spread out. He touched something on his shirt and said, "Williams?" There was a pause. "Two of you come in. The other stays out there in case someone tries to sneak by."

He must be talking on a radio, Brandon guessed. Sure enough, seconds later, two more soldiers arrived.

Suddenly, the main guy cocked his head to the side. After a moment, he said into his radio, "Check it out and report back." He took a step forward. "Time's up, everyone. On your feet. We're getting out of here."

The kids slowly got to their feet.

"Who's missing?" the man asked Brandon.

"What?" Brandon asked.

"Who's missing? There's someone not here."

Brandon looked around. All eleven kids and Miss Collins were there. "I don't know what you mean. Everyone's here."

The man took a step closer. "Don't lie to me!"

"I'm not lying. We're all here."

The man studied Brandon's face, then turned and walked several feet away. "Krieger, report." He paused. "Krieger, report." Another pause. He shot a look at the two newly arrived men. "Go."

They went back the way they'd come.

That's when it hit Brandon.

Chloe.

CHLOE AND MILLER were ready and waiting when the two men returned. Instead of luring them into the woods with a sound, they used the dead soldier's body, leaving his head sticking out from the tree line just far enough to be seen.

Like moths to a light, the two men rushed to their fallen comrade. Chloe and Miller were on them before they even knew what happened.

Four down.

"WILLIAMS?" JUDSON SAID.

No response.

"Williams, what the hell's going on?"

Still nothing.

What the fuck?

He glanced at McGrath and Torres. Both men looked concerned.

"Let's get everyone together," he ordered.

But before any of them could take a step, a shot rang out. McGrath fell to the ground, and Torres stumbled a few feet before joining him. Several of the kids screamed.

Not one shot, Judson realized. Two. He slipped behind a tree just as another bullet hit its trunk.

"Everyone get down!" Brandon Ash said. "Lie on the ground!"

Judson searched around, desperate. The girl who'd had to go to the bathroom was two feet away. He grabbed her and pulled her to his chest.

"Leave me alone!" she screamed, and started to wail.

"Let her go!" Brandon yelled.

Judson ignored him as the girl struggled in his arms. "Stop it or I'll break your arm."

Though her whimpering didn't stop, her thrashing ceased.

"Please," Brandon said again. "Let her go. You…you can take me instead."

Judson looked at the girl and then at Brandon. The boy was a lot bigger than she was, and would be much better as a shield.

"Fine. Get over here," he said.

"Let her go first."

"No way."

The boy hesitated a moment, then crawled over. Judson grabbed his arm and dropped the girl.

"Go to Miss Collins," Brandon told her.

The girl stood there like she didn't want to leave.

"Go on," Brandon said.

Tears streaming down her face, she nodded, and disappeared around the tree.

Judson yanked Brandon in front of him, and held him against his chest with his left arm.

"Come on out," a female voice called. "We know you're back there."

Who the hell is that?

His gaze darted all over the place. There had to be an escape somewhere, a way out of this mess.

There were enough trees that if he ran straight back, maybe they wouldn't be able to get a shot at him.

"You're wasting time," the woman said. "You're not getting away, so come on out."

Judson adjusted his hold on the boy, and whispered, "Follow my lead." He took a step forward.

The roar of the gun wasn't as surprising as the sensation of the bullet passing by only a few feet in front of him.

"I wouldn't, if I were you," a man said, his voice coming from the side.

Judson turned, putting Brandon between him and the shooter. The guy was about forty feet away, leaning out from behind a tree.

"Let the boy go," the man said.

Judson placed the muzzle of his gun against Brandon's head. "You let me out of here first, then he can go."

"What's going on?" the woman asked. She was closer now.

"He's got Brandon," the man replied. "Says if we let him get away, he'll let Brandon go."

Worried that she was going to sneak up behind him, Judson twisted around the tree, keeping Brandon in front of him. He was now out of sight of the man, but could see the woman. She was less than thirty feet away, her gun aimed at him. If she pulled the trigger, though, there was a very good chance she'd hit the kid first.

"Back off and let me go," he said.

"Brandon!" the little girl yelled.

"Get them out of here," the woman with the gun said to

the one Brandon had called Miss Collins.

Fear in her eyes, Miss Collins began ushering the kids away.

"Put your gun down," the woman said to Judson.

He pushed the barrel hard against Brandon's ear. "You put yours down. Both you *and* your friend. When I've put enough room between us, I'll let the kid go."

"And why should I trust you?"

"Because you have no choice."

She paused, looked toward where the other man had been standing, then back at Judson. "All right." She started to lower her gun to the ground.

Boom!

JOSIE WAS SURE she'd gone the wrong way.

When she found the house empty, she'd gone out the back, thinking it was the only direction everyone could have taken. She found trample marks on a bed of pine needles leading to the right, and assumed that was the way the others had gone. But since then, she had found no one.

She was about to turn back when she heard the gunshots. They were about a hundred yards ahead and to the left. She ran as fast as she could, then ducked into the cover of the woods at the first sign of movement. Peering around a tree, she saw Chloe, her gun raised in front of her. Scattered around her were several kids.

"Back off and let me go."

Josie's view of the speaker was blocked, but before she could even adjust her position, a little voice hollered, "Brandon!"

Brandon? Had he been hurt?

"Get them out of here," Chloe said.

Josie moved to her left for a better view. She froze. One of the soldiers had an arm around Brandon and was holding a gun against her brother's head.

"Put your gun down," Chloe said.

"You put yours down," he replied. "Both you *and* your

friend. When I've put enough room between us, I'll let the kid go."

Josie didn't believe that for a second. He was going to kill Brandon.

She lifted her newly acquired rifle to her shoulder, almost without thinking.

Breathe.

Hold.

Let a little out.

Squeeze.

CHLOE WHIRLED AROUND as the crack of a rifle filled the air. She aimed her gun toward the source of the shot. When she didn't see anything right away, she glanced back at Brandon and the soldier.

They were both lying on the ground.

No! She rushed over, heedless of the other shooter. As she dropped to her knees, she realized Brandon was trying to get out from under the man's arm. She pulled the limb to the side and Brandon rolled free.

"Are you all right?" she asked.

"Yeah. Yeah, I think so," he said.

The soldier was not, however. The shot had caught him squarely in the eye.

"Brandon?"

Chloe and Brandon turned. Josie stepped out between the trees, a rifle in her hand.

"Did…did you…was that…" Brandon said.

Josie dropped the gun as she ran to him. She wrapped her arms around him, and he wrapped his around hers.

"You're okay," she said. "You're okay."

"I'm okay. I'm fine."

Chloe climbed to her feet and scanned the forest. Though all seven men from the Project Eden team were dead, she couldn't help feeling like another would somehow show up any second.

Finally, she locked eyes with Miller and they both

breathed a sigh of relief.

When the Ash kids finally broke their hug, Chloe narrowed her eyes and said to Josie, “Thought I told you to stay back by the truck.”

“And I told you I knew how to shoot.”

A half laugh. “That, you did.”

Chloe threw her arms around both of them. Though it was a gross understatement, she said, “Good to see you, Brandon.”

“Good to see you, too.”

EVEN THOUGH THE majority of their group was now children, there were too many of them to all fit on the Resistance’s jet. But Chloe had an idea for how to deal with that. Before going back to the house, she and Miller stripped the fatigues off the soldiers, and used the transport truck to haul everyone down the mountain to Colorado Springs.

Instead of pulling up to their jet, they stopped next to the one belonging to Project Eden. Dressed in the fatigues, Miller entered the aircraft, and returned a couple minutes later with the two crew members who had been waiting on board. They locked the men inside a closet in the control tower complex. Given enough time, they’d be able to knock the door down. Chloe had wondered if she should kill them, too, but there had been enough death that day.

Finally, with Barry at the controls of the appropriated plane, and Harlan flying their original jet, they headed home, where they would increase the Resistance’s numbers by ten newly inoculated children, one newly inoculated adult, and the return of Brandon Ash.

31

LAS CRUCES, NEW MEXICO
4:59 PM MST

THERE HAD BEEN no report for hours from the team that had been sent to Colorado. Even the crew of the plane had not responded.

It was troubling, yes, but in the grand scheme of things, not something Perez could worry about. Others could figure out what happened and make the appropriate decision about what to do next. He needed to concentrate on the bigger picture, especially now that the time for the official cleanup phase had arrived.

"Are we ready?" he asked Claudia.

"Everything's set."

He watched the final seconds before the top of the hour click off on his computer's clock. When only two seconds remained, he said, "Begin."

32

AS THEY WALK through the offices of K-Ridge, Martina can't help but feel some of the luster of the radio world fall away. The place is a dump, and not the magical land of music she'd pictured when she was younger.

With her are Noreen, Riley, and Craig, the group now responsible for getting the station working. She can see they are equally unimpressed.

A flip of a light switch reveals that the building at least still has power.

The studio itself is a little better, though more cramped than she imagined. They turn some dials and push some buttons. A few light up, while others don't. At one point, feedback blares from a set of headphones lying next to the control board. Craig yanks down the control switch he just slid up.

"Sorry," he says.

On the wall, a digital clock reads 03:59:37 PM. This, Martina thinks, is the master clock the DJs used when they announced the time. How many times has this clock affected her life? More than once.

"Maybe there's an instruction manual somewhere?" Noreen says.

Martina thinks it would be more likely manuals plural, not singular, and probably written so only an engineer could understand them. But it's not a bad idea, and she's about to say so when they hear a voice from the other room.

They look at each other for a moment, and rush through the door.

The voice is coming out of a radio that must have been on when the station had stopped broadcasting.

"Did we do that?" Martina asks, wondering if they triggered a prerecorded show.

"Maybe," Craig says.

But as they listen, they realize it's nothing they did. The voice is coming from somewhere else, and what it says takes them all by surprise.

SANJAY AND KUSUM are sound asleep when someone knocks on the door of the dorm room they have claimed.

"Sanjay! Sanjay, wake up!"

Jeeval stirs from where she's been sleeping on the floor.

Ap. Ap.

The barks are halfhearted, but jarring nonetheless.

Sanjay opens his eyes, wanting nothing more than to sleep for another hour. He checks his watch—6:36 a.m.

"Sanjay!"

Now that he's more awake than asleep, he recognizes Naresh's voice. "What is it?"

"You have to come hear this."

"Hear what?"

"It is on the radio. Hurry. In the headmaster's house."

Both confused and curious, Sanjay gets up and starts to dress.

"Tell me if it's important," Kusum says from the bed. She rolls over and pulls his now unused pillow over her head.

When he gets to the house, he finds in addition to Naresh that Ritu and one of the children are there, too. Out of the speakers of the headmaster's stereo a voice is talking in Hindi.

"Is this a CD?" Sanjay asks.

"It's the radio," Naresh tells him.

"I woke early," Ritu says. "I wanted to hear some music. So I was trying to see if I could find a station that might still be playing some."

"And you found this?" Sanjay asks.

"No. Well, I mean, yes. This popped on. It's…it's on all the channels. Here." She turns the dial and sure enough, the same voice is speaking on other stations. "It is also in English. This is the third time through."

Sanjay listens to the voice, then looks at the others.

The astonishment in their faces mirrors his own.

I TRIED CALLING all the numbers in my contact list again. No one answered. I decided to go through the phone book, but after a few pages I just stopped because I was getting the same response, or rather, no response at all. Funny, I used to tell everyone that I was totally fine on my own and actually enjoy it. I've always considered that a strength, especially since I was planning on being a writer. I mean, what is *a writer but someone who spends most of her time alone. I may have been premature in that pronouncement, though. It would really, really (really) be nice if there was someone here to talk to. We could even have—*

Belinda stops typing mid-sentence and frowns. She's thinking too much.

"Poor lonely you," she says. "At least you're still breathing."

As she stretches, she realizes what she really needs is something to eat, so she goes down to the lounge. Tonight she decides to treat herself to a double dose of spicy shrimp Top Ramen. As the noodles and water heat up in the microwave, she wanders over to the window and looks outside, hoping to spot someone walking around. It's something she does every mealtime now.

And while, predictably, there is no one around, a flicker grabs her attention.

Her building is L-shaped, allowing her to see into the

windows on the other extension. In the lounge across the way and one floor down, the TV has been left on. She's noticed it before, but since the networks went off air, it has displayed nothing but black.

Now, though, she can see a person facing the camera, like a news reporter. Is the epidemic on the wane? Is life starting to come back to normal?

She walks quickly over to her lounge's TV and turns it on. She hovers her finger over the remote, thinking she'll have to hunt around to find the broadcast she saw, but it's unnecessary. The image of the man is on her screen.

Behind her, the microwave beeps to let her know her noodles are ready, but she doesn't hear it. All her attention is on the monitor.

ROBERT'S PLAN HAS not gone exactly as he'd hoped. While he has been sufficiently buzzed for the last several hours, he has yet to achieve the oblivion he wants the alcohol to bring on.

He isn't the only one who has been drinking. Many of the other resort staff members have been downing their fair share since news of Dominic's sacrifice spread. Many of the former guests of the resort, especially those who were thinking about returning to the mainland, sit around the bar stunned. Some have drinks in front of them, but most are sober.

Everyone knows if it wasn't for Dominic's selfless act, they would have all probably died. There is no talk of going back to the US now. They all realize that setting foot off Isabella Island means death. If Robert's mind were a little clearer, he would note that Dominic's actions not only saved everyone, but also brought the survivors closer together.

On the television above the bar, the classic movie channel they have been watching is still going strong. It's playing the old David Niven film, *Around the World in Eighty Days*. Phileas Fogg and Passepartout are on a train in the Wild West of the United States.

Robert barely registers it. The sound of the train, the dialogue, the music are all background noise. The sudden cessation of this noise, though, causes him to look up.

The train is gone. The West is gone. Phileas and Passepartout are gone.

In their place is a man in an image that most definitely was not shot in the 1950s. He is perhaps in his late forties, and stands in front of a gray wall. Hung on the wall is a flag—a field of blue with the white outlined globe of Earth in the center.

The flag of the United Nations.

Several others in the bar seem to notice, too. They move in behind Robert, their gaze fixed on the television.

For several seconds, the man simply stares straight out of the screen. Then he opens his mouth to speak.

THE FIRST QUESTION Brandon and Josie have as they reenter the Bunker is about their father. When Matt tells them he's awake, they break into a run, not stopping until they reach Captain Ash's room.

He is propped up in bed, his arm raised so that Dr. Gardiner can check the progress of his recovery. The second he sees his kids, he tries to swing his legs off the bed. His strength still leaves something to be desired, though, so it isn't difficult for the doctor to stop him.

It doesn't matter. The kids are at his side, hugging him. When he asks where they've been, they start to tell him, but their words collide with each other in a rush, so he asks them to slow down.

Chloe enters the room with Matt and says, "Well, look who's up."

Ash's smile broadens. He holds out his hand to her. "Chloe."

She takes it, gives it a squeeze, and lets go.

When he looks back at his kids, he says, "Why do I have a feeling I'm not going to like this story?"

"What story?" Matt asks.

"Where we've been," Brandon says.

"Doesn't matter where they've been," Chloe says. "They're here now. So at least you know the story has a happy ending."

The smirk on Ash's face is skeptical. "If that was supposed to make me feel better, it didn't."

A phone rings in the outer area beyond Ash's room. Lily Franklin picks up the call, listens for a moment, then yells, "Turn on the television!"

Chloe grabs the remote from the nightstand and flips on the TV.

As they listen to the man speak while standing in front of the UN flag, the tension in the room spikes. They know he's lying. They know he's not who he says he is. They know what his message really means.

When he finishes, the first one to speak is Matt.

"Oh, shit."

THE MESSAGE WAS prepared in every conceivable language that Project Eden thought necessary. Versions exist for both television and radio, and text versions have been posted on the Internet for those who might still have access.

The plan to broadcast the message around the world at the same time began years earlier, the work paying off nearly flawlessly as the code to execute is entered. There are a few minor glitches here and there, but these will be rectified presently.

The words unspool on a loop that will repeat for the next several weeks. Principal Director Perez has been assured that by the time it finishes, it will lead to at least ninety percent of those still alive being identified.

At that point, it will merely be a decision of who fits in the Project's plans for the future, and who does not.

> "MY NAME IS Gustavo Di Sarsina. I am the newly appointed secretary general of the United

Nations. You are all aware that our planet has been undergoing a catastrophe beyond anything we have ever experienced. The deaths from the Sage Flu are…incalculable. Billions have already died, and many more continue to do so. Friends, family, loved ones. In the span of ten days, the human race has gone from our normal, everyday existence to a desperate race for survival. If you are hearing this, it means you are one of the lucky ones.

"The good news is, help is now available. A vaccine has been developed, and we are in the process of producing it in large enough quantities so that all those who have survived can receive it. To that end, we need to determine exactly how many of us are left and where everyone is located.

"The problem we now face is one of communication. Many of the world's telecom systems have begun to shut down, and we fear the same is starting to happen with power grids worldwide. In an effort to work around this problem, we have set up various means by which you can reach us—Internet, shortwave radio, and even a phone number those of you still with service can try. And if none of those are available to you, we are setting up dozens of what we are calling survival stations throughout the world. These might require a difficult trip, but they are an option. Those of you watching television will see the information scrolling across the bottom of the screen. If you're listening on a radio, I will give you the numbers and addresses at the end of this message.

"This is the most important part. Whatever you have been doing to survive, continue to do so. The virus is still out there and contractible. Until you have been vaccinated, you must avoid contact with it at all costs. If you need to travel to one of the survival stations, wear protective clothing and stop for no one.

"While we at the UN have also been hit, we are still here. Our only goal now is to save everyone we can. As soon as the vaccine is ready, we will get it to you. After that, we will rise above the ashes of this horrible tragedy and ensure that this is not the end of the human race."

The Project Eden saga returns in 2013, with

Volume Five

EDEN RISING

17501472R00171

Printed in Great Britain
by Amazon